She ...
head ...

"Grace, I'm sorry if I stepped over the line."

"It's..." She waved her hand as if to brush the kiss away, and the gesture hit him like a punch to the gut.

"You work for me, Deke. And without my brother's extra pair of hands, I can't risk messing up and having you leave me shorthanded."

Her words sobered him. Work. She was all about work.

Sliding from the boulder, he held out his hand to help her down. He'd be lying if he said he wasn't disappointed by her decision, but he understood. She'd been looking out for her family for years before he came into her life. Wasn't he here because of that same loyalty to family? Grace wasn't the type to throw caution to the wind and start something with him that might affect the family business in a negative way. Made him admire her all the more for her stand, while at the same time, his heart wavered with a funny ache.

Dear Reader,

Welcome back to the Meet Me at the Altar series. In *His Honor, Her Family*, we continue spending time with the Matthews brothers. This book features Deke Matthews and a woman who is more than his match.

When a work tragedy has Deke rethinking his life, he takes a leave of absence and escapes to the mountains of North Georgia for much-needed solace. He wants silence and a chance to reflect on his future, including the law enforcement job that has been his entire focus. What he gets is Grace Harper.

Grace has always put her family first, despite her personal goal of escaping Golden, Georgia. Deke's arrival makes her question things, and soon the undeniable attraction Deke and Grace share brings about some great moments and difficult decisions.

Then there's the ongoing Matthews family quest to find out who, exactly, their widowed mother is dating. And the enchanting town of Golden. Nestled in the mountains, the colorful spot is full of rich characters and picturesque locations. If you love stories set in small towns, you'll fall for Golden.

There are so many twists and turns in life, but the secret is how we handle each upheaval thrown our way. Join me for Deke and Grace's journey as they discover the meanings of commitment, family and, most important, love.

Happy reading!

Tara

HEARTWARMING

His Honor, Her Family

USA TODAY Bestselling Author

Tara Randel

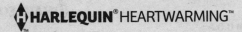

H HARLEQUIN® HEARTWARMING™

ISBN-13: 978-1-335-51056-3

His Honor, Her Family

Copyright © 2019 by Tara Spicer

Printed in U.S.A.

www.Harlequin.com

Tara Randel is an award-winning, *USA TODAY* bestselling author of fifteen novels. Family values, a bit of mystery and, of course, love and romance are her favorite themes, because she believes love is the greatest gift of all. Tara lives on the west coast of Florida, where gorgeous sunsets and beautiful weather inspire the creation of heartwarming stories. This is her eighth book for Harlequin Heartwarming. Visit Tara at tararandel.com and like her on Facebook at Tara Randel Books.

Books by Tara Randel

Harlequin Heartwarming

Meet Me at the Altar

The Lawman's Secret Vow

The Business of Weddings

His One and Only Bride
The Wedding March
The Bridal Bouquet
Honeysuckle Bride
Magnolia Bride
Orange Blossom Brides

Visit the Author Profile page
at Harlequin.com for more titles.

To my wonderful editor, Kathryn Lye.
Thanks so much for your insight and support.
It is a pleasure working with you.

CHAPTER ONE

GRACE HARPER LOOKED up from the paper-strewn desk as the office door opened, bringing with it a warm breeze blowing in leaves that had yet to be swept away from the outside entrance. A tall man strode to the counter with purpose. He removed his polarized sunglasses, his dark gaze meeting hers as he brushed a stray leaf from his short brown hair.

"I'm here about the job," he said, his deep voice succinct and to the point.

Thank goodness. She'd been back at the Put Your Feet Up vacation and rental business office for only two days. It was Wednesday and already she wanted to pull her hair out. As much as she desperately needed a new outdoor guide—*thanks for bailing, Nathan*—the idea of holding a job interview on top of straightening up the mess Mama had left behind was enough to give her a pounding headache. Which, she believed, was already knocking at her temples.

She sent him a pleasant smile. "What would you like to know?"

He nodded toward the door. "From the help-wanted sign out front advertising for a tour guide, and the fact that you offer outdoor vacations, I'm guessing you're shorthanded. So what would the job entail?"

"First, yes, we're shorthanded. My mother normally handles the office, but she was injured, so I'm filling in temporarily." She stuck out her hand. "Grace Harper."

Strong fingers enveloped hers. "Deke Matthews."

"Well, Mr. Matthews, I need someone who can hike, fish, canoe, kayak and zip-line, to start with." She handed him a brochure. "Our packages are listed here. I also need you to be able to manage a group of people and have first-aid knowledge."

He scanned the glossy paper in his hands. "Isn't it rather late to be hiring a guide with the summer season so close? It's already the end of May."

Biting the inside of her cheek, she wanted to scream, "Yes." Instead, she answered, "I'm afraid my mother's accident set us behind and our only other guide has been out of touch."

"I suppose you'll want someone to start right away?"

"That would be ideal."

He folded the brochure and met her gaze with his serious expression. "Then I'd like to apply."

"That would be fine, but I'd like to ask you a few questions first. Get an idea if you're a good match for the job."

"Go ahead."

"Do you have any experience in specific outdoor activities?"

"I was a senior counselor at summer camp when I was a teenager."

She swallowed in disappointment. "Anything more recent?"

"I've been hiking the Appalachian Trail for the past two weeks."

Okay, that was pretty hard-core outdoorsy stuff.

"Any experience leading tour groups?"

"No, but I like the outdoors. I think this will be a good fit for me."

She didn't need an employee who *thought* he was a good fit, she needed someone who knew what he was doing. And who would keep her from traipsing through the woods or venturing out on the lake. She was an attorney, for Pete's sake. Not a tour guide. Not anymore.

"Boating experience?"

"I can row."

"CPR?"

"Card-carrying."

She was about to roll her eyes at his direct

answers when she saw the very tiniest twinkle of humor in his dark eyes.

"Did I pass?"

Honestly, he was the only person to have inquired about the job since she posted the listing, so yeah, he passed. As long as his references checked out.

"If I think of any other qualifications," he said, "I'll add it to the work experience portion of the application."

"Right. The application. I'm sure I have one around here somewhere." Embarrassed by the fact that she had no idea where Mama kept the forms, she crossed the office area on her side of the counter that separated the open room, hoping it looked like she knew exactly what she was searching for. Odds were Mama hadn't touched the system Grace had put into place before leaving for her law career, so she moved to the filing cabinet and rifled through the folders, finding the correct form. Whispering a quiet thank-you under her breath, she removed the paper and carried it to the patiently waiting gentleman.

His eyes, a startling blue-gray she realized now, captured hers and for a moment she froze. Until one arched brow rose in a silent question.

"Yes?"

"Do you have a pen?"

"A—a pen," she stammered, annoyed at herself for losing her composure. Good grief. Yes, he was good-looking, but certainly not enough to crumble her iron control. She scurried back to the desk and snatched the one she'd been using. "Here you go."

A slight tug curved his lips as he took the pen.

Smoothing her pale pink, lightweight jacket, she asked, "Are you new to the area?"

"I'm going to be in Golden for a while."

Vague. But then again he didn't seem very chatty.

As her aspiring hire studied the form, Grace stretched her neck. She needed to get busy. The sooner she had Mama's life back on track, the sooner she could return to hers. "There are some outdoor tables on the sidewalk in front of Sit a Spell Coffee Shop if you'd care to fill out the application there. It's a lovely day and the air is always so fresh here in the mountains."

He glanced around the room. On his side of the counter, two ancient chairs were angled in the corner, a scratched table between them with outdoor magazines scattered on top. Oh, no, was that a cobweb on the ceiling? As he shifted, the wood floor creaked. She gazed at the walls, realizing for the first time that they needed fresh paint. Did the place look as run-down to him as it did to her?

She momentarily closed her eyes, picturing the office in its heyday. Clients coming and going, tour guides checking in, her parents managing the business together. There had been lots of good moments: doing homework after school with Faith right here at Mama's desk, Nathan underfoot as he played with his toy trucks. The times they piled into the bed of Daddy's pickup when he went out to the warehouse to check on a canoe or piece of camping equipment. Or her favorite, hiking trips up a trail in the north Georgia mountains on a sunny Sunday afternoon, just the five of them. It seemed like a dream now. Life had been fairly normal, until fate stepped in and her father couldn't resist an opportunity that landed him in jail.

Her lids flew open when he cleared his throat.

"I'll fill it out here at the counter."

"Then I'll leave you to it."

Turning on a very spiky heel, she faced the desk. The sight of the paperwork nearly had her groaning out loud. If her mother, Wanda Sue Harper, hadn't sprained her ankle after a fall, Grace would be in her downtown Atlanta office, planning court strategies and writing briefs. One frantic call and she'd put her life on hold for four weeks. Scrambling to line up family leave was tricky, but since she'd been with the firm for nearly a year, she was able to cover her open cases and come home.

It was like she'd never left.

She concentrated on the task at hand, but she was also a bit distracted by the lingering woodsy scent of the stranger. As she peeked at his broad shoulders, tanned skin and muscular frame, she decided he looked physically suited for the job. More than capable in a non-suit-and-tie sort of way. When he looked over and caught her gaze, she dropped her head to focus on the piles of paper in front of her.

Why was she even noticing anyway? Maybe because he'd come to a job interview wearing a long-sleeved T-shirt and worn jeans. Jeans. To a job interview! Despite his clothing choice, she found him extremely attractive. Odd, because she didn't go for the rugged type and never dated men who didn't dress with a bit of polish. Show her a man in a well-tailored suit and she was a goner. Better yet, put her in a professional office setting and she was one happy camper.

This time she did groan, eliciting another brief glance from the man before he returned his attention to answering questions and supplying data. Okay, back to his being athletic.

He seemed competent for the demands of the job, but the other requirements? She'd have to wait and see. She took a sip from her diet cola and then gathered up the vacation request forms she'd printed out when she'd arrived at the office. As soon as Mr. Matthews left, she'd read them over, along with returning calls and checking the website, as well as touching base with her uncle Roy, who oversaw the rental cabins. It was only ten in the morning and already she saw no end to her to-do list.

As she reached out to grab hold of the overdue bill folder she'd compiled, the front door flew open. She glanced up to find her worst nightmare perched on the threshold.

"Grace Marie Harper. When I heard you were back in town I had to come and see for myself."

The shrill voice of Lissy Ann Tremaine sent shivers over her spine, in a horror-movie, run-for-your-life kind of way. And why did everyone in town insist on using two first names?

"Hello, Lissy Ann."

The slim woman, her dark hair pulled back in a stylish updo, was dressed in a trendy blouse, slacks and peep-toe pumps and dripping in gold jewelry. She crossed the room, pushed her way to the counter, elbowing Mr. Matthews aside, and rested her designer purse on top.

"I heard your mama took a fall."

"You know those front steps. Real killers."

"So you've actually graced Golden with your presence." She stopped. Giggled. "Graced. Did you get that?"

Grace held back an eye roll but smiled. *Why?* she silently moaned. It was bad enough Lissy Ann and her insufferable husband had made her life miserable in high school. Did Grace have to deal with this woman as well as juggle her mother's doctor appointments and single-handedly run the family business?

"I'll be here until Mama can get back on her feet." Which Grace refused to do, remaining seated at the desk as she talked to her childhood...well, not friend.

Lissy Ann glanced around. Wrinkled her pert nose. "I suppose that's a good idea. You always did make this place work."

Which is exactly why she'd gone to law school and taken a job elsewhere, hoping her mother would finally accept the fact that this was her business, not Grace's.

"I hope you get things under control. We're having a huge, and I do mean huge, Summer Gold Celebration coming up. An entire week dedicated to merchant specials, making sure all the local lodging is booked solid, holding mini-events." She waved a hand with a huge honking diamond on it. "You know the drill. Your mama promised to get involved. The tourist numbers should be phenomenal so we need everyone in town working overtime to make Golden *the* hot vacation spot."

After dropping her conversation bomb, Lissy Ann looped her purse strap over her arm. "We can count on you, right, Grace?"

"Sure."

"I'll send the promotional materials right over."

"Oh, yay."

Lissy Ann huffed and left. The glass door panel rattled in the wake of her departure.

The silence felt good after having that unwelcome voice echoing off the rafters. Until a different voice said, "Friend?"

She'd almost forgotten Mr. Matthews was still in the room. "More like mortal enemy."

"I didn't know people really had those."

"If you had one, you'd know it…"

He tilted his head. "Sounds like big goings-on this summer."

"Lissy Ann is married to the head of the chamber of commerce. They have plans to put Golden on the map."

"You don't sound excited about it."

She shrugged. "I haven't been engaged in town functions for a while." With luck she'd be gone before the huge celebration. One could hope.

"I'm finished," he said, pushing the paper across the counter.

Grace rose, smoothing her skirt. Why she'd worn a work suit to the office today was anyone's guess. Folks weren't keen on formal clothing here in the mountain towns, going instead for a more laid-back look, except for Lissy Ann. By dressing professionally, Grace wouldn't let anyone forget for one minute the thriving law practice waiting for her seventy minutes south.

"Let's see," she said, lifting the completed paper. She noted his home address. "You live in Atlanta?"

"Decatur, but like I said, I'll be spending the summer in Golden."

She continued reading. He was thirty-one, three years older than her. She stopped short at his employment history, specifically when *special agent* popped out at her. "You work for the Georgia Bureau of Investigation?"

He nodded.

"Why on earth would you apply as an outdoor guide?" she blurted.

"Due to circumstances, I've taken a leave of absence from the bureau."

Should she ask what kind of circumstances? Like was he forced to take time off? Was he in some kind of trouble? She'd certainly find out when she checked his references, but in the meantime... Her eyes went wide when she continued reading. "You're a crime scene specialist?"

"You're familiar with GBI?"

"I'm an attorney. I work in Atlanta."

"An attorney?"

Why did it sound like Mr. Matthews spoke around something nasty tasting in his mouth?

"Yes, I'm surprised we didn't run into each other in court when I worked for the public defender's office."

"You don't work there now?"

"No. A private firm handling criminal cases."

His eyes became hooded. Uh-oh. Her suspicion meter went haywire.

"So," he asked, "do I get the job?"

Obviously his career was not a topic for conversation. She bit her lower lip. Did she hire him? He was qualified in a completely different line of work, but as he said, he'd taken a leave of absence. He needed a job. She needed an employee. Her brother, Nathan, had flaked out on her and her sister, Faith, was less than reliable these days, so to be honest, Grace was desperate. She couldn't do this alone and the tour schedule was quickly filling up. The cool, refreshing mountain air lured families and outdoor enthusiasts who wanted time away from the rush and summer heat of the big city. Spending time in a smaller town like Golden, which operated on mountain time, thereby alleviating stress, had become big business. She needed to help Mama by getting the season started and running smoothly.

"As I said, my mother is indisposed. I should run your application by her and see what she thinks. It'll also give me time to check your references."

He regarded her with an expression she couldn't decipher.

"I can promise you, I live a boring life. No past indiscretions to keep me from employment."

Maybe, but she wasn't willing to take any chances.

"So if your mother can't work and you have no one else to run the tours, do you have an idea of when you might come to your decision? If it's going to take a while, I'll need to apply elsewhere."

Logical question. Why was she suddenly stalling? "Technically I'm just taking care of the company until she can come back full-time. She's still the principal owner."

"But she transferred her authority to you?"

"For the time being."

"Unless you find me unqualified or you just don't like me, I don't see the holdup."

He didn't see the holdup? Who did he think he was?

"I don't mean to give you an ultimatum, but there are other businesses looking for help," he pointed out.

"Then perhaps you should apply at those other places, where, I might add, the owners will also want references."

"You'd send me away, even though you need me?"

"I never said I needed you."

His eyes gleamed. "But you do."

"I have other interviews lined up." *Liar.*

He rested his elbows on the scuffed countertop. "Until then do you plan on running the office and hiking up the mountain at the same time? Handling the town celebration by yourself?"

Why was she even arguing with him? She'd thought he might be the answer to her problem until he started questioning her methods. She hesitated until a voice in the back of her mind taunted, *Hire him so you can get back to Atlanta sooner than later.*

She couldn't allow herself to be sucked into family drama again. Her mother would try everything in her power to keep Grace in Golden. Hadn't it been an ongoing battle just to attend college and law school? If Mama could find a way to milk her injuries—very possible for Wanda Sue—Grace might end up back where she started, stuck in a town she'd dreamed of leaving since she was a teen. Everyone knew her here, knew the family's worst history and her part in it, a time when she'd been unable to manage events that had spun out of control. The sooner she was at her real job, assuming the firm didn't fire her if her mother didn't get back on track soon, the quicker she'd gain control of her life.

Still, telling Mr. Matthews to take his high-handedness and hit the road was on the tip of her tongue. Before she could utter the words, the phone rang. She held up a finger and snatched the wireless from the cradle. "Put Your Feet Up."

"Gracie, tell me you hired someone today."

"Mama, this isn't a good time."

"Buck Watkins down at the Jerky Shack said he saw a healthy man walk into the office. Did you talk to him?"

"I'm conducting an interview now."

"Can he take the job?"

"Yes, but—"

"Gracie, you always make everything so difficult."

Grace ignored a twinge at the not-so-subtle dig.

"I can't get ahold of Nathan and the first tour is in three days. How on earth will I deal with my injuries and not worry about the business if you don't get help soon."

Pile on the guilt trip, Mama.

"Let's discuss this later."

"Why? We'll still come to the same conclusion."

"I need to check his references first."

"Hire him now, check them later. If they don't pan out, you can fire him then, but for goodness' sake, don't let him slip through your fingers. We need him."

This was exactly why Grace had left Golden and the family company.

Turning from Mr. Matthews's curious expression, Grace closed her eyes and counted to ten. "I'll see you later," she said, ending the conversation.

Straightening her shoulders, she faced the man she was going to have to work with in the near future. "You're hired."

A smile broke the serious expression on his face. At the sight of his dimples, her breath stalled in her chest.

"That wasn't so hard."

Of all the… One, two, three…

"When do I start?"

"How about tomorrow? Nine in the morning."

"Works for me."

"Make sure you're on time," she said, rounding the desk as the phone started to ring again. As she reached for it, the front door closed behind her. Thankfully, she'd be heading back to her old life in a month. Then the family business, and all it entailed, was someone else's problem.

TAKING A SIP of hot coffee as he exited Sit a Spell Coffee Shop, Deke Matthews struggled to hold back a satisfied grin. Step number one taken care of. He'd landed a job and now had a cover story to justify hanging around Golden. Pleased with his progress, he pulled his cell phone from the back pocket of his jeans and hit speed dial.

"Deke, any success?" his brother Dylan promptly asked when he picked up.

"I got a job."

"That was fast."

"You know I always take care of matters in a timely manner."

"A trait I appreciate. Especially now."

Deke heard a rustling on the other end, then, "So what's your new profession?"

"Outdoor tour guide. Leading tourists up mountain trails, boating on the lake, that sort of thing."

"Sounds more like fun than work."

"Someone has to do it." Deke took another sip of the tasty almond-flavored coffee, swallowed, then asked, "Is Mom still in the dark?"

"Yes. And I plan on keeping it that way."

"Agreed."

"Derrick and Dante are on the same page, too."

"Still, this is Mom we're talking about. She has no clue?"

"No. James Tate has totally duped her."

Deke frowned. He hadn't met his mother's boyfriend yet. In fact, none of her boys had had the pleasure. That made him very wary of the guy. Along with the fact that his mother and Dylan lived in Florida, it made a quick pop-in to scope out the situation almost impossible. But their mother's recent behavior had set all the brothers into a tailspin.

First of all, this was their mother. She didn't date. Or at least hadn't, not since their father had died. In the years after Daryl Matthews's passing, she'd never once gone out with a man. Friend, romantic interest or otherwise. This Tate guy must have sold her an attractive story for her to finally move on from their father's cherished memory and try to hide it from her sons.

"Is she still giving you the runaround?"

"Every day."

At the frustrated tone of his brother's voice, Deke grinned. It took a lot to throw his brother Dylan off task, but Jasmine Matthews was good. Very good.

So were her sons. They'd learned from the best.

"I thought you had plans to run into them while they were on a date?" Deke reminded his brother.

"She caught wind of it and moved the location."

"Classic Mom."

Dylan let out a short laugh.

If there was one thing their mother was good at, it was bending her sons' wills to do her bidding. Not in an evil-queen kind of way. More like she'd mastered the art of manipulation after raising four boys. He guessed it was a survival tactic. But the Matthews boys loved their mother and would do anything to keep her safe. Even if it meant Deke detouring to Golden to follow a lead they'd uncovered about their mother's boyfriend.

At least that's what he told himself. Escaping from Atlanta had been the primary goal because the truth was much more complicated.

"Did you find the store yet?"

"I'll be passing it any minute."

At the intersection, Deke looked both ways before striding to the opposite side of the downtown street. A mix of busy storefronts and specialty boutiques lined each side of the avenue. As casually as possible, he stopped at the front window of a store named Blue Ridge Cottage. Shoppers milled about inside, but he couldn't see the store owner.

"It's just like the intel promised," Deke conveyed.

"Do you have a visual on the target?"

"No." As two older women exited the store, he nodded and moved on. "Give me time and I'll see what I can dig up."

"Are you sure you're up to this?"

Here it comes. "Why would you ask me that?"

"Because you escaped to the mountains."

"And that's a crime?"

Dylan's voice went tight. "That's what you do, Deke. Withdraw when you should be with people."

"I don't want to discuss this."

"You never do. Hiding away instead of confronting your past isn't good for you. You can't keep closing yourself off."

"Why not? It works for me." Deke shut his eyes and counted to ten. "Look, I told you I'd find something out about this mystery woman and I will."

"And then you'll deal?"

"Don't push me."

Deke went silent, pinching the bridge of his nose. Tired of the same refrain. He hated when his brothers pushed him to be social when he was better off with his own company.

"Listen, Deke. We're counting on you."

"No pressure, huh?"

"Never, brother. Gotta run."

Dylan ended the call and Deke replaced his phone in his back pocket. He walked over to a bench and lowered his lanky frame to the wooden seat.

Once Dylan had discovered their mother was dating, the brothers had decided to stick their noses in where they didn't belong. It was only fair play. Their mother would certainly do the same to them. Had done the same at one time or another in their relationships. She'd made it clear she wanted daughters and in order for that to happen, her sons needed to marry. They'd all disappointed her, she'd complained. Hadn't she set up impromptu meetings with single women or invited the "perfect" woman to dinner if one of his brothers planned to stop by her condo? It was a little trickier since he and Derrick lived in different states. Dylan and Dante had finally met their matches, but was his mother so lonely herself that she'd fallen for a guy no one knew anything about?

Deke loved his mother. Had felt helpless over the grief she'd tried to hide after their father's death. He wouldn't let some guy swoop in and take advantage of her. They also wouldn't violate any protocols and use their law enforcement jobs to do an extensive background check on the man just because they didn't trust him. When asked, Deke had gladly stepped in to try to find some easy answers.

The first break had come when James offered to do some work around their mother's condo. Curious, Dylan called the company James claimed he worked for. Turned out the place had never heard of him. After a little digging, Dylan suspected James Tate was not who he claimed to be, sending up huge red flags. Dylan laid it out for their mother, but she refused to heed his warning. She trusted James, she'd argued. He would never hurt her. There were things Dylan didn't know. And with that, she shut down further conversation on the subject.

More determined than ever to find out who this man really was, their younger brother, Dante, had pulled his new girlfriend into the loop. Eloise called in a favor and unearthed information they could actually use. They'd learned James regularly called a number here in Golden, which they traced to Blue Ridge Cottage. A young woman owned the shop. So who was she, exactly? And why did James call her? Since Deke was already up this way to hike the Appalachian Trail, once he was in range signal, Dylan had called and asked him to conduct the second part of their investigation. He was on leave of absence from his job, giving him the time to follow through on this lead.

Arriving in Golden, Deke wasn't sure what kind of job he'd find here. It wasn't a matter of being picky, but he did want something that would immerse him in the town so when he met the target it would seem natural. To her anyway. Working in a restaurant wasn't at the top of his list, so when he happened upon the help-wanted sign in the front window of Put Your Feet Up, his gut urged him to go in and inquire about the job.

Not only would being a guide be the perfect cover, he also enjoyed working outdoors. In many ways, he hoped this job would distract him from the recent events that had changed his life.

Across the street he could just see into the window of the Put Your Feet Up office. Miss Harper walked past the window, the sun lighting on her chin-length, blunt-cut blond hair. Clearly she'd hired him because she was desperate, not because of his witty repartee. The tourist season was upon them, which worked to his advantage, and since she couldn't be the guide and run the office at the same time, she was stuck with him. He took another sip of his coffee and savored the rich taste. Yeah, she hadn't been charmed by him—not that charm was his strong suit, he'd been told more than once—but he had to admit, when she'd mentioned she was a criminal lawyer, it was all he could do not to walk out the door. Probably would have, if this entire mission didn't focus on his mother.

A ding sounded from his pocket. He extracted his phone to find a text from his oldest brother, Derrick. Heard you got a job. Fast work.

What, had Dylan sent out a memo right away?

Another ding. Let me know if this is too much.

Deke clenched his jaw. He loved his brothers,

but their concern smothered him. He liked being alone. What was the big deal?

He typed, I can handle it.

While he waited for a response—because Derrick was not the kind to leave well enough alone—he pulled up his photo gallery. Scrolled through until he found a recent picture of his friend Brittany, with her husband and two young sons.

His hand trembled as her sunny smile tore at his heart.

It wasn't your fault, his inner voice asserted.

His chest squeezed tight and he could barely breathe.

A ding jarred his guilty memories. Call me if you need me, Derrick texted.

Deke didn't need his brother's, or anyone else's, help. He was dealing with the tragedy and he'd be fine. In time.

The idea of swallowing another mouthful of coffee made his stomach sour. He tossed the cup at the nearby trash can. It hit the edge, then tottered inside. Not a slam dunk, but then Deke wasn't exactly proficient in sports, even if he did excel in competition with his brothers. He'd do fine leading outdoor tours for the time being before deciding what to do with the next stage of his life, because going back to analyzing crime scenes when his investigation had put a good friend in a deadly situation wasn't an option right now. Sighing, he stretched his arms along the back of the hard bench, the warm sunshine beating down on him as he watched the happenings of Golden, Georgia.

He'd done his research before arriving in town. His brothers always razzed him about his geeky tendencies, but who did they come to first when they needed information about one thing or another in their lives? That's right. Him.

The town had been established around 1835 after a gold vein was discovered in the surrounding mountains about five years earlier. Folks had trekked to this beautiful spot of land, hoping to make a fortune. Gold mines popped up, much like the historical structure Deke had passed when he first drove into town. The US Mint built a branch in a neighboring town and produced gold coins. Eventually the rush slowed and those with gold fever moved on to California. From the signs posted on the curvy roads in the mountainous area, gold panning was a popular tourist attraction. He supposed he'd have to check it out before he left.

Golden's greater downtown consisted of six blocks of tree-lined sidewalks built on an increasing incline. There were gift shops, restaurants, lodging and a few professional offices.

The buildings were painted in vivid colors. Old-fashioned, ornate cast-iron lampposts lined the main street, supporting large planters overflowing with bright marigolds.

Once off the main street, there were further blocks of housing in all directions, but then the lots grew larger and farther apart as the thick woods and the slopes of the mountains took over the surrounding areas. Golden Lake was situated north of town, a popular tourist destination.

The pace was slow, the town folk friendly. Cars moved down the street in a leisurely fashion, unlike the massive traffic tangles he dealt with daily in Atlanta. He didn't miss the job, the place or the memories one little bit, but he couldn't stay away forever. At some point he'd have to return to the job. He'd need to give his superiors an answer on whether he wanted to continue working for the bureau or not, and as of right now, he couldn't truthfully say.

He wasn't posturing when he told Miss Harper working outdoors would be a good fit for him. He needed space from the events that had caused him to question not only his line of work, but life in general. Thinking about the tragedy left him with lots of questions and zero answers. Being outside in the fresh air and sunshine might help him discover what step to take next. If not…well, he'd deal with that later.

Miss Harper moved before the window again, this time stopping to gaze outside. He couldn't see her well from here, but he'd cataloged her details right after meeting her. Sparkling green eyes. Milky complexion. Probably only five and a half feet to his nearly six. Spunk, and plenty of it.

An attorney. What were the odds?

He'd freely admit he was biased when it came to his current personal struggle. She might be a criminal attorney, but that didn't mean she found ways to let killers go free. He knew he needed to work on the anger and yes, deep down, the guilt.

His new boss must have noticed him. She waved, then disappeared.

Yes, he'd make himself work with Miss Harper because this entire mission was about getting the truth for his mother. There was no way he'd let a criminal, if James Tate was indeed one, destroy another person he loved.

CHAPTER TWO

"MAMA, HOW MANY times do I have to tell you to stay put? Bagsy will be fine."

"Not if I don't feed him," her mother argued, hobbling with her wrapped ankle and cane across the scuffed linoleum flooring to the pantry. There was no stopping the woman when she worried about her fluffy, white feline companion. "He's all I've got."

How many times had Grace heard this refrain? She really thought she'd gotten past Mama's guilt trip, but apparently not. Her heart squeezed at the sight of the woman, face drawn and skin sallow, looking smaller than the last time Grace had seen her, if that was possible. Her mother was on the petite side, but in the last week she'd lost weight, concerning Grace even more.

"Mama, have you been eating?" she asked as she marched to the refrigerator and opened the door. Sure enough, the perishables Grace had brought over yesterday sat on the shelves, untouched.

Her mother waved her hand at Grace. "Don't worry over me."

"Right, like the way you don't fuss over Bagsy?"

"That's different. If I don't feed him, who will?"

"None of us will let him starve."

"If any of my children were around," she muttered under her breath.

"Really? Am I just a figment of your imagination?" Grace blew out a sigh. Call it oldest-child syndrome or the fact that Grace had managed her mother's life since their father had...left, it was the same song and dance.

The cat came running when her mother poured the dry food in a bowl, a grimace lining her face. After a quick pet on Bagsy's head, she sank down into a chair at the kitchen table and lifted her bruised and swollen foot to rest on another. "Sorry, Gracie. I know you came when I called. And Faith did stop by with a few prepared meals. I've been eating those."

"Glad to hear."

"Your sister has a lot going on, what with the babies being sick and Lyle out of a job again. I can't bother her."

No, but you can impose on my life.

Which wasn't a fair thought. Mama had been on her own for a few years now and had actually been doing well. She'd been running the company and taking care of her finances and seemed to be at peace with the past. Until Grace moved to Atlanta for good, Faith had to focus on her family and Nathan was…well, no one knew what Nathan was up to so that wasn't a good sign. Grace envisioned a visit from the police in the near future and held back a frown.

"So Faith has family issues. What about Nathan? Have you heard from him?"

"About a week before my fall. He called and said he'd be back for the first tour, but now I'm not so sure."

Grace pulled out a chair, slid it beside her mother's and sat. "Mama, I know you don't enjoy this conversation, but I'm going to ask you again. Why don't you consider selling the company?"

Her mother pressed her lips together and narrowed her eyes.

"This has been an ongoing discussion for some time. You can't avoid the truth forever."

"And what would that truth be, Gracie? That this family can't stick together long enough to make this business work? When your daddy gets back—"

"He's not coming back." He was never going to set foot in Golden again and it was Grace's fault.

"—things will be different." Tears clouded her mother's pretty green eyes. "Don't go sayin' things like that. He promised he'd come back to us."

Yeah, well, he'd lied.

He'd never even made the trip to Golden to say goodbye once his prison sentence was up two years ago, leaving her mother in limbo. They weren't divorced, and no matter how many times Grace assured her mother she could take care of the matter, her mother refused to file. Earl Harper had outright abandoned his wife. The coward walked away after his release from jail and never looked back. Grace was still picking up the pieces.

Knowing she would get nowhere with this tactic, she tried another. "Mama, Faith is always looking for some extra cash. Let her work a few hours a day at the office. She can bring the kids with her, just like you did when we were little."

"I don't know. She doesn't want to fight with Lyle about it."

Grace had a few choice words for Lyle, but voicing them was useless. The family business was less family and mostly Grace, no matter that she'd put steps in place before she left town to make running the company easier for all involved.

"Then let me talk to Nathan when he gets

back. Impress upon him once again his importance in the business."

"You know your brother. He's a free spirit."

An excuse for getting into hot water if ever there was one.

Her mother reached over and took Grace's hand. "You're the glue that holds this family together, Gracie. We can't do it without you."

Grace swallowed a groan. Fought back the frustrated tears stinging her eyes.

"I can't, Mama."

Sadness crossed her mother's face and she deflated right in front of Grace.

"But I promised I would stay until you're feeling better, and I will."

Her mother nodded and rose, shuffling into the living room.

Muttering the words she'd reserved for Lyle under her breath, Grace stood and walked to the kitchen window. The trees had finally sprouted tender green leaves. The mulberry bush on the side of the yard showed signs of bright purple berries, while orange butterfly weed and wild blue indigo bloomed haphazardly in the scraggly backyard. The small three-bedroom house sat on the top of a hill, the backyard sloping down to a creek that ran through the property.

When Grace had pulled up earlier, she'd sat in her sedan, blinking away moisture as she viewed her childhood home. It appeared as run-down as the Put Your Feet Up office. The house needed a fresh coat of paint and the concrete steps—which had crumbled, causing her mother's tumble and injury—needed replacing. After graduating law school, Grace had offered to have her mother move to Atlanta and live with her, especially when she landed a good-paying job. Her mother had balked, waiting for Daddy and all, so Grace moved out of the house and started a new life. Or at least she'd hoped to start a new life. Sometimes her family didn't make it easy.

The phone rang and Grace heard her mother say, "Faith, how are the babies?"

While her mother chatted, Grace strolled down the hallway to the bedrooms. Poking her head into her mother's room, she realized it hadn't changed in nearly thirty years. Same furnishings, although the quilt on the bed was different. The same comforting scent of Shalimar lingered in the room. Daddy had given a bottle to Mama one year for Christmas and she'd worn only that perfume ever since. Just one more indication of her mother's refusal to face the truth.

Backing out, she crossed the hall to her bedroom. Twin beds she and her sister had shared were now filled with Faith's children's toys. Grace stepped through the doorway, nearly tripping over a wooden block. With a smile, she bent to retrieve it, then tossed it in the toy chest that had been hers when they were all growing up. The waxy scent of crayons, reminding her how much she had enjoyed drawing, greeted her like an old friend. Not much had changed here either, except that the Harper children were grown adults with lives of their own.

Her mother's soothing voice carried down the hallway. Grace lowered herself to her twin bed, running her fingers over the worn coverlet designed with large pink-and-purple geometric shapes over a white background. A bittersweet sigh escaped her. She'd thought it was so cool when she'd picked it out at fifteen, shortly before Daddy left. It had been a big deal, the first grown-up decision she'd ever made. Little did she know it wouldn't be the last.

Spying a framed photo on the dresser, Grace rose and walked over to pick it up. The three of them, mugging for the camera. Grace with a tight smile, Faith all glammed up and Nathan grinning, an upper tooth missing.

"What happened to us?" she whispered.

They'd gotten along until the years after their father was incarcerated. Everyone blamed Grace but didn't balk when she'd taken over as the adult of the family. Faith had acted out and Nathan, well, it took time, but he finally decided to follow in their father's footsteps by engaging in questionable endeavors—not exactly illegal but definitely straddling the fence—hoping for a payout that never materialized. Lately, she dreaded coming home, always anxious about how her siblings would greet her. With a pang, Grace realized this was probably why Faith stayed away when Grace was in town.

"Gracie, come on in here," her mother called.

Replacing the picture, Grace squared her shoulders. Her heels echoed on the wood floor as she joined her mother.

"Faith said hello," her mother informed her as soon as she entered the room.

"I hope I get to see her while I'm here," Grace said, truly meaning it. The sisterly bond had been strong until they were in their teens. Faith, willful even then, accused Grace of trying to mother her. Grace had heard "You're not the boss of me" too many times to count.

It all came to a head one night when the girls were in high school. Grace had warned Faith about a party her sister wanted to attend. It was all over school that there would be alcohol. Their mother, in bed with the covers over her head, didn't have any opinion one way or the other if Faith went, so Grace stepped in, and, after an argument, forbade Faith from leaving the house. Which went over like a lead balloon. They yelled at each other, Faith calling Grace bossy and uptight, saying that no one wanted to be her friend. Grace tried to explain she didn't want Faith to get hurt. She recognized that the kids Faith had been hanging out with were nothing but trouble, but she couldn't convince Faith.

Faith sneaked out anyway and proceeded to get drunk. The cops busted the party and hauled the kids to the police department, mostly to scare them straight. Grace came to get her sister, thankful no charges were filed, and even though she never said I told you so, things were never the same between them. The sad truth was, Grace wanted to be Faith's sister, not her handler, but it hadn't worked out that way.

"She said she's—"

Grace held up a hand. "I know, busy."

Her mother averted her eyes.

"So if you're okay, I'm going to take off." Grace swallowed the thickness in her throat, picking up her purse from the sofa cushion. "I need to stop by the grocery store before heading to the cabin."

"I don't know why you won't stay here," her mother fussed. "I have a perfectly good spare room."

That was never going to happen. She'd stayed here last night and once was enough. After she had come in late from a long day of trying to figure out what was going on at Put Your Feet Up, her mother had filled her in on the local gossip before switching topics to cover what Grace could do while she was home. Eventually, she'd fallen asleep on the couch, waking the following morning with a crick in her neck and the guilt from the past weighing her down. If she had to stay in Golden, she needed her space or she'd go crazy, so the family cabin would be her refuge.

"Faith's kids use the bedroom when they come over. And Nathan will be back, eventually. Besides, I don't plan on being in town forever. Once you're feeling better, you can take over at the office."

"I don't know. These painkillers make me woozy."

"You'll be off them soon enough."

Her mother picked at a snagged piece of yarn hanging from her sweater sleeve.

Bending over, Grace placed a kiss on her mother's cheek. "I'll be back tomorrow."

"I'll be here," came the terse reply.

Grace had just made it to the front door when her mother stopped her. "Wait. I forgot to ask.

Did you hire the man who came to the office today?"

Turning, she said, "Yes, despite not running his references first."

"Myrna down at the coffee shop said he stopped in and is just the most polite young man."

"You're going by her word?"

"I've known Myrna and Delroy for twenty-five years. They wouldn't steer me wrong."

"Maybe not, but I still put in a request to speak to HR at his job."

"Last job, you mean?"

"No, current. Sort of. He's on a leave of absence."

Her mother frowned. "Odd."

"He works for the Georgia Bureau of Investigation."

Wide-eyed, her mother gasped. Yeah, cops weren't a favorite in this house since Daddy's arrest. "Tell him never mind."

"I will do no such thing. I hired him on your say-so. We need help and he looks more than capable for the job."

Capable was an understatement. More than once this afternoon she'd pictured him, broad shoulders, blue-gray eyes that captivated and drew her in, wondering who he was and what had happened in his life to bring him to her door. Or why her heart sped up when he smiled. Those dimples. Yikes. Then, just as quickly, she chastised herself for thinking about him. She wasn't in the market for a romance, no matter how handsome he was. Besides, she worked with lots of handsome men, she reasoned, even as an inner voice said, *Yeah, but they've never affected you this way.*

"But Gracie…"

"No *buts*, Mama. Unless he's done something heinous, he stays."

Her mother crossed her arms over her chest and pouted. It was all Grace could do not to laugh. "If you don't like my decisions you can return to the office and take over."

Wanda Sue dropped her arms. "Fine. He'll do."

"That's what I thought." She softened her voice. "Keep your phone nearby, okay? I love you, Mama."

"I love you, too, Gracie."

As she stepped outside, a breeze chilled her skin. She tugged her lightweight jacket closer. The month of May could still be cool in Golden, especially as the late-afternoon sun lowered in the sky, although it was beginning to stay lighter longer in the day now. She glanced at her watch and hustled to her car. She had enough time to hit the store and make it up to the cabin before dusk.

After power walking the small local grocery, she drove the five miles north of town to Golden Cabins. Her uncle Roy still owned and maintained the fifteen structures while the Put Your Feet Up office booked the rentals. This afternoon Grace had reserved the last available unit—the family cabin—just in time. By the end of the upcoming three-day holiday weekend, the vacation season would officially be under way.

She pulled off the main drag to the entrance. A wooden sign with bright gold letters welcomed guests. Gradually, the pavement receded to gravel and dirt. At the fork she turned left, leading her to the two cabins the family owned and used personally. Uncle Roy lived in one, and Grace's family used the other, renting it when it wasn't occupied. The rest of the rental units were to the right of the fork, away from the family. Spread out across ten acres, all the cabins had access to Golden Lake, which was within walking distance. Worn paths lined the property from years of tourists meandering through the majestic woods. At the very center of the property, where the river emptied into the lake, nature lovers could find a small waterfall. Even though Grace wasn't much for the outdoors after an ill-fated camping trip in high school, the falls were her most favorite spot on the entire planet.

With the window down and cool air rustling her hair, the ground crunched under the car tires until she pulled up to the dark cabin and parked. Removing her groceries, she noticed Uncle Roy's place was dark, too. He'd mentioned something about fishing until the guests arrived, so he still had a few days away.

Juggling her keys and groceries, she moved through the screened porch and unlocked the front door, then swiped the wall until her hand connected with the light switch. A bright overhead fixture illuminated the living room. Kicking the door closed with her foot, Grace carried the bags to the small kitchen and dropped them on the counter, then switched on another light before tossing her purse on the table and putting away the food that needed refrigeration. Once done, she opened the window to usher in the clean air. Her uncle had been gone when she'd called so the cabin hadn't been aired out. It still retained that closed-up smell.

She'd just opened the living room window and kicked off her shoes when the sound of shattering glass jolted her. Curious, she hurried to the window and peered outside. Only the hazy twilight greeted her. Shaking her head, she turned to go into the bedroom to change when she heard a loud thump. This time she went to the door and opened it.

The waning sun disappeared behind the mountains, causing shadows to linger over the densely wooded area surrounding the cabins. Just enough light flittered through the tree branches for her to catch sight of a particular shadow on the far side of her uncle's cabin.

She watched for a beat. Just as she was about to go back inside, she noticed a flicker of movement. Could it be a raccoon getting into mischief? Highly likely. She held her breath. Waited. Sure enough, the elusive movement caught her eye again. She blinked just to be sure, but something had stirred out there. She was certain of it.

Enough was enough.

She rushed straight to the utility closet in the kitchen and grabbed the best weapon she could wield, a broom. Yes, she was going next door to give those critters a piece of her mind. She'd sneak over and scare the party animals back into the woods where they belonged.

Holding the broom handle in a firm grasp, Grace detoured to her bedroom for a pair of flat shoes, then stormed through the screen door, down the steps and…stopped. What was she missing? Oh, yeah, a flashlight. She retraced her steps to find one, then came back outside.

After the day she'd had, she was ready to do battle.

The air had cooled even more since she'd been inside. Shivering, she gulped in several deep breaths of pine-scented air, debating the wisdom of her actions as the night grew darker. She rounded the corner of the cabin, heard a thud and a deep groan.

Okay, that was no animal. A burglar?

Quickly turning, she began running back to her cabin to call for help, something she should have done from the start, when she collided with a solid human body.

DEKE GRUNTED AT exactly the same time the woman who'd barreled into him screamed.

"Hold it," he yelled, hands outstretched as he saw an object moving toward his head. "I'm not going to hurt you."

The woman took a step back, brandishing her weapon in defensive mode before her.

"How do I know that?"

He recognized that voice. "Miss Harper?"

The broom lowered. A click, then a sudden flash of bright light blinded him.

"Mr. Matthews?" she asked as she aimed the flashlight directly at his face. "What are you doing here?"

"Trying to get into this cabin." He squinted

against the harsh light. "Mind lowering that thing?"

"Oh, right." She moved the beam to the ground. "I didn't see a car when I pulled up."

"I parked around back."

"I'm confused. My uncle lives here."

"He rented the cabin to me. I've been trying to find the key but it's not where he said he left it." Deke cradled his left hand. First he'd dropped a heavy planter on it while hunting for the key, then he'd knocked into a patio table. His fingers throbbed. He felt moisture and suspected he was bleeding.

"It's usually under the plant," his soon-to-be boss said.

"There's more than one in the back."

"No. It should be here in the front."

"I just looked."

She turned the light to the front porch, skipping over the large decorative planters to a small potted plant situated beside the steps.

"He said planter."

"Probably he just said plant."

She walked over, tipped the pot and sure enough, the light hit on a shiny silver key. She grabbed it and held it up. "See."

"I could have sworn he said planter."

"He's out fishing and when he's off by himself he usually chews tobacco. Maybe you misunderstood him." She held out the key. When he reached for it, she angled the light on his hand and gasped. "You're bleeding."

"Yeah," he said as the aftereffect of his inept search grew increasingly painful.

She took hold of his arm. "C'mon."

"Where are we going?"

"To my place. I have bandages."

"I'm okay, really. Now that I have the key I'll go inside and clean up."

Tugging on his arm, she said, "No way. I couldn't in good conscience let my newest employee bleed out."

"I'm hardly in danger of bleeding out."

"But we don't know that since it's dark and we can't properly see the damage."

Ignoring his protest, she dragged him across the property to a matching cabin. She had him inside in seconds flat, pointing left. "This way to the kitchen."

"Are you always this bossy?"

"Mostly."

In the bright light he could now see a gash across his palm. Two of his fingers were turning a faint purple.

"Goodness, what did you do?"

"I lost my balance when the planter fell on my hand and I bumped into the patio table. It toppled over and I cut myself on the edge of the glass top."

She took his hand, studied it for a second, then nudged him to the sink. "Rinse that off," she commanded, then disappeared. Moments later she reappeared with boxes of bandages, hydrogen peroxide, a small tube of what he guessed was some sort of salve and whatever else an injured man needed.

"Is it deep?" she asked as she dumped the supplies on the counter. "Should we go to the emergency room?"

He winced as the warm water trickled over the cut. "I don't think so."

"Any glass in it?"

"Not that I can see."

She took hold of his hand again. "Sure you don't need stitches?"

He tried not to be insulted. Stitches? For a medium-sized cut? "A butterfly will do."

She glanced up at him. "You're trying to act all manly, aren't you?"

"I am manly. And like I told you at the office earlier, I know first aid. A butterfly should be fine."

She fished through the box to find the bandage. "If you say so."

"Mind getting me a towel?" he asked when a thin line of red still ran off his hand.

She opened a drawer and pulled out a towel. He took it and covered his palm.

"That's going to hurt tomorrow," she informed him.

"It hurts right now."

She grinned. "Not so manly after all?"

He ignored the teasing.

Once his hand was dry, he lifted the towel to find the blood welling over the cut, but not gushing. He applied pressure again while she opened the bottle of peroxide. "This is going to sting," she warned.

"I know, but the cut needs to be cleaned." He removed the towel and braced himself. "Anytime you're ready."

Grace lowered his hand over the sink and poured. The muscle in his jaw jumped, but that was all the satisfaction he'd give her after she'd insulted his manliness. Yes, it hurt like crazy but he sucked in a deep breath.

"Sorry," she said.

"Uh-huh," he grunted.

Finished, she grabbed another towel and placed it over the cut. "Give that a few seconds to work and I'll place the bandage."

While she tidied up, Deke blew out a breath and rested his hip against the counter. With the worst part over, he now noticed his boss's blond hair glow under the harsh kitchen lighting. Her fair skin attested to her not personally leading the outdoor tours. He was intrigued by the softness that was in direct contrast to her very take-control attitude.

"So," he said, "you're a nurse, too?"

"No, but after years of working with vacation clients, I know first aid."

"Makes sense." He lifted the towel, glad to see the bleeding was minimal. "Let's get the bandage on now."

Grace unwrapped the butterfly and within seconds had it secure. Blood seeped around it.

"Still needs pressure."

Grabbing a box of gauze, she unrolled a long length and wrapped it around his palm with enough pressure to stanch any more blood flow. She tied it off, then looked up at him, a smile of victory curving her lips.

Their gazes met and held. A ripple of awareness took him by surprise. Yeah, he'd noticed how pretty his new boss was when he'd applied for the job, but this? This was a feeling he hadn't felt in far too long. He blinked as he tried to get his wayward thoughts under control. Her smile faded and she slowly backed away.

"Um, that should do for now," she said in a crisp tone as she packed away the supplies. "I suggest you see a doctor tomorrow."

"Thanks," he said, striving to get his voice under control. "For everything."

She nodded and tucked a strand of hair behind her ear. He inhaled a decidedly floral scent. Cherry blossom? Even her perfume suited her.

"I should get going," he finally said.

"Right." Grace led him to the door. "Sorry about nearly clobbering you in the head. I thought you were a raccoon. Or worse, a burglar."

"Serves me right for making a racket."

She tilted her head. "You're not very good at breaking and entering."

He grinned and silence hovered between them again.

"I should probably go get settled," he said again.

"Look, you don't have to come in tomorrow," she said, glancing down at his bandaged hand.

"It's okay. I'd like to learn about the company and find out what kinds of tours you have scheduled."

She nodded. "Then I'll bring the coffee. It's the least I can do."

"Thanks, Miss Harper."

"I think after tonight's events, you can call me Grace."

"Deke."

"I remember."

"Then I'll see you tomorrow, Grace."

She opened the door. "If you don't feel well during the night, don't hesitate to come over and wake me up."

"I can handle this."

"Then have a good night."

He nodded again and stepped outside to make his way to the cabin. As he walked across the loose gravel, then the damp grass, his eyes lit on a firepit between the two cabins, visible in the moonlight. The cool night air felt good on his heated face.

Dipping his good hand into his jeans pocket to remove the key he'd slid there after Grace had found it, he unlocked the door. He turned on the light switch and made his way around, familiarizing himself with his temporary home. When he'd finished, he went outside to bring in his duffel from the back of the Jeep Wrangler. By now, his head ached along with his hand. He found pain reliever in the bathroom, popped two and finally sank down on the couch in the living room.

Blowing out a breath, he muttered, "Great first impression, Matthews."

Getting cut might temporarily throw a snag in

his plans, but thankfully Miss Harper—Grace—hadn't told him he was fired before he started.

Grace. Even the name suited her. She was tough and caring, a surprising combination that he'd do well not to let get the better of him. He was here to lose himself in work, not notice his new boss.

CHAPTER THREE

THE NEXT MORNING, the rich scent of freshly brewed coffee greeted Deke as he walked into the office. Just what he needed after a miserable night of tossing and turning. His palm had throbbed, despite the pain relievers. After staring at the ceiling for hours, he'd gotten up at dawn to take a much-needed run through the woods. No sleep meant his mind was too busy obsessing over things he didn't have the power to change, mainly Britt's senseless death.

When he'd made his way along the path that skirted his side of the lake before veering off to the woods, he'd gotten his heart rate high enough that all he concentrated on was breathing. He'd returned to the cabin, soaking wet and winded, then cleaned up the mess he'd made on the back patio. He couldn't deny that the incredible scenery, tall pines and the water lapping the dank soil beside the lake, calmed his spirit. More so than Atlanta or even his childhood home in Florida. He needed to get his head in the game, not keep dwelling on the past. His brothers were depending on him to find infor-

mation on James Tate and he was determined
to carry through.

Grace was on the phone but pointed to the
cup waiting for him on the counter. As he removed the lid, a burst of steam escaped before
he took his first slug of the morning. Inwardly
sighing, he hoped the caffeine would soon do
its magic.

"Yes, sir, we have available openings for that
date." A frown pinched her pretty face. "I can't
promise that Nathan will be leading the group,
but I will certainly put him as your first choice.
Thanks so much for booking with Put Your
Feet Up vacations."

She jotted a few notes before looking up.
"We're getting busy."

"Good to hear."

She took her soda can and rose from the
desk. Again, she'd dressed in a power suit.
Yeah, he recognized one when he saw it. Today
she wore a navy waist-length jacket and pants,
with a white blouse. High-heeled pumps completed the look. Since he didn't have to dress
professionally for this job, he'd chosen a T-shirt,
jeans and boots for comfort over presentation.

"How's the hand this morning?" she asked,
nodding in that direction.

"Better." He'd tended to it when he got back
from the run, happy the cut wasn't going to

give him problems and that the bruised fingers were no worse than last night. "Not as deep as you would have thought." He held up his palm. "Just a large bandage today."

"Good. I felt really bad about what happened."

"It wasn't your fault."

"No, but it is my uncle's place."

"Serves me right for fumbling around in the dark."

She sized him up. "Why don't I think that's the case?"

"What do you mean?"

"I doubt you're the type that fumbles around. You came in here yesterday knowing exactly what you wanted and didn't back down." She took a sip of her drink, then said, "Somehow you made arrangements with my uncle to rent his place, which rarely happens. What are you, some kind of wizard?"

He chuckled at the suggestion. "More like a fact finder. I research, then apply the knowledge. In this case, Golden jobs and rentals."

"Hmm. A very cerebral approach to things."

"Guilty as charged." He took another bracing gulp of his coffee. "So, care to fill me in on the inner workings of the vacation business?"

"For your research?"

"If you want me to do a good job."

She lifted the hinged section of the counter and waved him into the office area. "I made some notes," she said as he passed by.

There was that cherry scent again. It seemed to have taken hold of his senses. Shaking off the notion that Grace was the one to conjure some sort of sorcery, he took a seat beside the desk and waited for her to get started.

She set her can aside and with nimble fingers took a printed paper from the top of the desk. "I pulled together a schedule. Memorial Day weekend is usually swamped with guests at the cabins, but most families do their own thing. I have two hikes scheduled for Saturday, a canoeing session on Sunday and a group zip-lining on Monday." She pulled a map from the folder, circling an area in red. "The hikes will be relatively easy. They're both at the same park, Crystalline Falls. It's a gradually inclining path from the footbridge up to the falls. Beautiful scenery. About a mile up and back."

"I passed the entrance to the park when I was driving around town the other day. I'll head out there later and check it out."

"Since it's Thursday, you have time to familiarize yourself with the terrain."

"Got it. Sunday's excursion?"

"Canoeing on Golden Lake. It's a bit tricky. Boaters will be out in full force because of the long holiday weekend, but most of the locals know to watch out for tourists. The canoes are stored at our warehouse just south of town. I'll take you over there so you can see the inventory."

"The canoes aren't in the water?"

"Not yet. Uncle Roy will tow them over when he gets back to town. There's a ramp and dock about a hundred feet to the north of our cabins, along with parking. We usually launch from there."

"I'll have a look later today." He read the next activity on the list and looked up. "I have to admit, I've never been zip-lining before."

"Don't worry too much. All you do is escort the group to Deep North Adventures. We have an agreement worked out with them, along with the company that offers river tubing packages and another offering horseback riding, to book our guests at a discount. They have trained staff to safely handle their equipment during the entire experience."

"I see. So your guides don't actually participate in all the activities?"

"You can if you want to, but it's not mandatory for the outsourced trips. A few years ago I realized it was easier to team up with other outdoor adventure companies in the area than try to do it all ourselves. It's really helped to pick up business for everyone involved."

"Smart."

"I thought so."

He grinned. Pretty and confident. A dangerous combination, if his lingering interest in her was any indication.

"You know, it just occurred to me," he said. "Put Your Feet Up is a misnomer. If anything, your tours keep people on the go, not relaxing."

She laughed. "True. The cabin you're staying in? My grandparents developed the land and built the cabins in the eighties. Uncle Roy took over and when my folks got married, my dad offered to assist by opening a booking office. Soon they expanded the business by offering local activities and the company grew from there."

"You mentioned your mother, but is your dad still involved?"

She hesitated, her eyes taking on a hooded look. Clearly he'd stumbled into something here.

"No. My father left for parts unknown years ago. That's why my mom runs the business."

"And you?"

"I help, as you can see. Mostly I worked here when I was growing up, then part-time while I was in college."

"But you came up with the business model?"

She blinked, surprised he mentioned it. "Yes. It wasn't really difficult to figure out ways to outsource some of the tours and still make a profit. For the most part people want someone else to arrange a tour, not make all the calls to different venues or worry about the costs or times. I do all that for a set fee."

"You?"

"I mean Mama."

At the heat in her voice, he backed off.

"What else should I know?"

Grace spent the next hour explaining the tour options and his responsibilities, answering questions and effortlessly fielding phone calls. She engaged with those on the other end of the line, laughing or reminiscing with prior clients. By the end of the conversation, he had to wonder why Golden didn't appeal to her anymore. She ran the office seamlessly.

After her last call, when she'd mentioned someone named Nathan again, he had to ask. "So, Nathan? Is he the reason you need a new guide?"

"Yes. And full disclosure, he's my brother. Unfortunately he took off a few weeks ago and my mother has only heard from him once. I have no idea when he'll be back."

"Noted. Anyone else in the family working here I should know about?"

"I have a sister, but she's not involved." She closed the thick folder and handed it to him. "I've enclosed employment forms you need to fill out and return to me. Any health issues I should be aware of?"

"For the most part, no. Allergies are about it." What his family thought was childhood asthma had sidelined him when he was a kid. While his brothers had been outside running around, he'd stayed indoors, reading as a way to make the hours pass. Turned out he retained everything he read, which gave him extensive knowledge on quite a few topics. Didn't hurt that he tended to be a geek. And he'd developed exceptional patience during that time.

Thankfully as he got older, the doctors realized it wasn't asthma but severe allergies. Since they'd worked out the right medication, he rarely experienced any problems. "During allergy season I fill a prescription and I'm good to go."

"Okay. I think that's it." She rose, grabbing a set of car keys from the desk. "Let's go visit the warehouse. We can leave through the back door once I lock up."

She smoothed her slacks, then headed to the front door, which nearly hit her as it opened.

A preppy-looking man with shiny blond hair styled in an expensive cut, a slick smile, a tan polo shirt and blue Dockers walked in. If Deke wasn't mistaken, he heard a muffled groan carry across the room.

"Grace Harper, it is you? Lissy Ann told me you were in town but I had to come by and see for myself."

"Why, Carter Tremaine, you've just made my day."

Was it his imagination or did her drawl suddenly grow more pronounced? Deke grinned at the fake enthusiasm of Grace's voice. He could see why when he glimpsed the outward disdain on the face of the other half of the well-dressed Tremaine couple. It perfectly mirrored his wife's expression yesterday.

"When you left Golden for the bright lights of Atlanta, we didn't think we'd ever see you again."

"As I'm sure you know, family matters brought me home."

"Shame about your mama's fall. Someone should really take care of that house of hers."

Grace's face turned red and her voice turned sharp. "What do you want, Carter?"

He handed her a large yellow envelope. "Lissy Ann compiled the information for the

Summer Gold Celebration. I'm sure you can pass it on to your mama and Nathan."

Grace hesitantly reached out to take the proffered envelope. "How neighborly of you both."

"We've invested in extensive publicity with the hopes of putting Golden on the go-to vacation map, and this celebration should seal the deal."

Grace stood before him not saying a word. If Deke didn't already dislike the visitor, he might almost feel sorry for him. Grace's stony silence threw the other man off.

"So, ah, can we depend on your commitment to the town and help during the celebration?"

"You'll have to discuss it with Mama when she gets back."

Carter looked skeptical. "But she's always on board with civic projects."

"Then there you go." She opened the door. "Thanks for stopping by."

Carter hesitated. "You both have a nice day." He shot a final glance at Deke and exited out the door.

Grace closed it behind him with more force than was necessary and quickly locked the door. She then stomped back to the desk with a decidedly ferocious frown. Tossed the envelope as she went.

"I take it you're not a fan of the husband either?"

She ran a hand through her hair. "Do you have people in your life whose mission it is to make you miserable?"

"Sometimes I feel like my brothers were put on this earth for the sole purpose of tormenting me."

Her eyes lit up over their common bond. "The Tremaines have been pains in my behind since high school."

"I'm guessing that's part of the reason you live in Atlanta?"

"Yes." In the overhead light, her green eyes sparkled. He liked her hair a bit ruffled, her cheeks bright with outrage. Made him want to kiss the stress away until she couldn't think of anything but him.

Whoa! Hold it. Yes, she intrigued him, but where had that thought come from? Thrown, he clutched the folder tighter.

"Let's get going before another town resident decides to stop in to confirm the rumors that I'm back in town."

She led him out the rear door to a narrow lane running behind the buildings in this block. They crossed over gravel to a small patch of grass, which then led to a public parking lot.

"Mind if I drive?" he asked. "I do better with directions if I navigate myself."

"Sure." She stopped short when she eyed the white vehicle he pointed to. "It doesn't have any doors."

"Yeah. It's a Wrangler."

He could almost see her brain calculating the distance from the ground to the seat. It was a bit of a climb to get in, but he had every faith she could manage it. Especially as she stared at the wide, silver side step, face etched with grim determination. Did she always approach life with such a take-all attitude? He and his brothers had been overly competitive growing up—still were today, truth be told—and he found himself wondering if she subscribed to the same philosophy. If so, this would make for a very interesting summer.

"Take hold of the grab handle and pull yourself up."

She shot him an incredulous glance. "Just like that?"

He chuckled. "Just like that." He couldn't wait to see this.

Blowing out a breath, she reached up for the handle, hefted her weight, tottered in her spiky shoes for a scary moment, then slung herself into the seat. She shot him a cocky smile. "What are you waiting for?"

Admiring her pluck, he jumped inside and started the ignition, and they were on their way.

As he pulled onto Main, she shouted directions over the loud engine. He drove through town, enjoying the cool temperatures and cloudless sky. With a sideward glance, he saw Grace's hair blowing in the wind while she uselessly tried to control it. Her tight, white knuckles grasped the handle for dear life as he took the turns. What a trouper. The idea of this woman, who had no use for nature, running her mother's outdoor adventure business struck him as a bit absurd, but he enjoyed the juxtaposition. Finally, a few miles outside town, she pointed down a winding road leading to a large warehouse nestled between tall pines and scraggly scrubs.

"Just pull up in front."

He did as she said, parked and followed her to the front door beside the large roll-up door beside it. Once inside she flipped on a light and led him to the center of the vast structure.

"Canoes and kayaks on this side." She pointed out the location. "Camping gear on the other."

The inventory was clearly laid out for easy access.

"There's a trailer on the other side of the building that's used to transport everything when needed. I didn't notice. Do you have a hitch on the Jeep?"

"Yes."

"Good." Her gaze encompassed the room. "Any questions?"

"Nope. You've covered everything."

Except why she didn't like being back in Golden, what was up with her family issues and why the Tremaines pushed her buttons. It wasn't his place to ask, even though he wanted to. He was here for one thing only, to get the dirt on James Tate and report back to his brothers. The Harper family dynamics were none of his concern.

Grace headed for the door. "Let's get back to the office."

As they started to leave, Deke noticed a few posters hanging on the wall, one featuring people water rafting and another of a campground at dusk, a fire flaring in a circle pit. He tried to picture Grace in either setting but had to admit he couldn't, not with her buttoned-up look.

"So what are the odds I can get you up the mountain or out on the lake?"

She snorted. "Zero to none."

He chuckled. "Good to know."

They walked back to the Jeep, Grace's expression resigned as she climbed in. "Let's get this over with," she said.

WHY ON EARTH anyone would enjoy traveling around in this hunk of metal was a mystery, Grace decided as Deke drove her back to the office. Every dip and bump jostled her and jarred her teeth. Thank goodness for the seat belt preventing her from sliding off the leather seat every time he took a turn. Her heels were not the best shoes to keep a good purchase on the floor and she just knew when they got back, her clothes would carry the odor of gas all day. She swore she'd gotten a bug in her teeth. A bug! Someone save her from the great outdoors.

Before long they pulled into the parking lot. As soon as Deke cut the engine, she swung down from his death machine. She shook her shoulders, smoothed her hair and faced him head-on. "Next time we take my car."

"Whatever you say, boss."

She wrinkled her nose. "Please, call me Grace. I don't plan on being here long enough to really be your boss."

He shrugged. "Grace it is."

They walked back to the office. His long stride made her pick up the pace to keep up. When she'd noticed his arm muscles flex as he'd steered the Wrangler, she'd had to force herself to look away. Yes, he was in good shape, and yes, he was good-looking. But he was an employee and she didn't mix business with pleasure. Even though his dark blue-gray eyes, which held a hint of sadness, made her curious. She chastised herself. She was in no position to ask about his secrets.

"Any other questions?" she asked.

"I think you covered everything."

"Once we're inside, I'll give you a key to the warehouse so you can get in whenever you need to." She unlocked the front door to the office and fished through the top drawer of the desk to hand him the key.

"Thanks. I think I'll go check out the path to Crystalline Falls."

"It's not taxing, but some of our clients misjudge how much of an incline they can handle."

She took a seat, hoping he'd leave so she could get some work done. Too much of his woodsy scent and masculinity for one morning. She needed to focus and with Deke around that was next to impossible.

"Quick question," he said. "Where's a good place for lunch?"

She rose, went to the counter and pulled a paper brochure from a clear plastic holder. "This lists all the stores and eateries in town. Depending on what you're hungry for, you can find it here."

"This helps a lot. I was going to walk back and forth along Main Street to familiarize myself with the area, but this gives me a heads-up." He opened the brochure to find a detailed map and scanned the information. "Golden seems to be quite a tourist destination."

"When I was a kid, there were only a few places for tourists to visit, but when Mr. Tremaine Sr., Carter's father, began promoting the town, it gradually grew to what you see today. We still have a long way to go to compete with some of the more established vacation spots."

"The son is following in the footsteps of the father?"

"Looks like that. The Tremaines are all about publicity, and the other important family in town, the Mastersons, are big into real estate." She might not like Carter and Lissy Ann, but she had to admit, they were committed to making Golden a premier tourist stop, which in turn kept her mother's finances in the black.

His head jerked up. "Masterson?"

"Yes." Her suspicion meter started clanging again. "Do you know them?"

"Maybe. I have a friend, Logan, in Atlanta with the same last name."

"He would be from the same family." She paused. "The wayward son."

"Huh," he said, then went back to the map. "Small world."

"I suppose." She tilted her head. "He never

mentioned Golden? I mean, since you decided to head up here to hike?"

"To be honest, I haven't seen Logan in about six months."

Made sense. She had to remind herself not everyone had ulterior motives.

"I see there are lots of shops listed up and down Main Street." He paused. "Jerky?"

"You'd be surprised what's been popular through the years. The buildings all remain the same. It's the type of businesses in each one that vary depending on current trends. Right now jerky and specialty sauces seem to be big sellers."

His perceptive gaze caught hers. "You have your finger on the beat of the business community, too?"

"From time to time." She would never admit it to her family, but yes, she kept up with the merchants in town. If only to help her mother, she'd convinced herself.

He continued reading. "Blue Ridge Cottage. What's that?"

"Handmade greeting and post cards, specialty stationery."

"Interesting." A moment later he looked up. "Tammy's Tiny World?"

"Miniature dollhouses and stuff like that." She frowned. "Why all the questions? Are you interested in a part-time job on top of your new full-time job to overlap with your leave-of-absence job?"

He chuckled. "Like I said, familiarizing myself with Golden."

He folded the brochure and stuffed it in his back pocket, not meeting her gaze. Was there something he wasn't telling her?

"Okay, I'm off," he announced. "I'll let myself out the back door."

"If you have any questions, call me. I'll be here all day."

He saluted her. "Later."

Settling in to work, she took some calls, but the office soon became too quiet. Normally she liked to work alone, but today, she was a bit antsy. Because of Deke? Didn't make sense, really. She'd worked with all kinds of well-built guys who were guides over the years. What was it about him that made her heart pick up speed whenever he was around? She pushed her thoughts from Deke, dressed in a T-shirt that molded to his muscles, to the attorneys she now worked with on a regular basis. Suits were the norm, and if they went for casual, it entailed losing the jacket but keeping the buttoned-up shirt and tie.

As she thought about that, her mind wandered to how fortunate she'd been to land a job at a popular firm and she hoped her leave of absence wouldn't jeopardize her future there. The timing was not ideal, but thankfully she'd already put in lots of overtime. She'd been taking care of her mother for so long that when she called, it was only natural that Grace came running.

Looking around the office, she realized how much of her heart and soul she'd poured into Put Your Feet Up. Not the physical space, which needed refreshing, but the spirit of the company. While the reminder was still fresh, she grabbed a piece of paper and made a quick list of the work to be done here at the office, as well as her mother's house. Once finished, she dropped her chin onto her upraised hand, pondering her attachment to the business.

If it hadn't been for her, her father's actions might never have come to light. And she wouldn't have had to grow up so quickly.

She'd overheard her father's conversation about deliveries and inadvertently mentioned it to her uncle. Soon after, the dirt hit the proverbial fan. Their father had been arrested when it was discovered that he and a buddy in town had decided to start a lucrative side business selling illegal recreational drugs. She learned later that Daddy was always looking for the next big moneymaker. Apparently her father wasn't that discerning. And he'd always been impatient. Not a great mix.

Then, after what seemed like a lengthy trial, he was sent away to prison. She often wondered if that was why she'd decided to focus on criminal law. Even though their lives had been upended by her father's bad decisions, the experience had left an indelible mark on her soul. She hadn't meant to cause problems, but she had gotten her father in hot water anyway. Maybe she could help others now.

But when her mother couldn't come to terms with the reality of her husband leaving, that left sixteen-year-old Grace, with the help of Uncle Roy, to step in. She'd be forever grateful to her bear of an uncle for guiding her in the early years. But Mama? Grace still didn't understand why the woman would let a teenager take over the family business instead of encouraging her to have a life. Her own life.

Yeah, it still smarted. She'd been involved in this company one way or another for most of her life. Was she destined to stay here forever? Shuddering at the thought, she realized she needed to get back to Atlanta as soon as possible.

Grace glanced at the phone. Reached over, hesitated, then tapped the numbers to the law firm, asking for her coworker Stacy when the receptionist answered.

"Hey, Stace. What's going on?"

"Swamped, as usual."

Guilt pressed on her shoulders. They'd been hired around the same time and now Stacy had to handle Grace's work as well as her own. "I'm sorry you had to take my cases."

"Don't even worry. Someday I'll need a favor and you'll owe me."

"You bet." Should she ask if there was any scuttlebutt that she was in danger of losing her position? "So it seems like it's still okay that I'm gone?"

"Yes. Things are running smoothly, don't worry." Grace heard voices in the background. "Look, I have to run."

"Thanks, Stacy," she said, but her friend had already ended the call. Grace stared at the receiver, then replaced it, a shiver of dread drifting over her skin. She shouldn't have called. Shouldn't have given in to her doubts. The partner who had interviewed her had been thrilled with her work at the public defender's office. Had given her the okay to take time off. Had assured her that family came first. She wanted to believe that...

The phone rang and she was soon caught up with vacation business. By three, she needed a change of scenery and decided to close up early. Maybe a walk by the lake would calm her nerves. Or the opposite, make her worry about what she was missing in Atlanta. Either way, she desperately wanted to head home.

She called her mother to see if she needed anything, but Wanda Sue informed her that some of her friends were going to bring dinner by the house. With her mother taken care of, Grace drove up the mountain. When she'd pulled up to the cabin, her mind had already created ten worst-case scenarios about her job, which quickly faded away when she spied a dusty, silver minivan that had seen better days parked in front. She eased to a stop. Only one person drove that make and color car with a deep dent in the back quarter panel.

She grabbed her purse from the passenger seat, opened the door and walked to the porch. She'd just stepped inside the screened enclosure when her sister appeared at the door, a baby on one hip, a toddler with his arms wrapped around her legs.

"Hey, sis. Mind some company?" Faith asked.

Just then the baby yelped out a loud wail followed by the little boy bursting into serious crying.

After the few days she'd had, Grace could relate.

CHAPTER FOUR

GRACE TRIED TO school her expression as she studied her sister. It had been almost a year since they'd crossed paths, but the changes in Faith were startling. Dark circles ringed her hazel eyes, tawny hair tangled around her wan face and her drool-stained, stretched T-shirt hung haphazardly over baggy shorts. What on earth had happened? Fatigue seemed to have washed the life out of her and Grace couldn't ignore the warning bells ringing in her head.

"Faith?"

Annoyance flashed in Faith's eyes at Grace's soft tone, a look Grace recognized from her sister's rebellious days, and she silently cringed.

"Don't mind me. I don't have the energy to dress up after mothering a six-month- and four-year-old all day."

"I didn't mean…" She could never get it right with Faith. "I just… You look beat."

Faith sent her a *really?* look.

Okay. Time to try another angle. "What are you doing here?"

"I don't mean to impose on you while you're in town, but Lyle has been beyond difficult lately, knocking down every idea I've come up with to solve our financial problems. I took off to find some space." Faith shot her a knowing look. "Apparently you had the same idea."

Grace closed the door behind her. "This has always been our go-to place."

Faith bounced her daughter. "If I'd known you were staying here, I'd have gone to Mama's."

"No, stay," Grace rushed to assure her. "Please." Hearing sniffles, she looked down at her nephew, clinging to his mother's leg for dear life. She knelt down. "Hey, John. What's with the tears?"

John tightened his grip on Faith's leg.

"Separation anxiety," Faith informed her. "This phase of child-rearing is wearing me out." She shifted Lacey again, bouncing up and down to get her daughter to calm down. Seemed both her children were on the same wavelength.

Grace rose. "What can I do?"

Faith nodded over her shoulder. "John's favorite truck is on the couch."

Grace tossed her purse on the sagging chair and fetched the toy. Once again on John's level, she held it out to him. "Here you go, buddy. Want to play cars?"

John sniffled, looked up at Faith, then eased his death grip. After a few tentative steps, he walked to Grace. Once the truck had his full attention, Grace rose, questions on the tip of her tongue.

"Let me get Lacey a bottle," Faith said. "Then we can talk."

"That'll give me a few minutes to change."

Grace disappeared into one of the two bedrooms and quickly shucked her work clothes for a hot pink T-shirt, denim shorts and pink sneakers, then quickly joined her sister in the kitchen.

Faith was preparing a bottle as Grace walked in and she handed Lacey to her while she finished the job. Inhaling the scent of powder and just plain baby, Grace tried to settle down her fussy niece.

"When Mama told me you were coming home, I should have known you'd escape here," Faith said loudly over Lacey's crying. "As soon as I stepped foot inside the cabin earlier today, I knew someone had aired out the place. Figured it was you after nosing around. Nice outfits, by the way."

"Thank you?"

Faith chuckled. "My first instinct was to leave, but I didn't want to go home to Lyle or explain to Mama that we aren't seeing eye to eye. Again."

"How long has this been going on?"

After testing the formula to make sure it was the correct temperature, Faith rubbed the nipple over Lacey's lips until the baby opened up and started drinking. Silence reigned. "Let's sit so I can keep an eye on John."

Heading back into the living room, Faith collected Lacey from Grace and took a seat in an armchair to feed her daughter, while Grace sat on the nearby couch, tucking one leg under the other.

"Uncle Roy didn't tell me you were staying here."

Grace grimaced. "Probably on purpose." Obviously their uncle thought the way to get the sisters speaking to each other again was to stick them in the same cabin. Talk about tough love.

"I can call him. See about moving over to his place."

"He rented his cabin."

Faith did a double take. "This is news. Since when?"

"A day ago."

"That doesn't sound like Uncle Roy."

"It might have something to do with a woman he met on his trip."

"A woman?"

"Long story, but when I thought someone was breaking into his cabin last night, I discovered a new tenant. When I called to confirm, Uncle Roy mentioned that he'd extended the trip." She grinned. "I heard a female voice in the background so I had to ask."

"Wow. I don't know whether to be pleased or confused. Since when did he start dating?"

Grace shrugged. "Beats me."

"I wonder if Mama knows."

"Are you kidding? If she did, we'd have gotten an earful by now." Grace picked at a thread in the couch fabric. "Besides, this is Golden. He probably wants to keep any potential romance private for now."

"I can sympathize. Privacy is hard-earned in Golden." Faith shifted in the chair. "I hate to admit this to you, but you're going to hear about it anyway." She took a deep breath, then blew it out in a hearty gust. "My bad decisions have finally come back to bite me. Big-time."

Shocked that Faith would admit her failings to her, Grace said, "You know I'd help you if you'd let me."

"Right." Sarcasm twisted her tone. "Like always. Grace to the rescue."

Grace opened her mouth to defend herself, then pursed her lips together, before saying, "Look, I don't want to fight. Since we're both staying here, can we agree on some kind of truce?"

More than anything Grace wanted to end the

impasse they'd been perpetuating since they were teens. With Daddy long gone, Mama needing help and Grace once again dropping everything to save the day—as they'd see it— her siblings would resent her for it.

Faith's tone was begrudging when she said, "I suppose we can handle a truce."

She'd been expecting an uphill battle. Faith's words came as a surprise. "I know things haven't been—"

"Pleasant?"

"—in a long time. I hate that we can't sit in the same room and carry on a conversation."

"Don't put that on me."

Dejection swamped Grace. "Are you ever going to let it go about Daddy?"

Faith could fix it right here, right now, by working with Grace instead of fighting her, but Grace worried old habits died hard.

"We were kids, Faith. Stuff happened. You have to know I never meant to get Daddy in trouble."

"Yeah, but he did and it changed everything."

"So I'm guilty forever?" Grace brushed her hair behind her ear. "Mama still expects Daddy to come waltzing through the door like nothing happened. You still hold a grudge for my part in that, and all the other things we fought about when we were kids. And Nathan…where is he by the way?"

"I have no clue."

"Great."

An uncomfortable silence blanketed the room. John filled it with his sunny chatter about cars and trucks while Lacey dozed off as her belly filled. Maybe it was time to leave the past where it belonged, in the past, and make strides toward becoming closer.

"We're family," Grace continued. "I know I'll mostly be working while I'm here, but I'd really like to catch up."

A strange look flitted over Faith's face. She opened her mouth and Grace waited on pins and needles to find out what was going on in her sister's mind when John carried his truck over to Grace. Frustration mounted as the moment passed and whatever Faith was going to say slipped away.

"Don't mind him," Faith said instead. "He's obsessed with anything on wheels, sleeping with his favorite truck and demanding to watch programs on television about heavy machinery."

Lacey had fallen asleep, snuggled against her mother. A rush of love for her niece consumed Grace. Reaching over, she ran a finger over the baby's soft skin. Lacey shifted and Faith rose to carry her to the crib she'd set up in the second bedroom. Grace was on the floor with John when she returned, racing his little cars around.

"Dirt," John said, holding up his truck.

"Code word for take me outside," Faith said. "Not now, John. Your sister is sleeping."

Not sure how Faith would react to Grace's suggestion, she said, "I can take him outside if it's okay with you. You look like you could use a breather."

Relief softened Faith's features. "Are you sure? My sister, the big-time attorney, actually asking to play with a four-year-old?"

She tried not to let the sarcasm in her sister's voice pinch her heart, but it did. "I wouldn't have asked if I didn't want to do this."

"Sure. But watch him closely. He takes off like a flash."

Grace rose, held out her hand and took John's smaller one in hers. "I may not be a runner, but I promise to keep an eye on him."

As Grace passed by Faith to get to the door, she stopped. "What were you going to say before John interrupted us?"

Tears clouded her sister's eyes. Instead of answering, she glanced away.

Grace touched her arm. "This is a safe place."

Faith blinked, straightened her shoulders and met Grace's gaze. "I'm a mother now. Time to own up to all the choices I've made."

"You don't have to do it alone."

"This is hard." She barked out a sharp laugh. "You always tried to look out for me, but I thought I knew better. Look how well that's worked out for me."

If Grace wanted to push for changes, now was her chance. "Faith, we're going to be in close quarters for a while. If there's something you want to say, just say it."

Faith ran a hand through her hair, her voice shaky when she said, "Give me a little time to sort it all out, okay, sis?"

"All the time you need."

With those words, Grace took John out to the path that led to the dirt lane, then headed toward the lake. She should be thankful that her sister wanted to talk, something they hadn't done in ages. Maybe living together was a blessing in disguise. As she listened to John's ongoing chatter, she hoped so.

GOOD GRIEF, WHAT was Faith feeding her son? And where could she buy whatever it was? The four-year-old had enough energy for a full platoon of men, with no signs of letting up soon.

They'd walked to the lake, then circled around to the play area. The sun was half-mast in the sky, which meant they'd be ready for dinner soon. Her stomach growled at the reminder.

"Okay, buddy. What do you say we head home?"

"No. I want to play truck."

"We have been."

He stomped his little foot, squeezed his face tight. "More."

Grace laughed. She couldn't help it. John was the spitting image of his mother when she was a child. "Good luck with that," she muttered under her breath, remembering how hard it was to corral Faith when her mind was made up. Seemed like karma was having a belly laugh about now.

"How about we get something to eat and come back later."

"No. Want to play."

"After dinner."

His brown eyes flashed. "No."

John had no sooner said the word than he streaked right past her. She turned in panic, ready to give chase, when she saw him dash right into a pair of long legs. Which belonged to her new employee.

"Slow down there, champ."

Her heart took a dizzy twirl when Deke waylaid her nephew. He smiled at the boy, revealing those dimples, which in turn made her chest squeeze tight. The sun caught the hidden highlights in his dark brown hair, and that woodsy scent of his tickled her nose. When his gaze met hers, well, she was nothing short of a goner.

This could be a problem.

"Hey," he said in greeting, his voice scratchy like he hadn't used it in hours. It definitely rubbed her the right way.

"Hi."

Their gaze held for a long moment before she felt John wrap his arm around her leg.

A glimmer of something—what, she couldn't say—crossed Deke's eyes before he covered his reaction. "I didn't know you have a son."

"Nephew. His name is John."

Grace reached down to take John's hand in hers. "This is Mr. Matthews."

John looked up at her with a frown. "Maffews?"

Deke chuckled. "How about Mr. Deke."

"Oh, I don't—"

"Deke," John shouted and took off. It was then she noticed the trailer full of canoes hitched to Deke's Jeep.

"That's Mr. Deke," Grace called as she hurried after him.

"I don't mind losing the 'Mr.'," Deke said as they followed the little boy.

"He should be learning manners," Grace argued.

"I think that's the least of your worries."

John stopped by the trailer, pointing up. "Boat," he proclaimed, tugging on Deke's jeans when they joined her nephew.

"That's right."

"Go for ride?"

"Not yet," Deke said. "I have to get them in the water first."

"And then we have to check with your mom," Grace added.

John wrinkled his freckled nose, but at least he didn't argue. Grateful for small miracles, Grace held back a smile and turned her attention to Deke. "What are you doing with the canoes?"

"Your uncle asked me to haul them to the lake."

Uncle Roy had called him? Without telling her?

"I figured I'd get ahead of the weekend rush by putting them in the water."

Unbidden, she heard herself ask, "Need some help?"

His brow rose. "I got the impression you were strictly office-bound."

Which had been the case until Mr. Tall, Dark and Outdoorsy walked into her place of business. Then all bets were off. "I've been known to wander into the great outdoors from time to time."

He eyed her, top of her head to her feet and back. A devastatingly handsome smile spread over his lips. She wanted to brush her hand over her hair to make sure she wasn't a mess, but she didn't want to seem obvious.

"I wouldn't refuse an extra pair of hands."

Oh, boy.

John jumped up and down. "I help."

Deke chuckled and tousled the boy's white-blond hair. "You bet, champ." He glanced at Grace. "Undo the straps?"

While Deke lowered the small gate at the back of the trailer, Grace unhooked the lines holding the canoes in place. Deke grabbed hold of one and slid it out. "Catch the end?"

"Sure." She hurried over, grabbing her end and hefting the weight of the canoe once it was in midair. Deke began walking backward to the ramp while Grace balanced her end, John skipping alongside them.

Her uncle had built a large enclosure abutting the water's edge to keep the canoes in one place during the season. This way they didn't float away, there was easy access when a trip was scheduled and they could lock them up when not in use. When they reached the ramp, Deke eased his end into the chilly water, guiding the boat into the enclosure. Grace bent down, side-stepping the ensuing splash as she let go.

"Now we go," John said.

"How about we empty the trailer first?" Deke suggested.

With a shrug, the youngster followed them back and forth, telling Deke all about his trucks until the last canoe was in the enclosure.

"That was easy," Grace said, hands on hips as she surveyed their work.

"Not so quick, sport. We have to transfer the paddles and then we're finished for the night."

"Fine, guide."

A smile hovered over his lips at her retort.

"Champ. Sport. I thought we were going for a nickname theme."

"Then add smart aleck to the list." He nodded over his shoulder to the Jeep.

They all trooped back to gather up the paddles, even letting John drag one behind him to keep him involved.

"I've got the lock in the Jeep." Deke jogged back to the vehicle, then returned with the metal lock. By this time, Grace and John had all the paddles in place.

"We make a good team," Deke remarked.

Grace blinked at him. Team? Odd. She felt like she'd always gone about her life alone.

"That surprises you?" Deke crouched down to secure the lock.

She wiped the startled expression from her face. "I'm used to working solo."

"That's no fun."

"You're a team player?" she asked, curious about the man who'd walked into her life just when she'd needed him.

"With three brothers you learn to work together or else it gets ugly."

She vaguely remembered those days. Before her father had gotten into trouble, when her family actually had fun together.

"Uncle Roy and I work together now. Or I should say, we did, until I moved to Atlanta. Faith chose another path, and Nathan?" She shrugged. "He may be my brother, but I have yet to figure him out. I thought he was interested in working with Mama. Guess I was wrong."

Deke yanked the lock to make sure it was solid. "So she called you?"

"As usual."

"Looks like you have the office well in hand."

"I've been running the business since I was sixteen."

He stood, the sun silhouetting his broad shoulders and lean build. Definitely not a stranger to hard work.

"Alone?"

Little ripples gently lapped the water's edge. John had found a muddy patch to run his truck in, talking to himself as he played. Grace breathed in the clean mountain air before answering.

"At first. Uncle Roy pitched in, but he has his own business to take care of. After time, my mother came around the office more and eventually I was able to get away to school."

"Let me guess. You hadn't planned on coming back to Golden."

"Is it that obvious?"

"Only when you get that look of panic in your eyes."

"Astute." She glanced away, not sure if she should be flattered or unnerved that he'd read her so easily. "I try not to let anyone notice, especially Mama. She doesn't understand why I don't practice law here in town, where I know everyone."

"Sometimes you have to get away. Make your mark."

They strolled over to John, who was making engine noises. "Why do I get the feeling you speak from experience?"

"A part of growing up, I guess."

Which her siblings had yet to do. Faith may be a mother, but she still acted like a sulky teen, fighting with her husband when they should be making their family work. And Nathan? Mama might call him a free spirit, but she thought he was just immature. It wasn't her job to fix their problems or make them grow up, no matter how much her mother might expect otherwise.

"C'mon, John. Let's go see Mommy."

They started down the path leading back to the cabins, the silence between them comfortable. With Deke she didn't need to make conversation, which she found relaxing. The pungent scent of rich earth grounded her as she stepped over twigs and clumps of dirt. The rev of a motorboat echoed from the lake. Shadows were just beginning to form as the sun sank lower in the sky.

As they crossed the tree line and the cabins came into view, Grace spied an oversize, gleaming red pickup parked next to her sedan.

"Oh, no," she muttered, taking John's hand again.

"Trouble?"

"Faith's husband. She's staying with me because she needed some time away."

She noticed the tension in Deke before he spoke. "So he shouldn't be here?"

"I don't know." Her nerves skirted to the edge. "Faith and I aren't close so she's never really confided in me, but I got the feeling things weren't good."

Just then, John noticed the truck. "Daddy," he exclaimed, pulling on Grace's hand as he tried to run ahead.

"Slow down, John."

Her nephew was having none of it. Once they reached the path to the screened porch, he broke loose. From inside, Grace could hear loud voices. "John," she called, her voice sharp with worry.

Deke placed his hand on her arm to stop her. With three long strides, he scooped up a fidgeting John and said in a low voice, "How about we surprise your dad?"

John looked at him. "Surprise!"

"Sure. Let's make it a game."

"I like games."

"Why don't you and Aunt Grace go across the way to my cabin. I'll go in and tell your dad you have a surprise for him." Deke placed a finger over his lips. "But you have to be quiet for this to work."

John wiggled in Deke's arms, running to Grace once his feet hit the ground. "C'mon, Aunt Grace," he said, grabbing her hand.

"Are you sure?" she asked Deke as John tugged her arm.

He nodded, his expression grave. "Don't worry."

Not worry? By the looks of it, Deke had

morphed into cop mode. She'd worked enough cases with police involved to recognize the way his body sprang into action, the way his intent gaze took in their surroundings. How could she not be concerned about her sister? At Deke's strident nod, she hurried John across the lane, leading the boy to the side of Deke's cabin. They'd just turned the corner when she heard a screen door slam, followed by angry voices. Once she had John safely in the backyard, a souped-up engine roared to life followed by the crunch of the dirt road beneath tires as Lyle drove away.

As the rumble faded she heard Deke call, "It's okay, Grace." His voice strong and confident. Squaring her shoulders, ready to meet trouble head-on, she lifted John to her hip and ran back to the cabin. Deke was in conversation with a shaken Faith.

"Are you okay?" Grace asked as soon as she was close to her sister.

Shadows hounded Faith's pretty hazel eyes. She ran a trembling hand through her tangled hair. John reached out for her and she grabbed hold of her son and squeezed tight.

"Where Daddy?" John asked, glancing around.

"He had to go to work, buddy," Faith told him.

"Work." John grinned as his little chest puffed. "We work."

Faith sent Grace a questioning glance.

"We put the canoes in the water."

"I'm hungry," John said, resting his head on Faith's shoulder.

"Right." Faith's voice was reedy when she said, "I don't have anything ready."

Grace stepped forward. "I bought a package of hot dogs. How about we cook them over the firepit."

"Fire, fire," John chanted.

"I'll put together the dogs and rolls, open a can of beans," Grace offered.

"I volunteer to gather the wood and get a good blaze going," Deke said.

Grace felt relief roll through her, grateful for his quick thinking and the immediate sense of safety he provided in a tense situation.

"Thank you," Faith whispered as a baby's wail sounded inside the cabin.

"Another hungry belly," Grace said, keeping a smile on her face when all she wanted to do was hug her sister. She clapped her hands. "Okay, everyone off to work. We'll meet at the firepit in ten minutes."

"Fire, fire," John chanted again.

As Deke headed in the direction of the in-ground pit to round up some kindling, Grace made her way back into the cabin. Not knowing what to expect, she stopped to view the living room, but nothing seemed out of place. While Faith took care of the baby, Grace went to the kitchen, gathering the makings for an impromptu hot dog dinner. She'd just opened a can of beans and emptied them into a pot when Faith joined her, bouncing Lacey on her hip.

"Are you really okay?" Grace asked as she turned the stove dial.

Faith averted her gaze. "Fine."

Grace stirred the beans. "What happened?"

Faith leaned against the counter, defeat making her look older than her twenty-five years. "Ongoing disagreement. Lyle wants to spend his paycheck on toys for his truck when I need to make sure I have food, formula and clothing for the kids."

"How long has this been going on?"

A harsh chuckle escaped Faith. "When has it not been going on?"

The beans and sauce came to a boil and Grace lowered the heat. "I wish you'd said something."

"Right. Like I'm going to tell Miss Perfect that I made a bad decision. You never liked Lyle anyway."

Grace knew Faith was upset, but her description, delivered in a mean-spirited tone, stung.

"It doesn't matter what I think about him. You're my sister and I care about you. And the children."

Faith crossed to the refrigerator to grab a premade formula bottle. "Which I've always given you a hard time about." She removed the top and placed it in the microwave.

"I never meant to control you," Grace said as she removed a few franks from the package to set on a plate. "I just worried."

The microwave beeped. Faith removed the bottle, tested it and gave it to Lacey. "I guess you get to say, 'I told you so.'"

"Is that what you think of me?"

Faith finally met her gaze, tears bright in her eyes. "I don't know what to think anymore," she whispered.

"Oh, Faith." Grace turned off the burner and enveloped her sister in a long-overdue hug, making sure not to squeeze the baby between them. Faith's shoulders shook as she sobbed, but Grace held on with every ounce of strength in her. Once the storm had passed, Faith stepped back, wiping her tearstained face.

"Wow," she said with a bitter-sounding laugh. "Some kind of mom I turned out to be."

Grace ran a finger over Lacey's downy hair. "You're a mom who cares about her children. That goes a long way in my book."

John chose that moment to come bursting into the kitchen. "Mommy! Hot dog, hot dog!"

"Give me a few minutes, buddy, then we'll go outside."

"Minutes, minutes," he repeated as he marched with military precision back into the living room.

Grace shook her head. "What's with all the chanting?"

Faith laughed with genuine humor. "He's four. What can I say?"

"Right. Well…" Reaching for a tray, Grace said, "We'll have dinner ready soon."

"Um, Grace?"

"Yes?"

"I appreciate your help, but I think we'll pass. I'm not in the mood for company so I'll fix John his dinner and you can join your friend. We'll eat in here."

"My friend?"

"I'm assuming that guy is your friend. Please don't tell me he's a stranger."

"No. I hired him to work at Put Your Feet Up."

"Thank goodness. You had me worried."

"Do you honestly think I'd be hanging out with a stranger?"

"Well, no, but Uncle Roy said the campgrounds were full this weekend."

"His name is Deke Matthews. He's going to be one of our guides this summer. He brought the canoes to the lake."

"That explains it. Although—" Faith's brow

wrinkled "—he did look kind of scary when Lyle brushed by him on his way to the truck. I'd followed Lyle outside and there was your... Deke, stone-cold staring us down."

"We heard you guys arguing when we came up the path. Deke is a cop and I guess he was ready for the worst."

"Cop?"

"Long story."

"Well, thankfully Lyle just passed him by."

Grace opened the bag of buns. "Is Lyle going to be a problem?"

"Probably."

"I'll let Deke know. He's staying at Uncle Roy's place."

"A guide and a cop? Well, then, I feel better having him close by."

Grace gathered up the tray of dinner supplies. "Me, too," she replied, for very different reasons.

CHAPTER FIVE

DEKE POKED THE logs burning in the circular stone hollow, sending a cascade of sparks into the air. Hearing footsteps, he looked up from fanning the flame. Grace, carrying a tray, walked his way, no sister or kids following.

"Where's the rest of your family?"

"Afraid it's just you and me?" she teased.

Yeah, he rather was. He liked Grace too much for comfort. "John conk out?"

"No, Faith."

He took the tray, inhaling the cherry scent that always accompanied her, and carried it to a wooden picnic table a few steps away.

"Is she okay?"

"She will be." Grace worried her lower lip. "I think."

"Marriage trouble?"

Grace picked up the metal skewers for the hot dogs and handed one to him. "To be honest, I'm not sure what's going on there. Lyle's rather flashy and Faith latched onto his attention from day one, jumping into the relationship before thinking. Lyle didn't have a dime, but convinced Faith they were going to hit the road and travel the country. Until she ended up pregnant and they settled in town." She reached for a hot dog and stopped midair. Let out a puff of air and dropped her hand to her side.

"Grace?"

"I was never very supportive. I guess I'd hoped Faith would grow out of her impulsiveness and start acting like an adult. Which she was forced to do once John arrived, but I could have been a better sister."

"I saw the concern on your face when her husband showed up. You looked like a mama bear ready to barge into the cabin and protect her."

"Not that she would have welcomed it." She sent him a rueful glance. "Too much history."

"Gotcha."

"But she's staying with me and we have a chance to fix things between us."

"Taking care of your mother, running the business and repairing a relationship? Tall order."

"It's what I do."

"And who takes care of you?"

Her confused gaze met his. "Who says I need taking care of?"

Oh, she needed someone to watch out for her, if that chip on her shoulder was any indication. Was he the man for the job? He thought he could be, if he didn't have so much weighing on his soul right now.

He held up a hand. "Just an observation."

"A wrong conclusion," she said, spearing a hot dog onto the skewer with more enthusiasm than necessary.

"So you have life all figured out?"

"I didn't say that."

He chuckled, taking the skewer she handed him.

"What about you, Deke? Do you have it all figured out?"

Far from it. Even on a good day. "We aren't talking about me."

She batted her eyelashes at him. "Oh, let's do."

A not-unpleasant pressure in his chest, one he hadn't experienced in a long time, reminded him that he was a man, enjoying an evening with a beautiful woman. It was so unexpected, he had to pause a few beats to realize what was happening.

"Deke?"

"Huh? Yeah, sorry. That little move of yours threw me."

"You mean the flirty look to get you to change the subject?" Her eyes sparkled in the waning light. "It worked, didn't it?"

He held up the skewer. "Touché."

"What do you say we eat?" She slid another hot dog on her skewer and settled into one of the Adirondack chairs scattered around the pit area. "I also heated up some beans. Not gourmet, but it'll do."

He dragged a chair beside her and sat, leaning over to angle the hot dog above the enthusiastic flames. "I'm not picky."

"Me neither." She waved away the smoke wafting in her direction. "I work long hours, so I'm pretty much happy with anything that's easy to fix."

"Same here."

"Looks like we're two dedicated professionals both on a leave of absence." She sent him a sideways glance. "What are the odds?"

Lower than she'd imagine, but he didn't need to spill the details concerning his mother. "Fate," he said instead.

She laughed. "You don't seem like a guy who puts stock in the unknown."

"I'm not, but you can't ignore the percentages."

"Ooh, a numbers guy." She handed him her skewer while she went to retrieve the tray of buns, condiments and beans, which she placed within reaching distance. He rotated both skewers to get the hot dogs evenly cooked, handing hers back when she returned. Once seated, she placed a bun and a scoop of steaming beans on a plate, handed it to him, then made a plate for herself. They continued cooking, plates resting on their knees.

"Well," she went on to say, "whatever the reason, I really have to thank you for showing up on my doorstep. If I hadn't hired you, I might have had to take over the excursions, and that's not my thing."

"Sitting behind a desk is?"

A big smile graced her face. "Absolutely."

Another chuckle escaped him. He hadn't laughed this much since...well, before the events that had brought him here.

"Why such a naysayer? Have a grudge against the great outdoors?"

She shrugged, but he didn't miss that her smile slipped or the rigid tension in her shoulders. "Not many great memories."

"Not athletic?"

"Not really, but I did enjoy sports when I was a kid."

"Like?"

"Softball. I love to hike. I never seemed to outgrow that activity."

"Doesn't sound so bad."

"It wasn't until high school." She averted her eyes. "I had a bit of a weight problem so it soured team sports for me."

This piece of news surprised him as she seemed toned and in good shape.

"I get it. I had severe allergies growing up, so I was late to the game when it came to the sports my brothers easily mastered. In my case, they encouraged me, so I caught up quickly."

"I stick with hiking. At least you can do that alone."

Which she probably did because solitary was easy. He knew from experience, but he didn't call her on it because that would have been hypocritical of him. "There are some beautiful trails around here."

"Right here on the grounds, too."

"You'll have to show me."

Her sunny smile returned. "I intend on keeping you too busy with tours. You won't have any free time." Grace glanced over her shoulder toward her uncle's cabin, where a single light shone in the living room. "Speaking of free time, do you expect any visitors while you're here?"

"Nope. Just me."

"Solo, huh?"

"I like it that way."

"Because...?" She held the word out, indicating she wanted an answer.

He shrugged. "Just do."

He noticed the frustrated expression in her

eyes and chuckled. Time to change the subject. Once the hot dogs were ready, Deke placed his in the bun and began eating. Before long, he helped himself to some beans.

"Tell me more about working for Put Your Feet Up," Deke said between bites, licking a dab of ketchup from his finger.

"Since we put the canoes in the lake, that's one job done. Hiking will just be a matter of you familiarizing yourself with the trails in the area. We coordinate with Deep North Adventures but they do most of the work. Adam and Colin are brothers who own the business."

"I imagine you know most everyone in town."

"If they run a business or if I went to school with them, then yes, I'm pretty well-informed." She slid him a sideways glance. "Is there anyone you're interested in knowing about?"

Yes, Serena Stanhope in particular, but he wasn't ready to show his hand yet. "I'm a cop. It's in my nature to want to know about everyone, including details of the town."

"About that. Being a cop, I mean." Grace placed her empty dish on the ground beside her feet. "You don't owe me any details, but why the leave of absence?"

Did he dare tell her? The sun had set, the air was warm and a beautiful woman sat beside him. A perfect time to let down his defenses. Confide his darkest secrets. He gazed her way, the flames flickering over her pretty features. The night cast a spell over them and even though he never thought he'd want to talk about Britt, about that horrible night, he found the whole sordid tale on the tip of his tongue.

"The last case I worked on didn't end well. A friend lost..." That darned lump lodged in his throat. He coughed to clear it.

"I'm sorry. Were you close?"

He hesitated. "Her name was Britt. We worked Forensics together."

"Job related, then?"

He nodded. "I still need some time to wrap my head around the events."

"I didn't mean to pry. I was curious after you filled out the employment application."

"I guess I did come across kind of vague."

"It's okay to—"

The screen door to Grace's cabin slammed, the sharp rap of wood against wood jolting them from the conversation. Grace jumped and looked over her shoulder. In the last vestiges of evening light, Deke rose as Faith strode toward them, her arms crossed tightly over her stomach. Grace must have sensed trouble because she stood.

"What is it?" Grace asked.

"Sorry to bother you. Mama called. She's all upset that you didn't answer your phone."

Grace patted her shorts pockets. "I must have left it in my purse and forgot about it when I took John for a walk."

"Well, she's called me three times. I told her you were busy, but you know Mama. You'd better call her."

Resignation flashed in Grace's eyes, along with a tiredness that went beyond physical. He understood the look, had seen it on his face too many times lately when he looked in the mirror.

"I'm going to have to cut our dinner short," she said, moving to gather up the plates, utensils and the pot of beans to replace on the tray.

He joined her, intending to help. Their shoulders brushed and a quick sense of yearning swept over him before Grace moved away.

"Can you help me carry these back to the cabin, Faith?"

Shaking off the moment, Deke stepped out of the way to let the sisters work. Taking the pot, Faith headed back. Grace hesitated before leaving. "I'm sorry. I need to check on my mother."

"You don't have to explain."

"I feel like I do."

"Does this happen often?"

"More than I'd like it to." She hefted the tray.

"I'll see you at the office tomorrow. We'll go over the weekend schedule one last time."

With a distracted nod, she hurried off.

Making sure she made it safely back to the cabin, Deke then set about putting out the fire before turning in for the night. A cloud of gray smoke puffed upward as he sprayed the pit down with water from a hose connected to a nearby spigot. He was headed to his cabin when he saw Grace hurry out to her car and take off.

As her taillights disappeared into the night, he scratched his head, wondering if this undercover mission to dig up information on his mother's boyfriend might not force Deke to look deep inside to figure out the next step in his life. Because when he was with Grace, he felt more alive than he deserved.

GRACE JOGGED UP the steps to her mother's house, knocking loudly once before pushing the door in. "Mama?"

"In the living room," came the terse reply.

Grace hurried in to find her mother in the armchair, her face pensive, twisting her fingers in the afghan covering her lap.

"What's wrong? Are you feeling ill? Is your injury bothering you?"

"No. I'm fine. Finally got the hang of maneuvering around on a twisted ankle."

"So you're doing better?"

"Seems that way."

"And your friends brought you dinner?"

"Yes."

"Then what's so urgent?"

"You didn't answer your phone."

Grace blinked. "I just called you before I left work. I'm sorry, but I left my phone in the cabin while I was outside."

Her mother sniffed, "You smell like smoke."

Grace wasn't going to explain herself. "Did you need something, Mama?"

She picked up the cordless phone on the armrest. "It's Nathan. I'm pretty sure he's gotten himself in trouble."

Grace's stomach sank. "What makes you think something's going on?"

"I heard from him once after my fall. I told him what was going on, how we needed him to come home. He said he'd be here soon, but tonight when he called to check in, I could hear the panic in his voice. And he was kind of whispering, like he was in a place where he couldn't talk out loud."

Grace ran a hand through her hair and took a seat on the couch. "Mama, that could be anywhere."

"I've tried calling him back, but his phone rings and rings and goes to voice mail."

"What did he say, exactly?"

Her mother squinted her eyes as if she were trying to remember the conversation word for word. "He said things had gone a little haywire and he wasn't sure when he'd be able to return. I asked him what things he was talking about, but he said not to worry. He had a plan and with a little more time, we'd be in good shape."

"What does that mean, 'good shape'?"

"Well...the business is doing okay but money's been a little tight on the personal side."

Her shoulders slumped. "Why didn't you tell me?"

"You've been after me to take responsibility for the business. I tried...but got a little behind and didn't want to tell you."

"Oh, Mama."

"Nathan wanted to fix it."

Nathan with a plan?

"You have no idea where he might have gone?"

"Gracie, you know how tight-lipped he is when he takes off."

She did. And that's what worried her the most.

"What should we do?" Her mother fretted.

She had to think. On the verge of a headache, Grace knew from experience this was going to be a long night. Rising, she headed for the kitchen. "How about I put on the water for tea?"

Her mother nodded, then picked up the phone and stared at it like it would ring just because she wanted it to. But this was Nathan they were talking about. Odds were he wouldn't call back tonight.

Odds. At that thought, Grace froze. Backtracked. "Mama, what if he's gambling again?"

The color leached from her mother's face. "I'd hope not, but after this call..."

The tension in her body nearly paralyzed Grace, but she continued her task of filling the kettle and turning on the burner. Last time Nathan had gotten involved with some unsavory characters—Uncle Roy's description—he'd lain low for months, on the run, until he'd managed to scrape together enough money to pay off his debt. Had he done it again? Lost big-time and would now suffer the consequences?

The tea whistle jerked her from her thoughts. Turning off the stove, she took two ceramic mugs from the cabinet and placed a tea bag in each, the comforting scent of apple spice calming her as she poured steaming water over them.

Back in the living room, she set one of the mugs on the table beside her mother. After taking a seat on the couch, she cradled the warm cup between her fingers, wishing the heat from the tea would warm her insides. She'd gone cold when they'd started discussing her brother's habit.

She didn't know what to do, whom to turn to. Uncle Roy was still on his long-deserved vacation. She didn't want to disturb him with the flimsy amount of information they currently possessed. Faith didn't need to be burdened by this. She had enough stress in her life. And Mama, as much as she'd like to help, couldn't hide the pleading expression in her eyes. Which told Grace everything she needed to know.

"What should we do, Gracie?"

The burden on her shoulders grew heavier, the band across her chest squeezing tighter. Finally, she reached for the cordless. Hit the redial button. The call went straight to voice mail. She tried three more times before her brother finally answered.

"Mama, stop calling."

"It's Grace. And I'll keep calling until you tell me what's going on."

A frustrated breath came through the phone. "Really? Mama called you?"

"What did you expect?"

In the background she heard voices but couldn't

get a sense of where he was. A poker game? Was he in another state or on a casino boat?

"I'm handling things, Grace."

"What things?"

"Look, I told Mama I'd get some money to help her out. She's gonna have medical bills."

"Yes, and we'll all work together to figure out the best course of action to pay them."

"You left Golden for your law practice, Gracie. Left us behind," her brother accused. "You shouldn't be involved."

"I already am. Who do you think is handling the office while you're off heaven knows where?"

"I'll be back soon."

"When? I had to hire a guide. We're booking up fast."

"I'm on a good streak. Just give me time."

She'd heard that refrain before. Right before a major loss. "Nathan, please. Just come home. We'll figure the finances out. You don't need to get yourself into a dangerous situation. We'll make ends meet."

"See, that's your problem. You want to rope me in. I need freedom."

This same old song and dance?

"Let me remind you, little brother, that you can have plenty of freedom if you do things legally."

"I can't do this with you right now."

She tamped down her annoyance and tempered her voice. "Then just come home, Nathan. We love you and need you."

She heard a noise on the other end.

"Did you just snort at me?"

"Since when have you ever needed help?"

The lone-ranger act she'd maintained for so long exhausted her and had to end. She couldn't keep up. "Now, Nathan. I need you now."

Silence greeted her. A shout went up and Nathan said, "Look, I gotta run. I…ah… I'll think about what you said." Then a click.

She lowered the phone and glanced at her mother.

"Well?"

"I don't know, Mama."

Her mother leaned over. Patted Grace's hand. "You tried."

"But was it enough to convince him?"

"Perhaps." Her mother sent her a quizzical look. "You've never told him, any of us, that you needed our help before."

Grace squirmed in her seat, still mired by the guilt she'd been carrying since her father's arrest. She was tired of taking care of the entire family alone. Her penance had gone on long enough. "I should have. But all these years after Daddy's arrest… I always feel like I have to make things right."

"You did. But in the process you let us all depend on you much too much."

She blinked at her mother.

"Yes, Gracie. I know I call upon you far too often." Her mother looked at her wrapped ankle. "Look at me, laid up and expecting you to do all the work. I know you'd rather be in Atlanta."

Did she? With everything going on, she hadn't thought about going back to her job in hours.

Her mother leaned back in the chair. "Maybe it's time the Harper family did a one-eighty."

Grace tried not to gape. "I know I didn't spike that tea of yours, so where is this new leaf coming from?"

"Your brother scares me, Gracie. Faith is a mess, even though she tries to cover it up. And you, atoning for what happened to your daddy? Roy was right. I shouldn't have called you."

Her heart twinged. "Uncle Roy said that?"

"Yes. Read me the riot act. Told me to get my head out of the sand."

"But you were injured. Of course I'd come home."

"And I appreciate that you were here as soon

as I called. Settled me back home and took care of me."

"Why do I hear a *but* coming?"

"It's hard. Wishing I hadn't wasted so much time pining for your daddy." She shook her head. "Give me a chance, Gracie, and I'll show you I can be a team player."

Just yesterday, Mama had been lamenting the fact that she wanted her husband to come home. Now this? The round and round made Grace's brain hurt. "Um…okay."

"Now head on back to the cabin and get some sleep."

Grace smothered a yawn. "No. I'll stay here tonight. Just in case."

A sly smile curved her mother's lips. "You know, I have an idea that will help you. Help all of us."

"Tell me what you have in—"

Her mother held up a hand but kept mum.

Was this all a ploy to keep Grace in Golden or was her mother's change of attitude a cosmic shift in the atmosphere? She found it hard to fall asleep with all the questions clamoring in her overactive mind.

CHAPTER SIX

MONDAY MORNING STARTED out relatively quiet, compared to the busy weekend Grace had endured, until the door opened and Lissy Ann traipsed into the Put Your Feet Up office.

"So we need to up our game," Lissy Ann announced, plunking her designer bag on the counter and removing a printed paper from a leather folder to pass to Grace. Afraid of what was in store for her, Grace took hold of the paper with the tips of her fingers like she was picking up a snake, with dread and caution.

"Changes?"

"It's an updated schedule." Lissy Ann tapped the paper with a manicured finger.

Grace hadn't had time to review the old schedule Lissy Ann had sent over yet. Between working on Saturday, spending some quality, if awkward, time with her sister and her children, then coming back to the office Sunday afternoon to undertake a thorough cleaning, she hadn't given the town festivities a second thought. Her new employee, however, had gotten second, third and fourth thoughts, especially after the night by the fire. She'd run into

Deke only once over the weekend, when she made sure to meet with the hiking tour before he had them pile into the van to drive to the scenic overlook.

He'd been well in command, ruggedly handsome in a T-shirt, shorts and boots, a knapsack hanging from his broad shoulders. Already tanned from spending time outdoors, probably from his days hiking the Appalachian Trail, he'd worn sunglasses and a wide-brimmed hat. She could have sworn his lips curved into an amused smile when she arrived at the parking lot behind the office to see the tour off. It was as if he thought her actions were predictable, like he knew she couldn't stand not being in charge and had to show up to make sure Deke got it right.

It wasn't that she didn't trust him, she assured herself. Yes, she might be a tad controlling, but this was his first tour and she needed to be proactive. Just because thoughts of the man had taken up residence in her brain wasn't a good reason to show up out of the blue, but she wouldn't scrutinize her actions too closely. Instead, she remembered how Deke had taken the lead a few days ago when Lyle showed up. She still couldn't get over how he'd known just what to do, his expression serious as he jumped into action with no concern for his well-being.

"Grace?"

Shaking off the direction of her thoughts, Grace felt her face heat and coughed to cover her reaction.

"As I was saying, the opening ceremonies for the Summer Gold Celebration start Saturday, but we need to keep the hype up on weekends throughout June and July, ending with a big blast in August."

"That's a lot of work."

"But worth it. We'll have tourists coming to town all summer long. We need the publicity to make us a premier destination."

And with any luck, Grace wouldn't be here. She'd be back in her Atlanta office, catching up on the work she'd left behind, delving into new cases and making up for lost time.

"So I was thinking about your walking tour."

Grace looked up from reading the schedule. Didn't like the gleeful expression in Lissy Ann's eyes. "What about it?"

Her mother had actually come up with the idea a few years ago. Inspired by a candlelight walk she'd heard about in another big city, she had suggested they do the same here in Golden. She and Grace had worked together gathering all the details about how the town was founded and planned a tour that focused on the history and original buildings that dated back to the first settlement. On Friday and Saturday nights during the tourist season and on special holiday weekends, they led visitors on a foot tour around Golden. It quickly became a hit, which proved her mother could really make this business work if she was 100 percent committed.

"Since you already focus on the history of Golden and how we're here because of the gold rush, the committee feels it would be in the town's best interest for you to dress in period costume during the celebration when you lead the tours. Just like your mama does."

"Wait. Did you say dress in period costumes?"

"I know you heard me the first time, Grace."

Yes, she had, and immediately analyzed the suggestion, thought through the logistics and came up with a big, fat no. "I'm afraid that won't work for me."

Lissy Ann shoved a hand on her slim hip. Today's outfit of a blouse in pastel pinks and greens with white capris and flat sandals reminded Grace of all the times in school when Lissy Ann had made fun of Grace's less-than-trendy wardrobe. Grace had hated the taunts, but she couldn't help her clothing choices. Her weight had fluctuated wildly back then, finally reaching a number on the scale that made her cry with embarrassment. And eventually, forced her to take a good look at what she was doing to herself. Pressure at home and trying to fit in at school when all the kids teased her about her jailbird daddy had pushed her to the edge until she got ahold of her inner demons and started eating healthily and exercising regularly.

Still, old memories haunted her. Her stomach clenched, but she ruthlessly pushed the reminders of the past away by smoothing the slimming charcoal pencil skirt she'd worn with a pale pink blouse and pumps. Grace lifted her chin even as her fingers trembled, silently daring Lissy Ann to argue with her.

"C'mon, Grace. This is for the good of Golden. It'll create more tourist attention for Put Your Feet Up, and you know it."

She did. Didn't mean she wanted to dress up in a stifling costume in the heat of the summer and relive the snickers behind her back.

"Besides, your mama signed off on it."

Grace swallowed a groan. It had been only a few days, but was this what her mother's cryptic promise to help the family business had entailed? *Give her some time*, her inner voice harkened. Time Grace didn't have, but she wasn't about to push her injured mother either. She'd just have to make do.

"I'll talk it over with her."

"Wonderful." Lissy Ann beamed. "I'm hoping you'll see the advantages of our plans, including the busy weekends."

"You do realize I won't be here."

Lissy Ann blinked. "And why not?"

"I work in Atlanta."

"So come home on the weekends."

Like she wanted to work all week, then come back to Golden and work the weekend. "It's not that simple. I put in long hours at the firm."

"Grace, I don't see why you had to run off. You can set up a practice right here in town, for heaven's sake. We could certainly use your expertise around here."

Oh, no. No, no, no.

"We all assumed you'd stay here anyway," Lissy Ann said, in more of a questioning tone, as if digging for details.

Which she wouldn't get.

"I like living in the city."

Lissy Ann shivered. "You'd never get me out of Golden."

The statement surprised Grace. "All I ever heard in high school was how you were going to travel the world. What happened?"

Picking at the strap of her bag, Lissy Ann averted her eyes. "I said a lot of things back then."

Never one to let things go, Grace prompted, "Like?"

"I was going to get a high-powered job. Marry well and have kids. Rule the town."

"You got the married and ruling part right."

Lissy Ann's gaze met hers. Grace expected a snarky reply, but instead Lissy Ann went on to say, "I admit I gave you a hard time, Grace, but I always knew you were going to make a name for yourself. I wasn't at all surprised you went to law school. You could debate circles around the rest of the team in high school."

Grace blinked. Was that a compliment?

"You went to college," she said, trying to include Lissy Ann's achievements in the conversation.

"For about five minutes. Carter wanted to get married and Mama and Daddy agreed..." Her hand cut through the air in a half-hearted wave as if she wanted to brush off her excuse but couldn't quite manage.

"Why didn't you tell them to wait?"

"Because we aren't all a big ball of confidence like you."

Grace let out a startled laugh. "Me?"

Lissy Ann rolled her shoulders. "You knew how to take care of yourself."

Because she'd had to.

"Look," Lissy Ann went on, "I know I was kind of...bossy to you—"

Try downright mean.

"—but I didn't think it bothered you." A bright sheen glimmered in Lissy Ann's eyes. "You didn't fight back."

Total and complete shock rendered Grace mute. Finally coming to her senses, she said, "Why would I? You were part of the popular crowd. I was the chubby girl whose daddy was in prison. I knew my place."

With a shrug, Lissy Ann tidied up the already neat pile of brochures on the counter. "Sometimes the people who hit it big in high school don't transition well into adulthood."

On the tails of that revelation, Grace took a closer look at Lissy Ann. Yes, she was dressed to the nines, but once she'd allowed herself to be real, it was evident Lissy Ann had her own ghosts haunting her. Her cheeks were sunken and she'd gone a little too far on the thin side. But her eyes… Grace glimpsed a sadness she'd never noticed before. Maybe because she hadn't tried.

"I don't know what to say."

"How about we forget this conversation ever took place." With jerky movements, Lissy Ann slung her purse over her arm and nodded to the schedule lying on the counter. "If you have any suggestions, let the committee know. We'd be happy for your input."

"Sure. Listen—"

"I really need to run. We'll talk again." Finger-waving goodbye, Lissy Ann escaped—yes, that's how Grace labeled it—from the office. Bewildered, Grace shook her head and sat down to get back to work.

She'd gotten through some paperwork when the phone rang. "Put Your Feet Up."

"Hey, Grace, it's Adam."

Her heart lurched. Adam owned Deep North Adventures, where Deke had taken a group zip-lining.

"Adam. Is everything okay?"

Deep male laughter sounded from the other end. "Don't trust your new guide?"

"No, it's not that. I just…"

"He's fine. The group is fine. It's Colin and I who have a problem."

Her chest eased with relief. "What's going on?"

"Remember the accounting software you convinced Colin we needed?"

"Sure. It's the best out there."

"Well, my brother seems to have jumbled it up already."

"I thought you ran the office and he took care of the tours."

"Normally. But we sort of got into an argument about our roles around here and he wanted to prove himself."

Grace bit back a laugh. "Say no more." The

Wright brothers were famous for scrapes they were sorry for later. She'd known them since elementary school, and when they'd all ended up in the tourist business, they'd worked together to promote their companies.

"Mind coming by to take a look?"

She glanced at the desk, mercifully free of the paperwork that had greeted her when she first arrived home, and said, "Sure. Today?"

"If that works for you."

"As a matter of fact, it does." She glanced at her watch. "How about eleven?"

"I'll be here."

This would give her a reasonable excuse to check up on Deke without being obvious. He might read her intentions the wrong way, but what did it matter? Adam had called her, not the other way around. Excuse or not, she couldn't deny she wanted to see Deke again.

She said goodbye, reaching for her purse when her cell phone rang. She recognized the caller ID and answered. "Uncle Roy. What's going on?"

"Not gonna make it back like I thought, Gracie."

"Did something happen?"

"Yep. I fell in love."

For the second time in one day, she couldn't speak.

"Maisy wants me to hang around a bit longer and I'm inclined to make her a happy woman."

"But what about the cabins? The summer tourists?"

"You've been handling the cabin rentals just fine."

"Until I have to leave." She ran a hand through her hair, imagining all the future work piling up in front of her. "Mama's still recovering. I can't manage your business as well as ours. For one thing, who will do the maintenance work on the cabins?"

"I called Roan. He said he'd cover the cabins for me as usual, and you got that new employee to do the tours. Besides, you've got perfectly capable siblings."

"Capable? Since when?"

"Grace," his voice warned.

"Nathan isn't back yet."

"He will be. And we both know Faith needs something to do, so ask her."

"Uncle Roy, I—"

"All you've been sayin' is that you need to get back to Atlanta. Can't do it if you ain't got any help."

He was right. Hadn't she come to the very same conclusion the night she'd spoken to Nathan? But in reality…

"Oh, and just so ya know, my cell reception's been spotty. Gotta run."

Grace moved the phone from her ear and stared at the screen.

This was not happening.

Everyone was out to get her. That was the only explanation for the way her life was going. Grabbing her purse, she locked the front door of the office and exited out the back, her mind running in twenty different directions. As she hurried to her sedan, her ankle turned on a loose rock and she nearly lost her balance.

"Slow down," she muttered under her breath. She reached the car, keys in hand, only to drop them before unlocking the door. As she kneeled to retrieve them, her purse slipped from her shoulder and landed on the ground, the contents scattering around her.

"Really?"

Mumbling to herself, she stuffed her belongings back into her bag and finally slid inside the car. Resting her head on the steering wheel, she took short, jerky breaths, trying to keep the ensuing panic at bay. Without success.

Okay. Conspiracy theory aside, she had way too much on her plate right now to flip out. She needed five minutes to gather her thoughts and put a plan in action, otherwise she was toast. After turning the key in the ignition, she pulled out of the parking spot. If she was going down, she thought on a grim note, why not take everyone with her, family and handsome new guide included?

DEKE LOOKED FROM his position on the zip-line platform to see Grace exit her car. Dressed in her usual professional outfit of skirt and blouse, she held her head high as she purposefully strode across the parking lot. Her blond hair shone in the bright sunlight and a smile curved her lips, but it was the confidence with which she carried herself that really seized his attention.

"Didn't take long," he said, mostly to himself, but Colin Wright heard him.

"What didn't take long?"

He nodded in Grace's direction. "My boss checking up on me."

Colin glanced over his shoulder as Grace started across the parking lot, his brother, Adam, meeting her halfway. He barked out a laugh.

"More like my brother's got a thing for her."

This piece of news grabbed Deke's attention. "Thing?"

"Yeah." Colin lounged against the wooden railing. In his early thirties, athletic, with an affable smile, he and Deke had hit it off right away. "We've known her forever, but since she became a big-shot lawyer, Adam thinks she's hot and is hoping for a chance with her."

"Does he have one?"

"Nah. Grace is strictly in the friend zone."

"But your brother is working on changing that status?"

"Won't work. Can't see those two together. They're too much alike." Colin straightened up. "Incoming."

Deke refocused the direction of his thoughts to get ready for the last tourist flying through the air, screaming at the top of her lungs in the final descent to the platform where he stood. Colin readied the brakes to bring the young woman to a safe stop.

They'd been at it for the last two hours, starting with Colin checking the pulley system, Deke checking harnesses and the all-important carabiner that hooked one to the other. Safety rules were reviewed, helmets passed out and secured on each guest before the group headed up the side of the mountain to the platform on the summit. Another Deep North Adventures guide went up to the top to get the guests started while Deke had elected to stay at the bottom, assisting them after their streak downhill, enjoying their enthusiastic shrieks and yells as they finished their ride.

Deke and Colin soon had all the tour guests out of the harnesses and back on solid ground in one piece. Excited chatter and laughs surrounded Deke, but he couldn't help searching for the lovely blonde who had been in his thoughts more often than he found comfortable. Because really, where could a relationship go with her? Eventually she was headed back to her law career, defending the very criminals he worked to put away. He knew better, yet found himself consciously seeking her out. What was wrong with that picture?

Besides, after getting the information he and his brothers needed, Deke wasn't sure which direction his life would lead. And while he mentally warned himself away from Grace, who was more than interesting and extremely attractive, the idea of another man also wanting to know her better didn't sit well.

He could almost hear Britt's amused laughter in his mind. She'd find his reaction to Grace hilarious, since she'd always tried to set him up with one of her friends and it never went anywhere.

The guests had moved inside the building for complimentary drinks as Deke helped Colin stow away the equipment. When finished, Colin slapped him on the back. "You were like a pro over there."

"I pick up things quickly." After reading everything he could find on zip-lining the night before, Deke had arrived ready to put his knowledge to work. Once Colin had gone over the mechanics with him, and after a ride down the line to better prepare himself before picking up the tour guests, he and Colin had worked well together. It wasn't an especially long ride down the mountainside, but he'd been more than ready for the challenges that lay ahead.

"You had a great group today." Colin closed the door on the shed. "Looks like most of them were experienced. Always helps."

"Grace said she partners with your outfit often."

"Yeah. She takes care of booking, we provide the entertainment."

"So we'll be working together again, I would imagine."

"Looks like. Gotta say, I'm glad you're here. Grace really needs some help until Nathan gets back, and, quite frankly, even when he starts working again."

"Trouble?"

"Not like he's negligent or anything. More like he has a short attention span. He was doing fine holding down the business before their mother got hurt."

"Why'd he take off?"

"Not really sure." The dark-haired man nodded to the building. "Want a drink before heading back to town?"

"Thanks."

The day had started out cool, but as the sun rose higher in the sky, the temperature had soared with it. Being in the thick woods had sheltered them from the heat, but now that they were back in the open parking lot, Deke's T-shirt clung to him. The morning's excursion had taken a lot of physical energy, but he found the guests made it less work and more fun. A word not found in his vocabulary lately.

"How'd you end up in Golden?" Colin asked, holding the door open to let Deke step inside.

"Chance." Which was true. It was just chance that he'd been hiking the Appalachian Trail when his brother got ahold of him. "I happened to be nearby and once I drove into Golden, I was intrigued."

"Was that before or after you met Grace?"

Deke chuckled. "Before."

The inside of the building was a good ten degrees cooler than outside. Deke followed the sound of voices down the hallway to a nicely appointed room with scattered tables, chairs and couches. Looked more like a coffeehouse than an outdoor adventure office.

"Good, because she's made it pretty clear

she's headed back to Atlanta as soon as her mom is better."

"Yeah, I got that impression."

Colin looked across the room to an open door. Deke followed his gaze, catching sight of Grace in animated conversation with Adam. He couldn't take his eyes off her, but to avoid needing to explain his fascination with the woman, he followed Colin to the drink station to grab a bottled water.

Guzzling the cool liquid, he scanned the room and took a silent head count of the guests. Didn't want to explain to Grace that he'd lost anyone. When his eyes settled on her again, Colin laughed.

"Sure you want to go there?" he asked.

"Excuse me?"

"Getting hung up on a woman whose life is elsewhere?"

Good question. He had enough on his plate living with guilt every day and getting the lay of the land so he could approach the target his brothers had sent him to find. Grace was a reminder of his failure as a cop. Not personally, since she hadn't worked on the case that had come back to haunt him. No, another lawyer had twisted the results of his hard work to get a violent criminal off on a technicality. What if he had to face Grace in the courtroom one day?

Would his animosity destroy their new friendship? Or would he let his budding attraction to her overcome his sense of duty?

His thoughts were getting ahead of him. "Maybe one day she'll settle down here."

"Doubt it." Colin pointed to the sliced oranges on the table. They both turned their backs on the room, filling small plates with slices. "Grace has had one foot out the door since high school."

"Still, she came back to help her mother."

"Shame, really." Colin took a swig of water and wiped his hand across his mouth. "She's good at running the business. Too bad she doesn't want to stick around and put out her shingle here in town."

"Colin Wright, are you telling tales about me?"

Deke held back a cringe at Grace's amused voice. Colin muttered, "Busted" under his breath, then turned with a big smile on his face. Deke did the same, his gaze meeting Grace's.

"I would never do that, darlin'," Colin assured her.

"Hmm, is that right? I bet you make that claim to all the women in your life."

"What can I say? I love the ladies."

"Problem is, you break too many hearts along the way."

"Not my intention," Colin replied. "I'm always up-front about not getting serious."

Grace rolled her eyes. "One day a good woman is going to steal your heart and you won't know what hit you."

Colin leaned over and planted a kiss on top of Grace's head. "But today is not that day." Popping the last orange slice in his mouth, he sauntered off to stop and chat with a few of the female guests.

"Some things never change."

Deke went to stand beside Grace as they watched Colin's antics. Her cherry fragrance drifted over him and he felt himself lured into her orbit. That wouldn't do. "So, ah, Colin said you guys go way back."

"Our parents did business together and we've carried on the work relationship."

"That's all it is?"

Grace whipped her head around, eyes round. "What are you asking?"

"You and Adam."

"Adam?" Her mouth flopped open and she floundered. "Me?"

"He's got a crush on you."

"What?" Her cheeks turned a cute shade of pink. "No he doesn't."

"Sure he does. And why wouldn't he? You're a smart, kind woman."

"I…but…we're friends."

"Colin implied that his brother has a thing for you."

She closed her eyes for long seconds before meeting his gaze. "Then it's one-sided." She tucked her hair behind her ear, shifting from one foot to the other. He'd really thrown her for a loop. When she spoke, her voice was low. "I really wish you hadn't said anything."

"Why?"

"That's information I could have done without. How am I going to work with him now?"

"I thought you were headed back to Atlanta?"

"I am, but in the meantime…"

He took her by the shoulders to face him. "In the meantime you act professionally."

Their gazes held for a long drawn-out moment. He noticed the flecks of gold in her green eyes the longer he stared. When she sighed, his legs felt a little off balance, especially when she sent him a shaky smile. Clearly she didn't want to hurt Adam, which sent his estimation of her skyrocketing.

"How'd you get so smart about one-sided relationships?" she asked.

He rolled his neck, ignoring the catch in his chest. "Lived one."

Interest flared in her eyes. "Really. Do tell."

He shrugged as a way to procrastinate in

order to corral his emotions. Thought about Britt and how they'd first bonded over forensic science, until she'd broken the cold hard truth to him.

"A woman I was once involved with told me I made a terrible boyfriend but a great friend."

At first he'd been hurt over Britt's declaration, but over time realized she was right. They'd managed a successful working relationship that had lasted right up until the day she died.

Guilt assailed him as a brief, searing picture of Britt's lifeless face flashed in his memory. He stepped away, not wanting to pull Grace into the swamp of regret with him.

She assessed him with intelligent eyes that were way too perceptive. "So what, one opinion is going to stop you from ever trying again?"

Surprised by her words, he felt the tension in his chest ease and allowed himself a small smile. "Is that an offer?"

Now it was her turn to look shocked. "I hadn't thought of it that way."

"That fact could send mixed signals, you know."

Her throat moved as she swallowed.

"Maybe Adam read you wrong."

"Adam should know better than to think romantic thoughts about me."

"And why is that?"

"I love my job first."

"There's something to be said about spontaneity."

"Yeah, it'll get you into a world of trouble."

"Jaded."

"Honest."

His gaze roamed over her face, taking in the green eyes, smooth skin and pink lips he found himself desperately wanting to taste. Oh, no. Put the brakes on. He hadn't come to Golden for romance, and he needed to remember that fact.

A sly sparkle lit her eyes and Deke knew he was in big trouble when he found himself playing along with the game. "Hmm. And if a guy walked into your life you couldn't resist?"

She considered the question. "I don't know. What does said guy have to offer that'll beat out my job?"

He looked up at the ceiling as if trying to come up with a witty answer. "Mystery. Adventure. Fun."

"That's all?"

He laughed. "Tough room."

"You started it," she said, pointing a finger at him.

"Yeah. And maybe I plan on finishing it."

CHAPTER SEVEN

DETERMINED TO FOCUS less on Grace and more on his mission, Deke decided to do a little recon on his first day off. Starting early Tuesday morning at Sit a Spell Coffee Shop, he shot the breeze with Delroy, while Myrna whipped up a latte that rivaled some of the popular coffee shops he'd frequented in bigger cities.

After solving the world's problems, he headed to the Jerky Shack, where he discussed the merits of smoked meat over a vegetarian diet with Buck. Deke wasn't about to win the argument since the bearded man took his meat seriously. From there he moved on to the T-Shirt Depot, then Hot Air, a shop featuring specialty blown-glass items. Amazed at the precise craftsmanship, he loitered at the counter watching a young man with a ponytail create a vase with different colors swirled together to make one impressive gift. Back on the street, he strolled to the crosswalk, enjoying the sun heating his T-shirt-clad shoulders, breathing in the fresh mountain air. Cars drove by, radios turned up loud enough for him to make out a song or two. Couples with strollers, retirees and curious tourists took advantage of the beautiful warm weather to make a day of it, browsing and walking through the historic downtown.

There was a method to his wanderings. Once he engaged the townspeople and established himself as a regular guy looking to make a living in a tourist town, he hoped tongues would loosen. He knew better than to ask directly about his target just yet. These folks weren't clueless. If he came in with probing questions about another merchant, he was sure they'd clam up quicker than a table of tightwads ignoring the dinner check. No, he had to bide his time, make his presence known and accepted, then work from there. Thankfully he'd learned the art of patience a long time ago. If his younger brother, Dante, were on the case, he'd have blown his cover by now. Deke couldn't let that happen. Not when he and his brothers were concerned about their mother's future.

When he first started his stroll that morning, he'd deliberately walked right past his place of employment. Mainly because he was snooping around the other shops until he reached his intended target, but he couldn't deny the other truth either. He was avoiding the Put Your Feet Up office for a reason.

After his lapse of *not* keeping things all business with Grace yesterday, he'd pulled back some. Although he enjoyed the flirting entirely too much, he'd since narrowed their conversations to the tours Grace had lined up, what equipment was needed for an outing— anything but acknowledge the elephant in the room. Which turned out to be his unexpected attraction to her and the intriguing fact that it didn't seem one-sided.

They'd clicked, there was no denying it. Question was, how did he fight these feelings for a woman who returned said feelings but was every kind of wrong for him?

With a shake of his head, he wondered if he was a glutton for punishment. What was he going to do? *Complete your mission*, replied his logical inner voice. The voice that had kept him levelheaded more times than he could count. Except the night he'd needed it most.

Running his hand through his hair, he pushed away the details of the past to focus on the reality of the present. He had work to do.

When the light changed, he moved with the flow of the pedestrian traffic to start his journey along the opposite side of the main drag. He strolled down Main Street, making sure to pop into each establishment, talking to the business owner. He found that most of the merchants already knew he worked for Grace— well, Grace's mother, he supposed. He chalked it up to small-town chatter. Living in Atlanta, anonymity was easily attained. Not here. Once you were accepted, folks wanted your life story. Since he'd proved to be helpful to Grace and her mother, he'd quickly become part of the tribe. Sure, guilt pinched at him a little bit at the pretense of his cover story, but he dismissed it, telling himself it would be worth it in the end. The lead Dylan had given him was strong and he had to carry this through for their mother's sake.

Stopping before the business in question, he took in the surroundings before heading inside. The Blue Ridge Cottage building was painted snow-white, while the door popped with a bright sapphire hue, along with matching window trim. When looking at the storefront, the entrance was on the right side with a big picture window to the left. The name of the store was stenciled on the window in thick, white lettering. The hours were posted on the door. A sandwich board on the sidewalk welcomed shoppers to stop in for custom-made cards.

Pushing his sunglasses on top of his head, Deke ventured inside. Right away he was met with a homey, inviting atmosphere. The crisp scent of paper reached his nose, then as he moved about, he noticed the subtle fragrance of lavender. One entire wall featured hand-drawn greeting and post cards. Tables were scattered about the showroom floor offering original stationery, fancy pens, bookmarks and a host of other related paper supplies.

Dodging the few customers admiring what was on offer, he stopped before a counter located in the rear of the shop. A moment later a woman entered from what he assumed was a storeroom. Tall, with startling blueberry eyes and long, straight black hair, she blinked when she noticed him. A welcoming smile spread across her pretty face.

"Good morning. Can I help you?"

"Just stopped in to say hi." He stuck out his hand. "Deke. I work for Put Your Feet Up."

Her eyes met his with an engaging warmth. "Yes, I'd heard Grace hired help. I'm Serena. Nice to meet you."

They shook hands and he angled his body to keep her in view but also take in the store. "Nice place."

"Thanks. I'm kind of partial to it."

"Do you do all the artwork?"

"Most of it. I outsource some, but mainly it's me."

"Been at it long?"

"A few years."

"Golden seems like a nice place to live and work."

"Thinking of settling here permanently?"

Was he? He hadn't arrived with that intention, but the town was growing on him. Along with the population. And one certain blonde dynamo. "I guess time will tell."

"It's perfect."

Deke chuckled. "I doubt any place is perfect."

"Well, as close as possible as far as I'm concerned."

He nodded. "Do you have family here?"

A wrapped box slipped out of her hand onto the counter. "Oh, my. I'm a bit clumsy today."

As he watched, Deke noticed a strained expression cross her face and her shoulders hike up. Interesting.

"I only ask because I'm getting to know everyone in town. Trying to catch up on everyone's story. You know the drill."

She averted her gaze. "Right. Because you work here now."

Had he hit a nerve asking about family? Gone was the perky shop owner of moments before. Time to dial it back.

"Exactly."

"Um, if you'll excuse me, I should help my customers."

"Oh, yeah. Don't let me keep you. Just wanted to pop in and introduce myself like I have been all over town."

Pulling herself together, she sent him a confident smile before stepping out from behind the counter to greet two browsing women. After taking another look around to appear curious about the store, Deke went back outside and headed to the next store. Once he felt he'd visited enough folks to seem legit, he crossed the street again, then strode through an alley to the parking lot on the back side of the buildings. He stopped a few feet from the Jeep, pulling his cell phone from the pocket of his jeans. Tapping a programmed number with his finger, he waited for Dylan to pick up.

"Tell me you have some news," his brother said.

"I made contact with the target."

"And?"

"Serena Stanhope is young, about our age. Owns her own business. No ring on her finger, so maybe a relative of Tate's instead of a romantic interest?"

"That would make sense. I finally met him and he really seems into Mom."

"I don't know whether to be happy about that or not."

"How about not for the time being. Reserve your opinion until we learn more."

"Agreed."

"What else did you uncover?"

"Not a whole lot since this was first contact, but in the course of our conversation I asked about family and that kind of rattled her. She turned wary after that."

"Like a person with something to hide?"

"Possible. I left before looking too suspicious."

"Good start. How is the job going?"

"I'm enjoying it, actually. I get to be outdoors and I gotta say, it's beautiful up here."

"And your boss?"

"Why would you ask about her?" he responded, much too quickly. "We're just working together."

"To see how the mission is going." Dylan took a long pause, making Deke sweat. "What other reason would I have?"

Right. It wasn't like he was going around telling people he was interested in Grace.

"Something you want to share?" Dylan asked, that I-know-you-brother tone in his voice.

"Only that I made contact and I'll go on from there."

"Sure that's it?"

"Positive."

Dylan laughed. "Okay. Keep me in the loop."

"I will."

They disconnected and with a muted groan, Deke slid his phone back into his pocket. His brother was way too perceptive. Of course, it didn't help that he sounded like he was over-compensating when Dylan asked about Grace. Not that he had anything to hide. *Yeah, right.*

He had to pull it together. Grace was not part of the detail.

Digging his keys from his pocket, he'd just gotten behind the wheel of his Jeep when the back door of Put Your Feet Up opened. Grace stepped out, so fresh and sunny in her white, sleeveless blouse and navy dress pants that his breath caught in his chest. She locked the door, then, fishing around in her purse, made her way toward him. Hoping she might not notice him, he found himself slumping in his seat, then wanted to smack himself. Why was he so jumpy? When she looked up, he was unable to turn away. A sultry smile graced her face when she registered his presence.

"Did I forget about a group?" she asked as she ambled his way in her high-heeled shoes.

Like she'd forget. Her mind was a steel trap. Something he admired about her.

He swallowed hard. "Nah. Just getting to know the townspeople."

"Why didn't you stop into the office first? I would have been glad to introduce you."

"You're always busy. I didn't want to disturb you."

She waved off his concern. "No bother."

"Well, I already made the rounds so…"

"Headed back to the cabin?"

An internal alarm he shouldn't ignore blared with urgency. *Danger, Deke Matthews.* "Yeah."

"Me, too. It was slow this morning so I decided to quit early."

"Tuesday's not a peak day?"

"No, so I can escape." She placed a hand over her eyes to shield them from the bright sunshine. "When we start up the walking tour next week, I'll be busy."

"I see."

She tilted her head. "Are you okay?"

He swallowed hard. "Sure. Why do you ask?"

"I don't know. You seem sort of tongue-tied."

"Talked to so many people this morning I've run out of words."

Her look said she didn't believe him, but she didn't press.

"So, ah, I'm going to the warehouse."

Her brow furrowed. "You said you were going to the cabin."

No way. Not if she was headed in the same direction and he'd be tempted to ask her to go for a walk in the woods or sit by the lake to while away a few hours. *Think, Matthews.* "I just remembered I need to get some extra paddles for the next canoe excursion. A client dropped one in the lake last time."

"It's your day off." Disappointment shadowed her eyes, but he didn't let that affect his decision to leave.

"I like to get a jump on things."

"Okay. See you later?"

"Maybe."

He started the Jeep, the engine loud enough to discourage further conversation, and backed out of the space. Grace still stood in the same spot, so he waved, then peeled out of the lot.

He'd investigated dangerous criminals, dealt with the handiwork of people who left behind devastation in their wake and apprehended bad guys without an ounce of fear, never cringing once. How was it Grace, feminine and smart, had him running for the hills because she'd affected him so deeply in so short a period of time?

GRACE WATCHED DEKE drive away. She didn't know whether to be amused or miffed.

Clearly something was up with him and she guessed it might have to do with the conversation they'd shared at Deep North Adventures. She'd been intrigued by Deke from the moment he'd stepped into her office a week ago, but she'd never thought she'd start having...

feelings for the man. And after their little by-play, she'd hoped he might be interested in her.

Her smile faded. Was it obvious that she was attracted to him? Then shouldn't she be glad she'd scared him off? The last thing she needed was one more link to a place that held too many bad memories.

"Great, just great," Grace muttered under her breath as she walked to her sedan. While daydreaming about Deke was a pleasurable pastime, right now, she had other things to worry about.

An hour ago she'd been on the phone discussing a tour package with a prospective client when her cell phone rang. Not able to get to it, she let the call go to voice mail, kicking herself afterward. Stacy, from the law office in Atlanta, had left a cryptic, two-word message. "Call me." Which Grace had done, immediately, only to hear Stacy's voice informing her that she was away from her desk and to please leave a message. Grace left a brief response, then waited for a call back. So far, nothing.

Knowing she'd be antsy until she found out what Stacy wanted, Grace took her cell from the front pocket of her purse and redialed, switching to speakerphone. She almost ran off the road to the cabin when Stacy answered right away.

"Stace, what's going on? Your call sounded serious."

"Hold on a sec," her friend said in a low, taut voice.

Grace's stomach took a nosedive. She didn't like secrets and behind-the-scenes maneuverings.

"Okay, I can talk," Stacy said a few seconds later. "I just needed to find a private spot in the office."

Grace tightened her hands on the steering wheel and waited.

"First of all, no one has said anything about your position being in jeopardy."

"What?" Grace practically screeched.

"But I wanted to tell you I was given the Sorrento case."

Chest squeezing like a vise, Grace pulled over to the shoulder of the road and braked.

"Come again?"

"Look, I know you put a lot of work into the case so far, but when questions came up in a meeting and the senior partners wanted to know the status, I covered for you." Stacy paused. "I offered to take over until you came back. Mr. Franks assured me I'd just be filling in for the time being, that you'd be back on board in a few weeks."

Which felt like an eternity since she was

only just over a week into her leave. Granted, this was only one case, but what if the partners grew tired of her delaying her cases? They could easily fire her since she hadn't worked there as long as the other attorneys. And Stacy was an up-and-comer, so was her friend being altruistic or looking out for number one? The thought made her nauseous.

"You just take care of your family and I'll hold down the fort here," Stacy went on when Grace remained quiet.

Hadn't Grace been doing that since she was a teenager? Bending over backward to make sure her family was taken care of? After all, they reminded her, if she hadn't ratted Daddy out they wouldn't be in this mess.

Tears burned behind her eyes because they were right. Even after she'd given them all the tools to successfully run the business without her, she was still trying to make up for what had happened with her father.

With a sharp shake of her head, she focused back on the present. "I… Thanks, Stacy."

"I have to run, but I'll be in touch. Oh, and just so you know, I went ahead and took the pertinent files from your desk. Talk to you soon."

Before Grace could respond, there was silence on the other end. If Stacy was taking files from her desk, were others? Not that Grace could complain, she wasn't there.

Stepping off the brake, she eased back onto the road, mind made up. She needed to get back to Atlanta sooner rather than later.

She pulled up to the cabin in time to catch her sister loading her children into the mini-van. "Where are you off to?" she asked as she stepped from her car.

"I've been trying to call you," Faith said, tension etched on her face.

Forcing herself to tamp down her annoyance, she said, "I was taking a work call."

"Mama needs us."

With a jolt of alarm, Grace hurried over to the van. "What happened?"

"She fell again," Faith said as she edged out of the back of the van after buckling John's car seat.

"How?"

"I think she said the front step. You never made arrangements to get it fixed."

Guilt washed over her. "I meant to call Roan but I got busy..."

"Let's go. She sounded pretty shaky when I talked to her."

Sliding into the passenger seat, Grace cringed when the van engine started up with knocking and coughing, black smoke puffing out of the exhaust. Once Faith backed out and started down the gravel road, the noises stopped, but the smoke continued.

"Faith, is something wrong with the van?"

A red flush stained her sister's face. "It's nothing."

"It's far from nothing. Has Lyle looked at it?"

"He's been busy."

With his own truck, Grace surmised. She sent a sidelong glance at her sister and, when she glimpsed the firm set of Faith's lips, decided not to continue the conversation. Instead she pulled out her phone and called Roan, asking him to stop by and take a look at the steps.

"When is he coming?" Faith asked.

"As soon as he can work it into his schedule."

"This is serious, Grace. He needs to put Mama first."

"He's busy." Grace rubbed her aching temple. "Between his regular stops and Uncle Roy hiring him to do maintenance while he's gone, Roan's swamped. But he said he'd get to it."

"I don't care. He should drop everything and see to Mama."

"Like you have?"

The minute the words slipped from her tongue, Grace grimaced.

"What's that supposed to mean?"

"You live right here in town, Faith. Surely

you could have made arrangements to have the steps fixed after Mama fell the first time."

Faith raised a brow. "And how do you expect me to do that when I have two kids to take care of?"

"It doesn't take that long to make a call. Do it while the kids are napping."

"Oh, that's easy for you to say. You with your cushy job—"

"—who has to drop everything when one of my family members has a problem they can't handle on their own."

"No one made you boss, Grace."

"Really? I seem to remember you taking off when we could have used your help at Put Your Feet Up. And where is Nathan? He should be here taking care of the business, not me."

"Don't put this off on me. If you hadn't turned Daddy—"

"Stop right there." She was getting tired of hearing the same accusations over and over as an excuse for just about everything that went wrong in their lives. "I didn't turn Daddy in. And have you all forgotten he willingly broke the law?"

Before Faith had a chance to answer, Grace noticed whimpering coming from the back seat. She twisted around to see John crying, fat tears rolling down his freckled cheeks.

"Now you upset my son," Faith berated her.

Leaning over to pat her nephew's knee, Grace murmured what she hoped were soothing words. At this moment, she needed them as much as John.

Thankfully they pulled up before their mother's house seconds later to find her sitting on the front steps, cradling her arm to her chest.

"Oh, no," Grace exclaimed as she bolted from the car. "Mama. Are you okay?"

"I think so. If it wasn't for the darned step."

"I should have had someone out here to fix it."

"Gracie, you can't do it all. I should have made arrangements. It's my house after all."

At her mother's admission, Grace stepped back and blinked.

"Did you fall on your arm?" Faith asked as she approached, Lacey on her hip, holding John's hand.

"I tried to keep from twisting my ankle again, so I sort of rolled onto my shoulder."

Grace closed her eyes. How could she have let this happen to her mother? A second time?

"We should get you to the hospital," Grace said, her stomach in knots.

"I'm sure it's nothing," her mother insisted,

but her face was pale. "I don't want to go back to that place."

"If not the hospital, at least let us take you to the clinic," Faith interjected.

"If you don't mind…"

"Grace," Faith instructed, "go get Mama's purse while I help her to the van."

Blinking at her sister, wondering if Faith was trying to prove she could handle an emergency after their argument, she then ran inside, gathered up the purse and a sweater, and hurried out to find her mother already buckled into the van. She jumped into the third row and they were off.

"Mama, what were you thinking?" Faith asked.

"I just went out for the mail."

"On your bandaged ankle?"

"I needed some fresh air," came her mutinous reply.

"Well, don't worry," Faith assured her. "We'll get that step fixed in no time so you don't have any more falls."

Grace silently fumed. Faith was definitely trying to prove a point. At the clinic her sister took charge of checking their mother in. Deciding not to fight this battle, Grace helped Wanda Sue over to a row of molded plastic chairs and sat with her. This was what she wanted, right?

For her siblings to step up to the plate? John wandered over. He stopped in front of Grace, sniffling. Her heart melted, and she scooped him up to nestle in her lap.

"Will Memaw be okay?"

Grace squeezed her nephew, who smelled of little boy, outdoors and baby shampoo. "Yes. Memaw will be fine."

Her mother patted John's knee in agreement and she felt him relax.

After twenty minutes, the nurse finally called her mother's name. Grace nodded to Faith, indicating she should be the one to go. Faith lifted her brow in surprise, but went with their mother and took the baby with her. Grace stayed put, John secure in her lap.

John twisted around to face her, his little finger tracing her cheek.

"You crying?"

Grace lifted her hand to feel her cheek. She had been so caught up in the newest crisis that she was indeed crying and hadn't noticed. Had Faith? Was that why she went so willingly with their mother?

"Yeah, buddy. I am."

"Why?" he asked, interest in his keen eyes.

She let out a short laugh. "Oh, my. That would be a long story to tell."

John cocked his head, then leaned over to

kiss her chin. "I kiss boo-boo and you feel better." His words brought another round of tears she didn't miss, or wipe away, this time. For once it felt good to let go of her emotions instead of bottling them up just to please everyone else.

An image of Deke flitted through her mind and she selfishly wished he wasn't here. There was something about his calming presence, his solid strength, that she wanted to draw from right now. Plus, his arm around her shoulder would be a welcome gesture. Blowing out a breath, she brushed away the fantasy.

This short reprieve wouldn't last long. Soon she'd know Mama's diagnosis and no doubt would remain in Golden for her entire leave. No early return to Atlanta. No salvaging her career, which kind of felt like a boat with a big, gaping hole, sinking under the water.

Time passed as she read John two children's books she found in the waiting room. She'd just started number three when the door opened. Her mother emerged first, a sling supporting her arm. Spirits sinking further, Grace put the book aside and took John to join the others.

"Well?"

"I bruised my shoulder. Nothing's broken, thank goodness, but the doctor says I'll be sore for a while."

"He wants to check her again in a few days," Faith added, the paperwork stuffed under her arm. Grace reached for it and, after a brief hesitation, Faith handed it over. She scanned the diagnosis, the fees and the prescription quickly before herding them back to the van.

"Mama, you shouldn't be alone," Grace said as Faith drove through town.

"It's no problem, Gracie. I'm used to it."

Another kick to the gut.

"Why don't you stay with us at the cabin tonight? Or we could all go stay at your house."

Faith sent her a sharp look in the rearview mirror but Grace ignored her.

"You wouldn't mind?"

"Not at all."

"Then let's go to the cabin. I've been cooped up in the house for so long, this will be like a family vacation. Memaw with her daughters and grandbabies."

"Party?" John asked as he clapped his little hands.

"Of course we can have a party," she answered, her spirits visibly rising.

"And this will give us time to talk about the business," Faith said quickly.

Grace stilled. "What about it?"

"Not here," her mother said, stopping the

conversation in its tracks, giving Grace a bad feeling.

When they reached the cabin, Grace got her mother settled on the couch, then ran back out to fill the prescription and stop for groceries. It was late afternoon now and Grace had to fight the after-work crowd in the stores. She finally made it home and the first thing she did was give her mother a pain pill. Changing out of the outfit she'd worn all day into a short-sleeved, yellow T-shirt and jeans, she joined her family for the spaghetti dinner Faith had prepared, waiting for the bombshell her sister was about to lob her way. It finally landed when they finished eating.

"So, Mama and I were talking," Faith said, pushing the last of her pasta around her plate. "She thinks it would be a good idea if I started working at the office."

Grace glanced at her mother. She'd actually listened to Grace's suggestion?

"You can teach Faith the ropes before leaving," her mother added. "Then if I need time off or something else happens, we won't rely on you so much."

Good idea in theory, but first she had to train her sister, who'd never shown the least bit of interest in the family company.

"Faith, this isn't something you can say you

want to do, then drop when you get bored," Grace warned.

Her sister visibly bristled. "I want to learn."

"Why now?"

"Why not now?"

There was more Faith wasn't saying, but with the don't-undermine-me look on her mother's face, Grace decided not to press her sister.

"After today, Mama clearly won't be back in the office as soon as we'd hoped. I can take up the slack."

Grace rubbed at her temples. The headache was returning. She looked at her mother. "Are you sure?"

"Yes, Grace. I want Faith in."

Her mother's decision would hopefully take some of the weight off Grace. Once things were under control here, she could return to Atlanta with a clean slate. Her spirits lifted until she glanced over to catch the fleeting indecision cross Faith's face and realized her escape hinged on her younger sister, who had never followed through on a promise in her life.

CHAPTER EIGHT

DEKE SAT ON the porch as dusk settled over the surrounding woods, listening to the loud scissor-snapping vibration of cicadas, thinking about the job, his mother's situation, the course of his life and Grace, whom he couldn't banish from his mind. The temperature had dropped after an extremely warm day, making for a pleasant evening. He'd just decided to check in with his brother Dylan when Grace rushed out of the cabin, slamming the screen door behind her.

Even though it was twilight, and she was a good distance away, he couldn't miss the tension in her shoulders, her determined pace eating up the ground as she stalked into the dense tree line. Despite his intentions of not inserting himself into her life, he stood, grabbed the flashlight he'd left on the porch and strode after her.

"Wait up," he called out when he was a few feet away.

Grace slowed down but didn't look happy to have her personal space invaded.

Racking his mind to come up with a good

conversation opener, he said, "Heard about your mother."

She stopped in her tracks, nearly tripping over an exposed tree root. "How?"

"I was at the warehouse with Roan when you called him."

She nodded, then continued walking.

"Is she okay?"

"Banged up her shoulder. She didn't break any bones, thank goodness, but she'll be sore for a few days."

"I saw a woman get out of the van with all of you earlier. Your mom?"

"Yes. She's staying with us tonight."

Apparently Grace was indulging only in small talk, so he'd take up the slack. "Roan said he'd take a look at your mother's front steps tonight."

Silence.

"Nice guy. Another admirer?"

She turned her head, eyes wide. "Uh, no. I'm not that popular."

"Just an observation."

"An incorrect one. Roan lost his wife a little over a year ago and he's still grieving. He and his daughter came home to Golden and my uncle hires him to help out here and there."

"Sorry to hear that."

"You probably noticed he's a man of few words."

"Yeah. What you told me explains it. He's got that...haunted look in his eyes."

One he understood all too well.

The light started to dim as they moved farther into the thick of the forest. Trees huddled closer together, the path became a little trickier to navigate with undergrowth and dead leaves scattered over the rich dirt.

"Where are you stomping off to?"

"My happy place." She shot him a pointed look. "Where I usually go to be alone."

He nearly chuckled at her disgruntled tone but decided she was already uptight and his laughing wouldn't go over well. "Then you won't mind me joining you?"

"You're a bright man. You know what *alone* means."

"I'm also bright enough to bring a flashlight. By the looks of things, you'll be walking home in the moonlight."

"I know my way by heart."

"Still doesn't hurt to be prepared."

"Fine, you can tag along as long as you're quiet."

"Works for me."

They walked for fifteen minutes. True to her word, Grace did know where she was going.

She kept to the path, knew when to duck under low-hanging branch limbs or step over fallen tree trunks. Before long he heard a gushing sound and noticed the scent of damp air. They passed into a clearing by a stream. A medium-sized waterfall took center stage.

Water tumbled over a ragged outcrop of rock into a lazy swirl before traveling downstream. Dry boulders were scattered around the water's edge. Grace climbed up on one and stretched her legs out as she viewed the splashing cascade glistening in the moonlight.

Following suit, he clambered up next to her. With a huff she scooted over.

"Nice happy place."

"I've always thought so."

"By the look on your face you came here to do some thinking."

She shrugged.

"Family?"

"Always."

He chuckled out loud. "I know the feeling."

She glanced over her shoulder at him. In the waning light her eyes were bright and inviting, her skin luminous. Her hair, mussed after the hike through the woods, framed her pretty face and he found himself wondering what it was about this woman he couldn't resist.

His perusal was interrupted when Grace

said, "Starting tomorrow there will be some changes at Put Your Feet Up."

He leaned closer, enjoying the warmth of her body heat and the scent of cherry blossoms. "Is that so?"

He felt her slump. "I'll be training my sister to work in the office."

"Is that a good thing?"

"I haven't decided yet."

"Because…?"

"Are you sure you're a forensic investigator?" She twisted to face him. "Seems like you'd make a better interrogator."

"Part of the charm."

"I suppose it wouldn't hurt to talk to you," she huffed. "Even though you work for us, you aren't related and I guess I need to vent."

"I can be as impartial as the next guy."

Looking away, she focused on the surging waterfall. Long seconds ticked by and he started to wonder if she'd trust him enough to reveal whatever was bothering her. He might regret it later, but he really wanted her to lean on him right now because he doubted she let her guard down very often.

"If it makes you feel any better, I understand tricky family dynamics," he said in way of encouragement. "Believe me, my brothers and I have gotten into hearty disagreements from time to time. We're competitive to a fault and try to outdo each other on a regular basis, but I know I can rely on them no matter what's going on in my life." He paused. Thought of his father, a man he'd looked up to, even after he'd been gone for many years. "I guess because my dad always made sure to treat each one of us differently. He picked up on our interests and took special time with each of us. Gave us confidence no matter what road we traveled down."

"And your interest was?"

"Books. Science." Deke smiled at a memory. "He used to take me to museums. Just the two of us, nerding out. I never really fit into a steady group of friends, but my dad made sure to let me know I was loved."

"That's wonderful for you. My father wasn't quite so invested."

"I noticed there was no Mr. Harper around to give your mom a hand."

Her body tensed, and he would have given anything to see her expressive eyes. "Took off for parts unknown after finishing a stint in prison."

Okay, that was unexpected.

Pinching the bridge of her nose, she said, "After I put him there."

"Whoa. Back up."

She let out a big sigh and inched a little closer to him. "Well, technically I didn't put him there. My mouth did."

"You aren't a very coherent storyteller."

"It's a time in my life I don't usually get all nostalgic over."

"So what happened?"

"One day I came to the office after school and overheard my dad talking on the phone. I was in the hallway leading to the rear door, so he never saw me, but he was talking to someone about a delivery. He said it was coming from Atlanta and they had to meet the truck up at Bailey's Trail at midnight. I thought that was weird because we didn't normally have anything delivered to the office and midnight was way too late for a hike in the woods. Then my dad said he had a major buyer, which seemed off. Buyer for what? When I finally walked into the office, he gave me a big hug and asked me to tell my mother he wouldn't be home for dinner, that he had an errand to run."

As she told the story, she leaned into him, probably unaware she was doing so. Deke stayed still, not wanting her to come to her senses and move away. He hated to see this normally in-control, vibrant woman beating herself up over her father's actions.

"He'd been missing dinner, scheduled tour

trips and other family outings often, and my mom was always miffed at him. I just shrugged off my dad's request, hating to bring Mama bad news. Later that afternoon Uncle Roy and a bunch of his buddies came by the office and he'd asked where my dad was. I told him I didn't know, but that he was going after a delivery later and my uncle's face turned a funny shade of red. He asked when and where, and I told him. That night, my dad got busted for dealing drugs."

"And you had no idea?"

"No. I was fifteen. Naive about the world. Other than the fact that my parents were arguing a lot, I was just like any high school kid."

"What happened then?"

"He was arrested, stood trial, got sentenced to time in prison. No one ever admitted who tipped off the police. My mother retreated, still in denial to this day. My uncle, who suspected what my dad had been up to but could never prove anything until our conversation, poured himself into running both our business and the cabins. Faith rebelled and Nathan followed in Daddy's footsteps."

"Selling drugs?"

"No, finding the easy way out. Apparently my dad got tired of the day-to-day grind and wanted a fast way to make money. He got hooked up with a guy he used to know from the next town and they decided to funnel drugs into Golden, which didn't go well with local law enforcement or the residents. My family became outcasts after that, until the trial proved only my father was part of the drug business. I took over Put Your Feet Up shortly afterward."

"I get it now."

"Get what?"

"Why you're a criminal attorney."

"That obvious?"

"Now that I know your story, it makes sense."

"So if I were to know your story, I'd understand why you became a cop?"

He rested his chin on top of her head. "My dad was police commissioner. All my brothers are in law enforcement."

Making space between them, she said, "Who'd have thought, the daughter of a criminal sitting here chatting the night away with the son of an upstanding policeman."

"Doesn't make us perfect."

"Bet you didn't have kids making your life miserable in school."

"I was bookish and quiet. They picked on me anyway."

"Did your brothers stand up for you?"

"I never let them know, but if I had, they would have intervened."

"Must be nice."

"Your family isn't so bad."

"Really? Faith took off and Nathan goofed off. No relying on them then or now."

"Maybe your sister working in the office will change things. For the better."

"I'm not holding my breath. Faith is usually all about Faith."

"She has her own family now. Hopefully her priorities have changed."

Grace stared at the water. "I guess I'll find out."

They went silent for a time, both caught up in their own thoughts. Deke would definitely have to deflect swapping family details if he wanted to keep the reason he was in Golden a secret, but sharing stories had given him a new insight into the woman he found more fascinating every moment he spent with her.

Grace eased back against him. "What a pair."

Deke fingered the ends of her hair, enjoying the soft silky strands sliding across his skin.

"So, is there a significant other in your life?" He had to ask. "Hiding out in Atlanta maybe?"

"Right. Between my family woes and my work hours, who has time to date?" She rested her head on his shoulder. "You?"

"No one serious."

"What about that friend you talked about?"

His stomach jolted. Here was an opportunity to open up about what had happened, to ease his guilty conscience. Instead he went for easy. "Her name was Britt. We tried to date once, but were better off as friends. I actually introduced Britt to her future husband and they clicked in a way she and I never did."

Truth be told, he'd been jealous and hurt, but as time went on, he realized Britt was right. He became buddies with her husband and he'd been adopted into the family as Uncle Deke after the birth of her sons. In a way, she still owned a tiny piece of his heart. Not in a romantic way, he'd come to realize, but part of a loving friendship he missed terribly. He'd never found anyone to fill that void, until now. In a short time, Grace had touched those empty places inside him.

He shifted, moving Grace so she faced him. Yeah, she did it for him. Her eyes glittered in the sliver of moonlight filtering through the leafy tree limbs. Her gaze met his and when he saw approval there, he didn't hesitate. He leaned down. Covered her lips with a gentle brush. She inched forward, placing her delicate hands on his chest. His heart raced beneath her palms, so he kissed her again, this time with greater intention. She went soft against him, returning his kiss with an ardor of her own. He forgot why he was in Golden, the personal conversation they'd just shared here in the middle of the woods and why going this far was probably not a smart idea. All he was capable of recognizing was how Grace made his blood speed through his veins. She touched him in a way no one had ever done—how, he couldn't begin to explain. She was so wrong for him, this attorney who defended criminals and took care of her family above all else, leaving no room for others in her life. Yet this kiss couldn't have felt more right.

He would have kept tasting her lips for hours if she hadn't pulled away, her voice breathy when she said, "I, um, think we should head back."

"Grace, I'm sorry if I stepped over the line."

"It's…" She waved her hand as if to brush the kiss away, but the gesture hit him like a punch to the gut.

"You work for me, Deke. And without Nathan, I can't risk messing up and having you leave me shorthanded."

Her words sobered him. Work. She was all about work.

Sliding off the boulder, he held out his hand to help her down. He'd be lying if he said he wasn't disappointed by her decision, but he understood. She'd been looking out for her family for years before he came into her life. Wasn't he here because of that same loyalty to family? Grace wasn't the type to throw caution to the wind and start something with him that might affect the family business in a negative way. It made him admire her all the more for her stand, while at the same time his heart wavered with a funny ache.

As she started along the path, he flicked on the flashlight to illuminate the trail.

"Maybe if you decide to go back to Atlanta and your old job, we can see where this leads," she said, her voice muted as she led the way.

He stepped on a twig and it snapped, just like the mood. If they were both back in Atlanta that meant she'd be defending criminals he was trying to put away. And how exactly would that lead to moving closer? He'd be betraying Britt's memory, and right now, he couldn't take that step.

"We'll see," he said, tempering his tone. He noticed her shoulders tense and realized he'd driven a spike between them and the tender moment they'd just shared.

"WHY CAN'T YOU just file the request form like I showed you?" Grace asked after correcting Faith for the third time Wednesday morning.

"I don't see what the big deal is."

"The deal is we have a pipeline so the booking requests don't get lost."

"I can remember."

"Really. With Lacey crying and John wandering off?"

"So it's not ideal, but I want to learn, Grace."

"Then please follow the protocol I've put into place."

"Fine." Her sister muttered under her breath, taking the printed request and making a grand show of placing it in the right slot on the shelf on the wall.

The phone rang and Faith grabbed it. "Hello."

Grace closed her eyes and counted to ten.

"Ah, I mean Put Your Feet Up."

Grace lifted one eyelid and squinted at her sister, who was hunting for a pen. Grace had just placed the ones scattered across the desktop back into the holder.

"Yes, we have boats."

Grace cringed again. Mouthed, "Canoes."

"Right canoe trips. I'd be happy to give you the information."

Faith rattled off the packages from the detailed notebook Grace had stayed up late last night preparing. Once she'd returned to the cabin after a terse goodbye to Deke, her mother had informed her that Faith was starting work first thing the next morning. Then she'd gone to sleep in Grace's bed. Since the lumpy couch was going to keep her up anyway, she'd stayed busy until three that morning, detailing vacation packages, costs and schedules. Thankfully Faith had read through it a few times and was booking tours with Grace's assistance.

They had both dressed in a skirt and blouse for work today, but Grace noticed the frayed cuffs Faith tried to hide. Were things worse than Faith let on? Lyle hadn't been back to the cabin and Grace didn't know if Faith had enough money to get by. A sobering thought. Suddenly Faith's situation took on a whole new light.

Taking a breather, she went to the small office fridge and removed two juice boxes. She pulled up a chair, opened the straw and stuck it in the cardboard container to hand to her nephew. "I think we deserve a break."

John dropped the truck he'd been running across the floor, sound effects and all, and sat back. "Yeah. We workeded hard."

Grace grinned and sipped the sugary juice after inserting her straw. She could have gone for another soda right now, but she didn't dare leave Faith alone.

"Mommy do good?" John asked.

Surprised by the question, Grace nodded. "Yes. Why would you ask?"

"We said an extra prayer last night. Mommy do good and make you happy."

Her heart twisted as she glanced from John's sincere face to her sister's. She was trying desperately to follow Grace's instructions. Instead of sniping, Grace should cut her some slack.

"Yes. Thank you for contacting us," Faith finished up the call. She filled out the form, stared at it for a few moments, then tossed it across the desktop.

Grace loudly cleared her throat.

"Come on, Grace, you are so fussy," she said as the office door opened.

"She may be fussy but she runs the best vacation outfit in north Georgia."

"Nathan," Faith screeched and ran around the counter to hug their baby brother.

His dark blond hair was longer than the last time Grace had seen him, his face pale from lack of sun. Once he was back outdoors, he'd tan quickly. Grace rose slowly, making her way toward the happy reunion.

Her brother's brown eyes, so much like their father's, searched her face as she approached before he pulled her into a bear hug. She had to admit, it was good to see the doofus, so she returned the hug with gusto. Then stepped away and slapped him on the shoulder. "Where have you been?"

"Here and there," he answered cryptically, getting down on one knee to open his arms for John, who beelined toward him and wrapped his little arms around Nathan's neck.

"How are you doing, buddy?"

"Got a new truck."

Nathan ruffled John's hair. "Good for you."

John returned to his toys, leaving Nathan without anyone to hide behind, which was good because Grace had plenty to say.

"Nathan, we need to get you up to speed. While you were—"

He placed a finger over her mouth and she swatted it away. "What are you doing?"

"Stopping your tirade before it begins."

She slammed her hands on her hips.

"Look, I know you all don't appreciate me being MIA. But I'm back, ready to work and to look after Mama."

Grace wasn't sure she believed him but wasn't going to argue. They needed another tour guide.

"Fine. I'll skip the lecture."

He grinned, all easygoing and not a care in the world, but Grace didn't miss the shadows lurking in the depths of his eyes. She knew her brother well enough to accept he would never confide in her, so she crossed her fingers and hoped for the best.

"Heard you hired help. A cop? Really, Grace?"

"He was the only one to apply for the job and since I couldn't locate you, it worked out." She frowned. "How did you know he was a cop?"

"Mama."

Hmm. Seems her family members had had more conversations than her mother had disclosed.

"Mama may not be thrilled about a cop in the midst, but I don't care. Deke is doing a great job."

Nathan laughed. "Yeah, Mama wasn't happy about him being the police, even though she told you to hire him."

Grace rolled her eyes.

"Since he's here to stay, we'll work it out." He glanced around the office. "Something looks different."

"I cleaned," Grace answered.

"No, more…" His eyes lit on Faith. "You're working here?"

"You didn't know?"

"I haven't spoken to Mama in a few days."

So Grace was right, Mama had been keeping Nathan up to speed.

Faith's jaw tensed. "Got a problem with that, little brother?"

"Are you kidding?" A big smile crossed his face. "This is great. I always wanted you to join us but you were busy with the kids. And then Lyle..." He broke off, a frown creasing his brow.

Faith stared at him, eyes round with surprise. "Why didn't you say anything?"

He shrugged. "Doesn't matter. You're here now."

"See, Grace? Someone is glad I'm working."

"I never said—" She stopped short. Sighed. Her protests would only land on deaf ears.

Nathan rubbed his hands together. "So, where do I start?"

Grace rounded the desk. "Let's see what's scheduled." She pulled up the calendar on the computer and was about to update Nathan when the back door opened. Deke, tall, strong, solid and way too good-looking for her peace of mind, strode into the office. He sent Grace a nerve-tingling smile before his perceptive eyes assessed the situation.

He took a step toward Nathan, hand out. "You must be the third Harper."

Nathan took his hand to shake, standing taller as he gave Deke a once-over. "Yep, and now that I'm back we'll have to divvy up the work."

"Sounds good to me." He handed Grace a clipboard and keys. "All hikers accounted for and the van is parked out back."

"Thanks."

Their fingers brushed as she took the board. Controlling the shiver that wanted to skate up and down her arms, she sent a covert glance toward her siblings. She'd never hear the end of it if they suspected she was attracted to Deke. Pointing at the calendar on the screen, she scooted out of the way when Deke moved so close his arm brushed hers. Good grief, what was wrong with her today? This was the first time she'd seen him since the kiss in the woods last night. A kiss she hadn't stopped thinking about.

Before long, Deke and Nathan were working on the allocation of tours while Faith carried on with phone calls. Finding herself not needed, she sat down near John, who stood and crawled into her lap.

"Boat?"

She wasn't sure what he was talking about, but when she noticed John staring at Deke, she remembered the day they'd carried the canoes to the lake. "You want to go out on the boat?"

John bounced up and down. "Boat. Boat."

What had she done?

Deke came over to kneel before her nephew, close enough for her to smell his crisp, woodsy scent. Her toes curled in her sensible pumps.

"You remember taking the canoes to the lake?"

John nodded, his eyes big. "Mama, let's go on lake?"

Faith bit her bottom lip. "I don't know, John."

Deke rose. "We have life vests his size and if you give us the okay, we won't venture far from shore."

"I suppose…"

"Boat. Boat."

Grace hid a grin. Oh, Faith had a child just like her.

"Okay, but only if you go, too, Grace."

Alarm bells clattered in her head. "I can't leave. We're working."

"And you haven't had a moment to do anything fun since you got here."

True, but the lake? With Deke? "I'm here to work. Not have fun."

"I can handle the office for a few hours," Faith assured her. Testing her, maybe?

"And since this afternoon is free," Nathan chimed in, "I can catch up with Mama and get ready for the next tour."

Were her siblings ganging up on her?

Deke glanced her way. "You'd let your nephew down?"

As if on cue, John looked up at her with wide, brown eyes.

"Sheesh. Okay. I'll go."

John jumped from her lap, clapping his hands.

Deke's smile took her breath away and suddenly a canoe trip on the lake seemed more than just about pleasing John.

"Give me about thirty minutes to get things ready," he said, then faced Nathan. "If you have a few minutes, I'd like to run an idea by you."

"Sure." Nathan hugged his sisters again, then slapped Deke on the shoulder. "So, what's on your mind?"

As the guys left, deep in conversation, Grace turned, ready to finish up so she could head back to the cabin and change for the excursion on the lake. She stopped short when Faith's knowing eyes met hers, sparkling with humor.

"What?"

"I see how it is."

Grace shook her head. "How what is?" *Please, please, please don't say it.*

"You and Deke?"

She said it.

"It's not what you think."

"Really? You didn't just get all gooey when he promised to take John on the lake?"

"It was nice of him."

"Nice." Faith snorted. "I saw you melt."

Grace rolled her shoulders. "I'm not having this conversation with you."

"Fine, but sis?"

"Yes?"

"It's about time you stop being all about work and let yourself get involved with a nice guy."

Was that what she was doing? Getting involved with Deke? From the look on Faith's face, her sister thought so.

She couldn't argue either.

Yikes. I'm in trouble here.

CHAPTER NINE

"HURRY, AUNT GRACE." John stood in the doorway, bouncing from one sneakered foot to the other.

"Hold your horses," she answered, scouring Faith's closet for the pair of boat shoes her sister had offered for the lake excursion. Since Grace had brought a limited wardrobe for her stay in Golden, and canoe trips weren't penciled into her day planner, she'd worried about having the right footwear. What she hadn't expected to find was what she believed to be all of Faith's worldly possessions stored here at the cabin.

"Found them," she sang out, slipping her feet into the canvas shoes. Taking a step back, she perused the closet, then scanned Faith's room. Unopened boxes were stacked in the corner, squeezed tightly beside the crib. Twin beds worked for Faith and John. On a hunch, Grace checked the dresser to find it packed with John's clothing.

Faith wasn't just here for a time-out with her husband. By the looks of it, she'd moved in permanently. Was this the reason for her sudden interest in the family business? As she investigated, Grace spotted a framed photograph of Faith and the kids. She crossed the room to pick it up, deciding it looked fairly recent.

John hammed it up for the camera, Lacey shared a gummy grin. Faith? No amount of makeup could hide the dark circles under her eyes. Hmm. No husband or father in the shot. This couldn't be good, but it explained why her sister had shown up here, willing to share the cabin with Grace. Had Faith left Lyle?

"Aunt Grace," John yelled from the living room, only to be shushed by his grandmother.

She replaced the picture. Making a mental note to get answers from her sister later, she smoothed the T-shirt she'd pulled on over shorts.

"Let's go," Grace said as she entered the other room, grabbing a pair of sunglasses from the coffee table. "We shouldn't be long," she assured her mother, who was trying to rub sunscreen on a squirming John.

"Be careful. John's so little, I don't want him falling in the lake."

The Harpers had learned early on that things happened out of your control, but it wasn't like Grace wouldn't be vigilant with her nephew.

A knock sounded on the screen door, followed by a deep voice. "Don't worry, Mrs. Harper. John's in good hands."

Tingles skittered over her skin as Grace's gaze jerked to the door. There stood Deke, still in the same T-shirt and cargo shorts from earlier, sunglasses perched on top of his head, smiling at her mother. He didn't share smiles often, but when he did, watch out.

Spreading leftover lotion on her forearm, her mother walked over to open the door. "Come on in."

Grace hurried to follow. Her mother hadn't met the newest employee yet, and since she had a thing about cops, Grace wasn't sure if she'd behave. "Mama, this is Deke Matthews."

"Figured as much."

Deke stepped into the living room, all broad shoulders, tanned skin and gorgeous dark blue-gray eyes, filling the room with his presence. He continued smiling at her mother. To win her favor, Grace wondered?

"Mrs. Harper. I was hoping we'd meet soon."

"Please, call me Wanda Sue." She tucked a chunk of graying hair behind her ear. "You've most likely heard I'm out of commission."

"Yes, ma'am, but I thought perhaps you'd be working soon. The way your children talk about you, it sounds like they really miss you at the office."

Grace could have sworn her mother blushed. "Why, that's so sweet of you to say."

"I only speak the truth."

Another trait Grace found wildly attractive, after dealing with her truth-elusive family.

As Deke and Mama spoke, Grace realized her mother was more animated. She'd already gotten rid of the sling and only grimaced as she moved her shoulder. Grace hadn't seen a glimpse of this woman since she'd handed the day-to-day running of the office over to her mother before moving to Atlanta.

Tears pinched Grace's eyes.

"So, are you guys ready?" Deke asked, turning his attention on her.

Under his steady gaze, Grace momentarily forgot what he was talking about. She shook her head. "Yes." Held out a hand to her nephew. "John?"

"Boat. Boat."

Deke chuckled. "One-track mind."

Her mother held the door open as they all strolled outside, her gaze straying to John as the earlier concern returned to her eyes.

"Don't worry, Wanda Sue," Deke assured her, giving the older woman's hand a quick squeeze. Deke certainly had a way of putting people at ease. Grace had seen it firsthand with the clients. And he'd managed to make her feel pretty calm a time or two. But to soothe her overanxious mother? His small gesture touched her deeply.

"Grace and I have this covered."

At his inclusion of her, Grace's heart took a nosedive. She was in more trouble than she thought.

"Silly of me, I know," her mother went on to say.

"I get it," Deke replied. "Family is important."

"Why yes, it is."

"Boat," John piped up.

"We won't be long, Mama." Grace kissed her mother's soft cheek then followed the guys outside. John was already rattling out question after question, which Deke answered patiently in an even tone.

The afternoon was just short of gorgeous. Fresh air filled Grace's lungs. Fluffy white clouds drifted in a crystalline blue sky. Black-eyed Susans popped up along the way, adding a splash of color to the well-worn path to the dock. As they drew closer, they could hear the water lapping against the lake's edge. For the first time in ages, she was actually going to enjoy an outing in the great outdoors.

They'd just reached the dock when the growling rev of an engine caught their attention. As it grew louder, Grace squinted, making out the souped-up truck rolling in their direction. The path they had taken from the cabin meandered through the foliage, whereas the truck had used the access road.

"Oh, no," she muttered.

"Trouble?" Deke asked.

"Oh, yeah." She tamped down her temper. "It's Lyle. Faith's not-great husband."

She started to take a step in the direction of the now-idling truck when Deke grabbed her arm. "Slow down. Let him tell us why he's here before jumping to any conclusions."

Sheesh. He was getting to know her pretty well.

The cab door opened, sunlight reflecting off the shiny red paint. Lyle jumped down, his boots kicking up dust from the dirt lane.

"There's my boy."

John, who had been studying the canoes, heard his father's voice and turned. "Daddy!"

Before Grace could catch him, John bolted toward Lyle. Deke moved to stand next to her, a heavy hand on her shoulder keeping her still.

Taking a calming breath, she moderated her tone, "Lyle, what are you doing here?"

He shot Grace a disgruntled look. "Can't stop by to see my boy?"

"I didn't say that."

"I got rights."

Oh, boy, that didn't sound good. Grace was

now convinced that Faith's marriage was in deeper trouble than she'd let on.

Deke stepped forward and held out his hand. "Deke Matthews. We didn't introduce ourselves the other day."

Lyle stared at him in silence, like he didn't understand the concept of common courtesy. Which he probably didn't. She'd never liked the way he treated Faith, and since her sister's recent actions were beginning to come clear, she held her tongue.

"Grace and I were just getting ready to take John out on the lake."

Lyle glanced over at her and wrinkled his nose like he smelled something bad. "Really? Not worried about getting your hair wet, Gracie?"

She ground her back teeth.

"Daddy, come on boat?"

Lyle glanced down at his son. "I'm here to pick you up," he answered.

Before Grace could jump into the conversation, Deke straightened his shoulders, pushed his sunglasses up on his head and leveled Lyle with the kind of cool stare she imagined made criminals nervous.

"Is that so?"

Lyle's bravado slipped a fraction. "Check with Faith if you don't believe me."

"Trust me, we will." He turned to Grace. "Let's go back to the cabin."

Right. She didn't have her phone on her, and by the shift of Lyle's eyes, she didn't know if he was telling them a story or not.

"Fine," he agreed, slamming the truck door closed.

"Nice truck," Deke said, rubbing his chin. "That the proper frame height?"

Lyle did a double take. "Sure it is."

"Looks a little high."

"Naw, I…uh…it's fine."

"If you say so."

Grace didn't know vehicle regulations, but from Deke's questions, he certainly did. His gaze met hers and when he nodded ever so slightly, she took his cue.

"I'm sure it's safe enough to take a toddler for a ride, don't you think, Deke?" Grace asked, her voice as sweet as honey.

Hiding a smile as Lyle flinched, Grace watched him try to divert attention from the truck by lifting John onto his shoulders. The little boy cried out in glee.

Her mother came out of the cabin as soon as they walked up, a frown creasing her brow. "Faith called to tell us Lyle would be here to collect John."

Lyle sent her a told-you-so smile.

Deke crossed strong arms over his broad chest, his voice ringing with authority. "I'm assuming you have the appropriate child car seat in the truck?"

Lyle frowned at Deke. "What are you, some kinda cop?"

"Actually, I am."

Lyle's face paled a shade. "I got the car seat. Stop hounding me."

Grace recognized the ornery glint in Lyle's eyes and laid her hand on Deke's muscular arm. Faith had given her husband permission to pick up their son. No one here might like it, but he wasn't breaking any laws.

She held out her arms, taking John from his father. Cuddling him close, she inhaled sunscreen and little boy, raining kisses on his face.

"Ew. Aunt Grace, stop."

"What? You don't like my kisses?"

He pushed her away, breaking into peals of laughter.

"We gotta go," Lyle cut in.

Deke nodded. "Memorized your license plate," he said, ruffling John's hair after Grace set him down.

"Got it," Lyle grumbled.

"We'll go out in the canoe another time," Grace promised.

John's face fell. "No boat?"

"Not today, son."

"But I want to."

Lyle tried to lead him back to the truck. "C'mon. We'll get some ice cream."

Feet planted firmly in place, John crossed his arms and pouted. "No."

Grace had seen his temper tantrums. This wasn't going to be pretty.

"Let me get the truck," Lyle said, taking off in a sprint.

Deke knelt beside John, said something low in his ear. The boy nodded. When it became apparent John wasn't going to pitch a fit, the truck arrived and they made sure Lyle strapped John safely into the car seat. What had started out as an idyllic afternoon was now marred by a rumbling engine and gas exhaust. The riotous clatter didn't fade until Lyle turned onto the main road, tires screeching as he hit the asphalt.

Grace winced and slipped her arm over her mother's shoulders. "He'll be okay."

Her mother patted Grace's hand. "I'd best call Faith and tell her that Lyle did stop by." She stepped from Grace's arm and stared down Deke. "Don't usually have much use for cops," she said, "but you'll do."

Deke choked on a laugh. "Thanks?"

"High praise," Grace said as she watched her

mother limp back into the cabin, needing the cane only for longer trips.

"I get that your family didn't like your dad being arrested, but really?"

She held up her hands and shrugged. "What can I say? The Harpers know how to hold a grudge."

"Remind me never to get on your bad side."

"Keep doing a good job and you have nothing to worry about."

He sent her a wary look, to which she responded with a big smile.

"Now that we've established you're scary, let's get that canoe in the water."

Grace did a double take. "Wait. We don't have to go now that John can't come."

"You backing out on me?"

"No. I mean…we were doing this for my nephew."

"And it's a shame he's going to miss out, but we don't have to." He tilted his head. "It's a beautiful day. You've already left the office. Why not enjoy a few hours of relaxation?"

"I appreciate the offer, but I…uh…think I'll go hang out with my mother."

She started to walk away when his next words stopped her in her tracks.

"Afraid to be alone with me?"

Yes. She composed her features and turned.

Threw a little sass into her voice. "Why would you think that?"

"John's gone and you're walking away. That leads me to the conclusion that you don't want to spend time with me."

"It's not that."

One brow rose.

"Okay, maybe it is."

"Because I kissed you?"

Her face grew hot. "Wow, that was quite a leap."

Deke's perceptive gaze captured and held hers. The truth lingered in the depths, along with a dare.

She squared her shoulders. "Don't flatter yourself."

He sauntered in her direction, his long legs eating the distance between them. "What if I promise to keep my lips away from yours?"

The dimples that appeared when he smiled so confidently did her in. Her stomach dipped and her heart protested. Problem was, she wanted to taste his lips again. Wanted the jolt of adrenaline that came only from his touch. The intensity of her feelings for the man scared her way more than paddling out into the middle of Golden Lake.

"Look, we'll make this a kiss-free zone. What do you say?" He lowered his sunglasses over his eyes and crossed his arms over his chest.

She cleared her throat, excitement mixing with dread. "Fine."

He swept out one arm in the direction of the dock. "After you."

Jutting her chin, she marched back to the ramp next to the canoe enclosure. "You can do this," she said under her breath, swearing she heard Deke's chuckle behind her. All she had to do was put one foot in front of the other. She'd faced down determined, hard-line prosecutors and won her cases. Surely she could handle one afternoon on the lake with her handsome employee.

Working together, they had the canoe half on the shore and half in the water. He tossed her an orange PFD, and after securing it in place, she took her single-bladed paddle to store at her end of the boat until they slipped completely into the water. Grace carefully duck-walked down the middle of the canoe, hands gripped to the sides as the boat swayed.

"Doing good," Deke praised.

"I think I know how to get into a canoe," she scoffed, then stood and turned to face him, nearly losing her balance in the process.

"Whoa. Watch it there, Captain. Keep your

center of gravity low so you don't tumble overboard."

Embarrassed, she lowered her stance, stepped over her seat and sat, facing forward. She looked over her shoulder to see Deke don his PFD and then toss a pack into the boat. One foot in the canoe and one on the ground, he pushed off before getting settled in his seat. They were paddling in perfect coordination in no time. It had been years since Grace had been in a canoe. It took some time to balance her weight, sway with the motion and remember just which stroke to use. All while she felt Deke's eyes on her back.

They settled into a steady rhythm, Grace setting the pace. As the boat skimmed the lake, water sprayed around them, cool on her heated skin. Minutes rushed by as all Grace thought about was the sun on her shoulders and the water around her, as far as the eye could see. The muscles in her arms protested quickly, reminding her that she had to get back to the gym. She wasn't sure how far they'd traveled, but they were in the middle of the lake when she heard Deke's voice call out, "Let's take a short break."

"No, I'm good."

"Grace, we could use some water. It's pretty calm right here so let's stop."

"Fine."

Pulling her paddle from the water, she rested it beside her, then swung her feet over the seat to turn and face Deke. He was rustling inside his pack. After removing a bottle of water, he tossed it to her. Her fingers slipped on the slick bottle and she fumbled, afraid it might go overboard. Her movements rocked the boat, and as soon as she caught the bottle, she immediately dropped it to brace her hands on the sides of the canoe.

"Just calm down, Grace. We're okay."

She cracked open the cap and glared in his direction. "Do not make fun of me."

"I wouldn't even consider it." He took a long swig of his water. Grace watched the muscles in his throat work and swallowed hard. He lowered the bottle and nodded to her.

Oh. Right. Water break. She lifted the bottle and nearly moaned out load as the cool liquid slid down her parched throat.

"Remind me again why you don't like the outdoors?"

She pointed the bottle at him. "Wise guy canoe mates like you."

He chuckled and took another drink.

Grace scanned the shoreline. Cabins and vacation homes dotted the landscape. Various watercraft scurried over the lake in the distance.

Tree limbs canopied the water at the shore, leaves spread out to create a natural umbrella.

"It's peaceful out here," she finally said. "I couldn't tell you the last time I was out on a boat."

Deke nodded, keeping his thoughts to himself. She'd noticed the way he would change the subject to focus on her instead of revealing any tidbits about his life.

"So tell me, what did you say to my nephew that took his attention away from the lake?"

"I reminded him that big boys are polite and listen to adults."

She practically snorted. "I can't believe he went along with that."

Deke shrugged. "I also told him his dad came first."

"Is that some guy code?"

"No." He paused. "Spending time with one's father is important."

"Let me guess, like you did with your dad?"

"I wouldn't trade it for anything. He guided me into the man I am today."

Grace took another sip of water, watching the emotions play over Deke's face. How she wished she'd had a father like his, had the knowledge that her father loved her. She'd never been quite sure how her father really felt about his family.

A shout went out as a catamaran sluiced by, a bunch of rowdy boys waving at them.

"Did you go boating with your brothers?" she asked as the waves rippled around them, gently rocking the canoe.

"Grew up on the coast in Florida. Pretty much lived in the water."

"Explains your expertise."

"Like you had any doubts? I told you I could canoe when you hired me."

"No doubts. You seem to be a man of your word."

"Seem?"

She shrugged. "Okay, are. As far as I can tell."

"You keep contradicting yourself."

"So sue me."

That one lifted brow said so much.

Time to turn the tables. "You seem to know a lot about me. Tell me something about you. You mentioned you didn't have a lot of friends. Why not?"

"I ended up escaping into books instead of running around outdoors with my brothers. I guess that's when I got used to being alone."

"Or lonely?" she asked.

"I never really equated being solitary with being lonely. I'm comfortable being by myself. Never needed a bunch of people around to make me feel whole. Guess I'm just wired that way."

She pointed to his oar. "Well, it looks like you caught up to your brothers. You can paddle a mean boat."

"I'm also a fast learner."

"I can see that. But what I really want to know is what brought you here. Not a vague answer but the real story."

He rested his elbows on his knees and gazed over the water. Was quiet for so long Grace didn't think he'd answer. When he looked at her, she couldn't decipher the expression in his eyes, but heard the pain in his voice when he said, "I blew my last case and Britt died because of it."

HE IGNORED GRACE'S sharp intake of air, determined to soldier on with the story. It had been haunting him for weeks now, keeping him awake at night, flashing into his mind at different times during the day. He didn't want to be the sole owner of the truth any longer.

"Britt died at the hands of a recently acquitted criminal who'd been released when his slick lawyer discovered a technicality. The case where I was the lead forensic investigator."

"Oh, Deke. I'm so sorry."

He nodded, his throat too thick for words.

"What happened?"

He took another long drink. Stalled a few more moments. He'd opened the door, might as well keep going.

"We got a call to a murder scene. We were short-staffed and I'd just worked a double shift." Deke's hands fisted. He'd been so sure he had all the evidence needed to convict the criminal who had forced his way into a home and brutally killed the occupant. After all, nearly every crime scene he'd been at brought a conviction. Why would this time be different? "My team and I worked the scene like we normally would."

"But?"

He focused on the sparkling water. "The case was pretty contentious. When we got to court, it came to light that the latent fingerprints extracted from the scene had been mislabeled by a member of my team. It became a technicality that was exploited unfairly." He ran a hand over his head, his hair damp from the splashing water while they were paddling. "I've gone over that night in my head hundreds of times, run through all the standard procedures, positive we did everything by the book." Yes, he'd been overworked when he caught the case, which was no excuse. The perp practically admitted to wrongdoing, but had Deke thought he was tougher and smarter than everyone else? The possibility taunted him day and night.

"I know that extenuating circumstances come into play during a trial," Grace said. "Granted, I haven't known you for long, but you seem like a very competent individual, so I imagine your work as an investigator is solid. Maybe it was just a fluke."

"I don't believe in flukes. We messed up. And I accepted responsibility for it." As he admitted the truth, the weight on his shoulders lifted for the first time in weeks.

"Are you sure?"

"Yes. The defense attorney noticed the mistake and jumped all over it."

"It's not like your team meant to make a mistake."

Tone grave, he said, "But we did."

Anyone else looking at the situation might suggest that Deke had no control over what happened next. He would disagree. "If the murderer hadn't gone free, he wouldn't have shown up at the bureau to exact revenge at the same time Britt was leaving work to head home to her family." He glanced at Grace. "She's gone because of me."

"Oh, Deke."

A speedboat zoomed up, preventing further conversation, which suited Deke just fine. The canoe rolled in the violent wake. Grace yelped, gripping the sides with white knuckles. He used the diversion to blink away the heat welling behind his eyes. Once they'd ridden the wake, the boat settled down, as well as his emotions.

"You okay?" he asked.

"Better than you, I'd imagine."

"Look, I'm not entirely sure why I dumped all that on you, but we don't need to dwell on my life's mistake." He'd said what he needed to say. Didn't want to rehash the memory over and over.

A slight smile curved her lips. "You're welcome."

That's what he liked about Grace. She got him enough to know he was finished spilling his guts. That, and she knew when to introduce humor into the conversation.

He felt a reluctant grin work its way over his lips. "Thanks."

Add kissing to the list of things he liked about her and it pretty much summed up his growing feelings for Grace.

"Anytime." She took her paddle in hand again and glanced at him. "But, Deke?"

He swallowed a groan.

"You can't hold on to the guilt forever. You had no idea how the court decision would set the series of events in motion."

"Easy for you to say." The guilt rose up and tackled him, just like it had the day he'd learned Britt had died.

"It is. It took me years to realize I wasn't the reason my father got arrested. He was guilty. He would have been caught eventually, whether I mentioned where he was going to my uncle or not. And that perp? The one who got away? He was a murderer. You didn't push him over the edge. He was already there."

He wanted to believe her words. He truly did.

"Time, Deke. Trust me, it takes time to let go of the guilt."

He nodded, unable to speak past the lump in his throat. He watched Grace swivel to face forward in her seat. They both placed their paddles in the water at the same time.

"Ready?" she called over her shoulder.

Was he? Somehow the answer seemed way more weighty than just the okay to get the boat moving again. "Let's go."

They glided over the water, evading speeding vessels and sailboats with folks yelling out happy greetings, making good time back to the dock. He could have spent the entire day on the water, letting the sun and waves take his cares away. But he'd noticed Grace straining, her arms probably jelly after the nautical miles they'd covered. "Slow down," he yelled, earning a thankful grin as she turned her head toward him.

"How much longer?" she called.

"Couple hundred feet."

"I'm starved. How about dinner tonight? My treat."

Deke's stomach rumbled. "I'll take you up on that."

"Great, you fire up the logs in the pit and I'll make burgers."

"Sounds like a plan." A plan he could live with. Spending the day with Grace had lifted his spirits in a way he'd never imagined possible. Had him thinking maybe he could find the means to forgive himself.

They hadn't moved much farther when Deke noticed Grace struggling.

"I think something's snagged my paddle." As Grace began to panic, her actions became jerky.

"What are you hung up on?"

"Can't tell. Maybe if I stand—"

"No," he shouted as she lifted herself from the seat and tugged on the paddle. The canoe dipped precariously, but she quickly sank back down, keeping them from tipping over.

"Nice save," he said as the boat leveled out. He positioned his paddle to guide them to the ramp. Looking ahead to check the distance, he slowed. But Grace had risen again.

"Not yet. We aren't—"

Too late, she tumbled over the side and into the water. Seconds later she surfaced, sputtering and holding the paddle over her head, just as Deke was ready to jump in after her.

"Wh-what happened?"

"You stood up."

"I was trying to get the paddle loose."

"Next time try to free it without standing up."

"Next time? Oh, no, there will be no next time." She fluttered about in the water as the canoe drifted and finally banked on shallow ground.

"Ew. Gross." She shivered, making her way to shore. "It feels like my feet are wrapped up in old clothes."

"It's only leaves," he said as he stepped from the canoe, pulling it on shore and then wading into the water. Grace stumbled toward him. Meeting where the water was waist high, he held out his hand, ready to assist her to dry land. When her hand was secure in his, she yanked back with all her strength, pulled his PFD with her other hand and dragged him into the water with her.

"What the—"

Hilarious laughter greeted him as he lost his footing and ended up floundering beside her.

Righting himself, he wrapped an arm around her and they floated deeper into the cool, inviting waters.

"What was that for?" he asked.

"For convincing me to get into the canoe in the first place. I told you. I'm not outdoorsy."

He tugged her closer. "Really? I think you protest too much."

As they treaded water, their legs tangled, but Deke made no move to back away. Their body heat mingled and before he realized what had happened, she'd slipped her arms around his neck and brought her face close to his.

"My hero," she whispered against his lips.

"I don't think it constitutes being a hero when you were wily enough to drag me into the water."

Her eyes grew serious. "Not this. Your job. What you do in order to protect others. That makes you a hero."

"I don't—"

She placed a finger over his lips to silence him, then leaned in and replaced it with her soft lips. His hands circled her waist, drawing her against his chest. She nearly took his breath away, not only with her words but how she kissed him as if he were the most important thing in her world. Because, if he were honest, he was beginning to feel like that about her.

Grace broke away, her eyes shining as she smiled at him.

"What do you say we change into some dry clothes," he suggested, voice raspy with emotion.

"I say lead the way."

Taking her hand, they trudged out of the water. After placing the canoe back in the enclosure, he said, "We still on for dinner?"

"I'm not sure. Not after you dumped me in the water."

"You stood up."

Her eyes sparkled with amusement. "You should have warned me again."

"I tried but you were already pitching over the side. It was too late."

"And that's supposed to make me feel better?"

He chuckled as they began walking back to the cabins, water squishing in their shoes, clothes dripping lake water. "You promised dinner and there's no getting out of it."

"You're right. I offered." She squeezed the moisture from her T-shirt. "Seven. I'll meet you at the firepit."

At the cabins, they parted ways. He watched Grace, a smile hovering over his lips. His chest went tight, not from the usual pain he'd been living with, but something else entirely. Taking a moment to decipher the strange feeling overwhelming him, he realized he felt lighthearted. In his confiding in Grace, in her not judging him, instead speaking positive words, Grace had given him an unexpected gift. Hope. With a joyful hop in his step, he jogged to the cabin, fervently clutching this optimism close while at the same time choosing to ignore the inner voice taunting, *How long can this last?*

CHAPTER TEN

STEAMING COFFEE CUP in hand, Deke stood in front of Blue Ridge Cottage the next morning, mentally reviewing his strategy to fish information out of Serena Stanhope. He'd texted Dylan beforehand, mostly to let his brother know he hadn't fallen down on the job. He'd been busy. First, with work, then, figuring out his mixed emotions about letting Grace deeper into his life. Their professional goals did not intersect, except maybe in the courtroom, which Deke didn't want to consider.

He still couldn't believe he'd mentioned his last case to Grace. Yes, she'd gently pushed, but he didn't have to respond. He'd grown adept at deflecting his feelings, but there was something about her that had grabbed hold of his heart and he didn't want to walk away until he saw how this played out. Risky? Maybe. He'd never opened up to Britt as quickly when they'd first become friends, but for once in his life he was willing to put his emotions out there and see what happened. He might admit to being solitary, but he wanted Grace and all it entailed.

And if the spark in their kisses was any indication, this attraction wasn't totally one-sided.

Back to the plan at hand. He took a sip, savored the dark blend, getting his game face in place. The day had dawned cool, great for running through the dense woods surrounding the cabin. He'd found a well-worn path that led to the lake the second day he'd arrived. His runs had become a daily ritual he enjoyed, especially in the quiet dawn when he shoved all of life's concerns away. This morning, he'd watched the water lighten from a dark blue as sunlight painted the sky. After a childhood spent cooped up inside with allergies, being able to enjoy nature still filled him with gratitude and appreciation.

Of course, the outdoors was the place where he'd kissed Grace, twice, so there was that.

His phone rang, dragging him from his ruminations, and he checked the caller ID. Groaned when he saw it was Derrick. Taking a bracing breath—because this was Derrick—he answered the phone with trepidation.

"What's going on, bro?" How like his older brother to bypass the pleasantries and get right to the crux of the conversation.

"Not much. Working."

"Good. Good."

Silence. His brother had a way of dragging

things out of his siblings that was as impressive as it was annoying.

"Any news on the investigation?"

"As usual, your timing is perfect. I'm standing in front of the shop now."

Serena appeared inside to unlock the front door. She looked up, noticed Deke and waved.

"With a plan?"

"A loose one. I'll steer the conversation and see what happens."

"Is she pretty?"

Deke's radar went up at Derrick's deceptively casual tone. "The suspect?"

"Your boss."

How? How did his brother pick up on these things? "Why would you ask me that question?"

"Because instead of telling me about your investigation, the first thing you mentioned was the guide job."

"Hey, I needed a cover."

"Sure. And you also need a life. I get the feeling you're finding one in Golden."

Deke ground his back teeth at Derrick's smug analysis.

"So…tell me about your boss."

Taking a sip to stall, he decided there was no point trying to run his brother off track. He'd just snoop on his own. This way Deke could control the narrative.

"Her name is Grace and she's an attorney."

"Interesting. Go on."

"She's pretty. A go-getter. And a nurturer, even though she'd never admit it."

"Hmm. Quite a detailed description."

"You asked."

Deke heard the humor in his brother's voice. "Indeed I did."

"Why do you do this?"

"Because it's fun."

Deke shook his head, fighting the smile hovering over his lips. "You're the one who needs a life."

"I have one. A very good one, in fact."

Deke went in for the kill. "Except for the fact that you've never found Hannah."

Silence. Senior year, Derrick's high school sweetheart had left town in the dead of the night with her family. Derrick had searched, but never found her. He acted like her sudden disappearance didn't still bother him to this day, but Deke sensed otherwise.

This time Derrick sounded annoyed. "Low."

"Turnabout." Guilt swirled in Deke's stomach. "Yeah. I'm sorry. I hate when anyone noses in my business."

"I realize that, but I also know this solitary

thing isn't good for you. Go out and enjoy your life."

"You know that's not my thing."

"More like you're afraid to try."

The deep nagging sense that his brother was right unnerved Deke. Grace had already managed to nudge him from his comfort zone.

When he didn't answer, Derrick piped up. "Keep us in the loop after you speak to Serena Stanhope today."

"You know I will."

"Look, I get that you're happy alone, you don't want to put yourself out there, blah, blah, blah. But Grace would be lucky to have you. That's all I'm gonna say."

Deke chuckled. "That's all? Why am I sure you're lying?"

"Later, bro."

Shaking his head, Deke returned his phone to his back pocket, took a bracing sip of the phenomenally good coffee that Myrna at Sit a Spell had whipped up for him—this alone could keep him in Golden forever—then squared his shoulders and went into cop mode.

A bell tinkled overhead as he moved into the retail space. The soothing scent of lavender greeted him and once again he was impressed with the elegant yet inviting interior.

"Be right with you," came Serena's voice from the back.

Since most businesses along Main Street had just opened, tourists weren't out and about yet, giving Deke the perfect chance to speak to Serena without interruption. As she walked from the back room, she slowed her pace upon seeing him, her blue eyes wide, her long, straight black hair swirling around her shoulders, but she quickly regrouped and pasted a wide smile on her face.

"Deke. Nice to see you again."

He strolled toward her, pasting an equally pleasant smile on his face. "Same here. I have some free time this morning so I came here to ask for your help."

Her brow wrinkled. "Me?"

"Yes. My mother's birthday is coming up and I'd like to get her a present. She loves writing her friends, so I thought your shop was a perfect place to start."

What he imagined to be relief eased the tension from her face.

"What did you have in mind?"

Glancing around the store brimming with inventory, he said, "I'm not really sure."

She stepped from behind the counter and headed to a rustic hutch filled with colorful boxes and doodads. "I keep all the notepads, stationery and similar items on this side of the store." She pointed at the far wall. "You can find a card over there."

"Okay. So what do you recommend?"

"You said she likes to write to friends, so I would go with a nice stationery set." She took a few packaged boxes from the hutch. "They're all custom-made and have a special pen included. Here are just a few."

"Is it okay if I set my coffee cup here?" he asked, indicating an empty table nearby.

"Sure. We use this area for specialty classes so it'll be fine."

"What kind of classes?" he asked, as he accepted the boxes from her.

"Calligraphy. Penmanship. Creating your own card designs, that sort of thing."

"Nice."

"I think so. Everyone is always so busy sending messages on their phones, it's like we've lost the art of personalizing our correspondence." She sighed. "Guess it's my way of going back to a less hectic way of life."

"Looks like it's worked." He studied the boxes, one with a bird theme, the next, flowers and the third, an outline of the mountain landscape. "These are great. Where do you get your inspiration?"

"Locally. I love it here in the mountains."

"It's growing on me, too."

In the short time he'd been here, Golden had somehow gotten under his skin. Or was it the inhabitants of the town? Mainly, one Grace Harper.

He spent the next ten minutes looking around before settling on a stationery set and card, the flower theme evoking images of the floral shop where his mother lived and breathed. He placed the items on the counter.

"All set?" Serena asked as she looked up from a spreadsheet.

"I am. Thanks for the suggestions."

"All part of the service." She carefully wrapped the box in sparkly tissue and placed it in a navy blue bag with the store logo printed on an oval white sticker—the outline of the mountains around the sketch of a small cottage and the store name.

Time to move ahead with the plan.

Two women had just come in, chatting about a special order. Moving around the store as Serena finished bagging up his purchases, he made the motion of tripping, then tilted his coffee cup just enough that the liquid dribbled on his hand.

"Great," he uttered, making a big production of shaking his hand. Serena hurried over.

"Are you okay?"

"I spilled my coffee with my clumsy move. Do you have a restroom where I can clean up?"

"Sure. In the back to the right."

"Thanks." He glanced over to the women watching them. "Why don't you help these ladies. We can finish my transaction when I come back."

"Of course."

While Serena went off to help her customers, Deke disappeared into the back room. He scanned the area, discovering a storeroom, small office and bathroom. He hurried to rinse off his hands and threw the cup away, quietly returning to the office.

Small workspace, but neat. He quickly looked for any clue that would tie Serena to James Tate. Nothing obvious, not that he suspected this to be easy. He flipped through some papers, all store related. Time was running out as he heard the women finish up their order. His glance caught on a scattering of pictures pinned to a corkboard on the wall. On closer inspection, he found several of Serena with a group of people. A cottage nestled in the pines. A photo of her with an older man's arm wrapped around her shoulders. Pulling his phone from his pocket, he snapped them all. He'd just re-entered the main part of the store as Serena turned in his direction.

"I was just coming back to check on you."

He held up his hands. "Nothing a little soap and water couldn't fix."

"Let me finish your order."

While Serena added up the prices, Deke said, "I think my mother would love this place." He handed Serena two twenties when she announced the final total.

"Tell her to stop by."

"She lives in Florida, so unless she comes to visit, I'll have to describe your shop to her."

He noticed her hands tremble just the slightest bit as she returned his change.

"Florida. How nice."

"I was hoping to get her up here, but she just started dating a man, so the chances are probably slim. At least for a while. Maybe they'll come for a visit together."

She tucked a strand of her dark, poker-straight hair behind an ear. "That would be nice for you."

"Do you have family around here?"

Her eyes narrowed. "That's rather personal."

"Just being friendly." He tilted his head and pulled up a concerned expression. "Sorry if I overstepped."

"No. I…ah." She waved a hand in front of her. "Don't mind me. And for the record, no family around here."

He pointed to the bag. "I thought maybe the sketch was a family home."

"More of a legacy."

He waited for an explanation but she didn't elaborate. Figuring he'd gotten as much as he could for one day, he said, "I'll be sure to bring both my mom and her friend here if they get up this way."

The chimes tingled as the door opened. A woman Serena's age hurried inside. "Sorry I'm late."

Serena nodded to the woman and handed Deke the bag with his purchases. "Thanks for stopping in."

He took the bag and held it up. "I can guarantee I'll be back."

With a smile, he turned to leave the store, hearing Serena say, "Heidi, good. I have some calls I need to make. Can you take over?"

"Sure, boss."

Calls? To contact James Tate, maybe? If only he had a way of eavesdropping.

Serena stepped out of view, and unless he wanted to appear suspicious, he had to be on his way. Out on the sidewalk, he took one last look into the store. The new arrival was busy behind the counter. So, no way to find out what Serena was up to.

Taking a moment to send the pictures to

Dylan, he left a text message. Check these out. Not much to go on, but a start. Plus, he'd planted some seeds of discomfort. Job done for today, he strode a few steps before glancing across the street. Stopped short when he noticed Grace standing in the window of Put Your Feet Up. When he met her gaze, she lifted her hand and pointed to her wrist as if to say, *Look at the time. You need to be somewhere.*

The corners of his lips tipped up. Bossy. Nodding, he strode to the crosswalk and joined her in the office moments later.

"I was just about to call you," she said in greeting, standing by the desk. "The guests for the zip-line adventure are due here in fifteen minutes."

"I thought I was free until this afternoon."

"Faith didn't send you the updated schedule?"

"No." He set the bag on the counter and pulled out his phone. Tapped the screen to bring up his email. "Nope."

Grace's face slowly turned red. "She must have forgotten."

"Don't worry about it. I'm here and ready to work."

An arched brow rose. "Really? We're not cutting into your shopping time?"

He smothered a chuckle at her disgruntled expression. "I have a life, you know."

"True." She picked up a pen and tapped it on the desktop. "So, Serena waited on you?"

"Yes. She helped me pick out a gift."

She bit her bottom lip. He'd come to know her well enough by now to imagine she was dying to ask who the gift was for but didn't want to come off as overly pushy. Or wait. Was she more curious about his conversation with Serena than the recipient of the gift? Now he had to find out.

"Nice woman," he said. "She's created quite a pleasant atmosphere in her store."

"She is. I don't know her well, but we've chatted from time to time."

"So she's not one of the original merchants in town?"

"No. She moved into the space about two years ago."

"A transplant like me?"

"I guess." She stopped tapping. "So did you talk about what you have in common?"

"And if we did?"

"I… You…"

He laughed. Couldn't help it, really. Grace's interrogation skills were sadly lacking. Also, he hadn't enjoyed himself like this in a very long time.

He found himself wondering what she was like in court. Did she possess a take-no-prisoners attitude? Ask relentless questions to make her case? Or was she quiet but authoritative? And why should he care, since one of the reasons he'd escaped here was to get away from all things law enforcement and trial related.

She slammed her hands on her hips. "What?"

"I find it amusing that you're so concerned about my visit with Serena."

"Well, you work for me. I'm responsible for all my employees."

"Enough to dig into their personal lives? Who they're dating?"

Her eyes went wide. "You're dating Serena?"

"Jealous?"

JEALOUS? GRACE?

She waited for the smug expression to leave his ridiculously handsome face, but he continued grinning at her.

Drat. She was jealous.

"I'm not jealous."

Except her tight chest said otherwise.

"Could have fooled me."

How could she not be after their kiss at the lake yesterday? She'd have to be dead not to feel something, and last time she checked, her heart was still beating. Overtime, apparently, for this man.

And not just the kiss. He'd opened up to her. Even in the short time she'd come to know him, she understood how hard that had been for him. So, feelings for Deke? Big-time. But she'd never, ever, admit she was jealous.

"Okay, I am a little curious, but no way am I jealous."

"Because that would mean you have feelings for me." His grin grew bigger. "As a concerned boss and all."

"Funny."

"This really is."

She rounded the desk to walk to the counter. "It's just…after our time on the lake yesterday, I thought we'd connected."

"We did."

She hated to have to spell it out, but there didn't seem to be any other way to get to the truth. "But you want to play the field?"

"Are you kidding? Right now I have enough trouble just keeping up with you."

She felt a reluctant grin tug at her lips. "I'm special like that."

Deke ran a hand over his short hair and didn't meet her gaze. "Very special, so let me assure you, you have nothing to worry about."

Sweet, he thought she was special. How

long had it been since she'd tried to have a relationship but sabotaged it by putting her career or family first? Her dismal dating experiences spoke volumes. Deke certainly had her full attention and she planned on holding on to that for the foreseeable future. Did that mean more kisses? At the thought, she wanted to do the happy dance right there on the spot, because yeah, she could see more kisses in the future. Maybe they'd meet at the lakeshore at midnight. Or by the firepit under the stars. But more than that, she could talk to Deke. Really talk to him, and that was pretty equal to his amazing kisses.

Wondering if her thoughts were mirrored on her face, she tried to read his expression, then realized he hadn't looked at her when he said she had nothing to worry about. Which made her worry. He was avoiding her gaze for a reason. Why? What was he hiding?

Giving herself mental whiplash, she took a few seconds to stop and think about what he'd said. He'd said *she* had nothing to worry about. Which meant…

"But someone else needs to worry? Serena?"

Surprise crossed his face. "Very astute."

"Lawyer."

"You do have that working for you."

She pressed her hands to her stomach. "Are you in some kind of trouble?"

"Me?"

"Sure. You show up out of the blue, looking for a job. Then you…wait. You didn't just show up here on a whim, did you?"

A sheepish expression crossed his face.

"You came to Golden on purpose?"

"Yes."

"Because of that trial you told me about?"

"No. A family issue."

Relief swept through her. She didn't want to think about trouble following Deke here and what that would mean for her hometown. Although why she would be relieved when she planned on leaving soon was beside the point. Her family still lived here after all.

"Is this thing with Serena serious?"

His broad shoulders rose as he exhaled a breath. "I don't even know if Serena is involved in the problem. It's a lead my brother asked me to follow up."

"And since you're on a leave of absence—"

"And already up here hiking the Appalachian Trail."

"—you decided to infiltrate my town."

His brow creased. "You make my actions sound nefarious."

"If you'd fill me in…"

"I can't. Not right now." His steady gaze met hers. "But I trust you, Grace."

Even though Deke had revealed himself yesterday, she sensed he didn't say those words easily or often. The tightness in her chest eased and she found herself touched that he'd confided in her, even if it wasn't the entire story.

"Okay. How about this? You tell me when you can, and in the meantime I'll do a little reconnaissance for you. Like I said, I don't know Serena well, but we are friendly. If you give me a direction to follow, I'll see what I can find out."

After a long, charged moment, he said, "I can do that." He moved closer to the counter and suddenly she was engulfed in his woodsy scent. "See what you can find out about her family or if she's involved with anyone from out of state."

"Deal." She held out her hand and he took it. After a firm shake, she tried to remove it from his grip, but he held fast. She looked up, getting lost in his dark blue-gray eyes. His thumb brushed over her skin and it was all she could do to control a runaway shiver.

When he finally let go, she brushed her hands off. "I think we'll make a good team."

"I'm counting on it."

"Sure beats worrying about my own family for once," she said with a grimace.

"They don't need your concern, Grace. They need to stand on their own feet."

"Easy for you to say, but remember, Faith didn't send you the memo about this morning's tour group."

"She probably has a good reason for forgetting. She's a mother with two kids and it doesn't look like her husband is any help."

Guilt pressed on her shoulders, but she stood her ground. "You just made my point."

"I'm not arguing the point because right now I have a tour to meet up with." He grinned at her. "Unless you want to take over?"

She shivered. "Please." Picking up a form, she handed it to him. "The Kelly and Pope families. They're vacationing here together. Mr. Pope called to let me know they're running late."

Having read the form, Deke looked up, curiosity clear in his eyes. "Okay, then you can tell me why you dislike the outdoors so much."

"It's not dislike, really. And it's not all outdoors. More like some bad memories that linger after all these years."

"Nothing could be that bad that you wouldn't take advantage of the beautiful weather and scenery here."

"You'd be wrong." She'd boxed up those memories years ago and hidden them where they belonged, in the past.

He rested a hip against the counter. "I shared."

She sighed. Yes, he had.

Resting both hands on the counter, she closed her eyes. Conjured up the high school trip that had ended in embarrassment. Right on cue, her stomach started swirling, but she met his gaze.

"Short story. Senior camping trip. I was surprised by Lissy Ann's invitation to hang out with her friends. I sat with them around the campfire, hiked the park with them. One evening a few of us were allowed to take a path up the mountain to the lookout. It was getting dark when Lissy Ann realized she'd forgotten her flashlight and asked me to run back to our camp to get it. Carter was leading the group and she insisted she couldn't leave his side, which was not unusual since they were always glued together. Thankful that she'd included me with her friends, I went on the errand."

His strong hand covered hers. "Let me guess. You never met up with them."

She carelessly lifted one shoulder, trying to hide how much the memory still bothered her. "No one was at the lookout when I arrived. Once I realized I'd been duped, I decided to return to camp, only it was getting darker and

I got turned around and took the wrong path. It was spooky and I swear I could hear animals coming for me, so I froze. Spent hours curled up under some bushes until the teachers found me. When I eventually got back to the campsite, I didn't miss the kids' eyes on me or the laughter at my expense.

"I ducked into the restroom and overheard a few girls who'd come in laugh over Lissy Ann's treatment of me. The chubby girl with the convict father." She shook her head as if the physical movement could keep the tears at bay. "Got so nauseous I threw up. When I finally ventured outside, I did my best to pretend their whispers didn't bother me, but obviously they did."

"Now I understand why you were less than overjoyed to see Lissy Ann the day she stopped by."

Grace shoved the memories back in the box. "I thought I'd gotten over it, but it all links up with those memories of being teased because of my family. But that doesn't explain why she wants to be friends now."

"Want my opinion?"

"I shared, so yeah."

He chuckled. "You're successful. Not only as an attorney, but your family business has done well. I'd venture a guess and say she's disappointed at how things turned out for herself. Reconnecting could be her way of apologizing."

"We did kind of discuss our past when she stopped in the other day."

He leaned toward her, his masculine scent engulfing her again. "Now that you've figured it out, you have no reason not to love being outdoors."

"Don't push it, Matthews. I may incorrectly lump all outdoor activities with being left in the woods at night, on top of being teased, but it's my issue to deal with." His genuine smile sent tingly sensations over her skin in a way she didn't want to examine. "But I'll be heading back to Atlanta soon, so I suppose it doesn't matter in the big picture."

At her reminder, he removed his hand, taking his warmth with it. The room suddenly turned cold. At the loss of his touch or the idea of going back to her career?

"Except to your family," he went on to say.

"I've left the tools for them to succeed. If Faith focuses and Nathan spends more time working than scheming, Put Your Feet Up should be fine. If they can't commit, then my mother should consider selling."

A dark brow arched. "You'd advise her to sell?"

She clasped her hands together. "I already have. She refuses to even consider the idea."

"Let me ask you something."

"Okay."

"Do you really want them to succeed?"

His words startled her. "What kind of question is that? Of course I do."

He held up a hand. "Hear me out. You've been the one to take care of the family for so long, maybe you don't really think there's any way they can possibly manage without you."

"That's always been the plan. I've made sure they knew I would eventually leave to practice law away from Golden."

"Yet you come running every time they need you?"

"Are you suggesting I like it when they mess up?"

"No, but control is powerful and can be difficult to let go."

"I have no…" She stopped. Was Deke right? She complained when they needed her, but dropped everything to bail them out of their messes. "Wow. I'm an enabler."

"I don't know about that, but I can see you've spent a lot of time and put a great deal of thought into this business. It's part of who you are, Grace, just like being an attorney is also who you are. You can't have one without the other or separate them."

She'd never considered her life like that.

"If you act like they can't do anything without you, you're subconsciously saying you expect them to fail, and they will. But you've given them everything they need to run this business. It's time you stepped back and let them. For real this time."

The back door opened and voices carried up front.

"The clients," Grace said, relief and disappointment mingling at the reprieve.

Deke's serious gaze pierced hers. "And here's my last piece of advice. If your family takes over, you can focus on your own life for once. That means more time with me."

That said, he lifted the counter partition, squeezing her shoulder as he passed by to greet the guests and get them on their way. She touched the spot, wishing he didn't have to rush off. He'd opened the door to a topic she'd never wanted to delve into and didn't want to go through alone. He grabbed the van keys, nodded goodbye and ushered the group outside, the words shared between them hovering in the air.

Focus on your own life for once.

Grace's shoulders slumped. She'd never

placed the spotlight on herself before. Was almost afraid to try.

More time with me.

Did she want more time with Deke? If she were honest, yes, lots of it, in any way, shape or form. Evidently he was on board. The question was, would she dare take advantage of his suggestion?

CHAPTER ELEVEN

BRIGHT AND EARLY Friday morning, Grace was reviewing the tour schedule for the next week when she heard the back door open. Running a hand over her hair—because it could be Deke coming in to work after all—she stopped mid-motion. Okay, so she liked when he saw her at her best, but honestly, he'd managed to see her at her worst far too often. Lowering her hand, she was surprised when Nathan walked in from the hallway, carrying a large tote bag.

She checked her watch, then stared at him. "It's nine o'clock in the morning. You don't have a group. Why are you awake?"

His hair looked shaggier than usual, like he'd just rolled out of bed. "There's a change in guides today."

She glanced at the schedule. "What are you talking about? I haven't made any changes."

"No, but Mr. Newton has."

"Come again?"

"He called me thirty minutes ago. Seems he wants an additional guide to go along with the youth group. I told him you'd be happy to fill in."

Mr. Newton had been bringing inner-city

kids to the mountains for as long as she could remember. They'd always given his organization a special discount and made sure to show the kids a good time.

"I'm not a guide, Nathan."

"No one would ever confuse you for one." Her brother chuckled in his raspy morning voice. "But are you willing to lose a longtime client because you're stubborn?"

She rubbed her forehead. "You're going to have to explain."

Nathan pulled a chair out, sank down and lifted his feet to rest on the desk. "Mr. Newton is bringing a coed group this morning. Apparently he wants both a male and female guide for the mix of kids. Deke had already signed on and the last time I checked I'm not a female so..." He held out his hand to indicate Grace was the next choice.

Grace considered her options and came up empty. Faith certainly couldn't do it, not unless she found a babysitter. And since she brought the children to the office because she couldn't afford one, that put her out of the running. And Mama was out of commission. As much as she could come up with many different reasons not to be in the outdoors, Grace was the only one available.

Resigned, she said, "I'm the guide."

"You got it."

She glanced at her watch again. "You could have called instead of driving over. I need to run back to the cabin for a change of clothes."

He hefted the bag and tossed it on the desk. "No need. Since I was at Mama's, I packed for you."

She stood to unzip the bag and riffle through it. "I don't recall leaving anything there. I can't—" She stopped short when she pulled a pair of jeans and a long-sleeved, red-and-black plaid shirt from the bag. Recognized them from the last time she'd lived at home. "Nathan, I don't even know if these clothes are my size."

He yawned. "I remember seeing you wear them before, so I figured they'd still fit."

Surprised by his efficiency, she dug farther, finding an old pair of hiking boots, thick socks and, under those, a small backpack. "You've thought of everything."

"I'm handy once in a while."

She took the socks in her hand to unroll them, admiring the fact that her brother had the foresight to look ahead and plan for her. "I'd say more often than that."

He dropped his head back and closed his eyes.

"Why do you do that?"

His head jerked up. "Do what?"

"Sell yourself short. You're good at this, Nathan. Remember, I see the books every month. You've increased business. I get that Mama let her finances go, but why drop your life here and run off?"

"You wouldn't understand."

"Try me."

He dropped his feet to the floor, aiming a serious gaze her way. "I get…antsy, Grace. Like there's something out there I'm missing by staying in Golden. So I try to earn some extra cash to go after an adventure."

Grace snorted—she wouldn't exactly call his gambling habit earning money—but she got it. She'd wanted out of Golden, set a goal and met it. But what bothered her was the fact that he seemed to be following in their father's footsteps and they all knew how that turned out.

"Why haven't you ever told me?"

He sent her a get-real glance. "You've always known what you wanted, Grace. You've always been in control. That's a tough act to follow."

She swallowed hard. Nathan was right. He didn't say so with malice or envy, just knew that's how things were.

Her conversation with Deke rang in her ears. Had she held her siblings back, all in the name of doing what was best for them? Or was it for her? "I'm sorry, Nathan. When I handed the business over to you and Mama, I should have kept my nose out of it."

"Is that even possible?"

"I don't know. But I also never tried."

The room went silent as they both considered the direction of the discussion. Grace stared out the front window, watching people come and go on the sidewalk, wondering if their lives were as muddled as her own.

"Nathan, you can have adventure right here in Golden. If you put half as much passion into the business as you do into chasing the next exciting thing, you'd fulfill that longing."

He dropped his head. "I don't know, Grace. Maybe that ship has sailed."

"I don't agree. You can do this, Nathan."

He stood. "I guess we'll see. Once Mama is okay and you leave, I'll be back at the helm."

She rose, skirting the desk to touch his arm. "Will you at least give it one hundred percent? If, after that, you decide staying in Golden isn't for you, we can discuss next steps."

"Like selling?"

Her face flamed.

"Mama mentioned it."

"As a last option."

He nodded. "Look, I have some things to tie up first. By the time you head back to Atlanta, I should be square."

Suspicion twisted her stomach. Nathan was way too nonchalant. "Square how?"

He dropped a kiss on her head. Stepped back and flashed her an easygoing smile. "Don't worry, sis. I have things under control."

So why didn't his assurance leave her convinced? Because this was Nathan and his track record was less than stellar.

"Deke should be here in twenty and then you two are meeting the bus at the public parking lot at the bottom of Crystalline Falls."

Right. Back to work. She'd done what she could, hoping what she'd said had gotten through to her brother. The ball was in his court now.

He took off and Grace changed into her casual clothes. It felt strange, dressing down after she'd become used to selecting outfits that suited the law office. She had to admit, the jeans were more comfortable than she'd remembered. The loose plaid shirt gave her room to breathe and thankfully the boots were a custom fit. She might suffer with a few blisters at the end of the day, but getting away from the office and family issues it entailed suddenly appealed. Especially since she'd be spending those hours with Deke.

He made her forget to worry about her job status. Made her think on her toes, waiting for a casual brush of the hand or a long stare that took her breath away. Romance was definitely the last thing she'd expected when she'd come home to Golden. She still wasn't sure it was in the cards for her. Instead of trying to figure it all out, she decided to stay present and enjoy every moment with Deke before she went back to her real life.

She'd just exited the restroom when Faith arrived, struggling to open the back door while she juggled the baby and an oversize diaper bag while answering John's fifty questions. Grace rushed over to lend a hand. Once Faith noticed her, she stopped short.

"This is the Put Your Feet Up office, right?" Faith craned her neck to look around, like the surroundings were foreign to her and she was trying to judge where she was. "Because I've never seen my sister dressed for work like this."

"Ha, ha."

Faith chuckled. "Really, Grace? Did the raccoons run off with your wardrobe?"

Grace explained the guide situation, which elicited a big belly laugh from Faith. "Priceless." After setting Lacey in the mini playpen and unpacking John's toy trucks, she pulled out her phone and aimed it at Grace.

Grace slammed a hand on her hip. "Just what do you think you're doing?"

"I need proof. No one will believe you're actually going out on a tour."

She finally recognized the absurdity of the situation and laughed. "It's been a very long time."

"Since you were in college. And even then you didn't go willingly."

Grace averted her gaze. "Today is different."

Faith immediately zeroed in on her mood. "Because of Deke?"

Yes, because of Deke.

"Because my family is working with me and as a team we've handled the situation. I'm proud of you guys." She leaned her hip against the desk. "Nathan and I had a good talk this morning and here you are, all set for the day. Once Mama is A-okay, the Harper family should be back on their feet."

A faint shadow crossed Faith's eyes but quickly disappeared. "Thanks, Grace. For giving me a chance."

"And thanks for putting up with my bossing."

Faith grinned. "You aren't the easiest person to work with."

"Shockingly, you aren't the first to tell me so."

John rose from the floor to stand by his mother. "Aunt Grace is the boss," he said matter-of-factly.

"And how do you know this?" Faith asked.

"She told me."

At John's words, the sisters shared a laugh. He shrugged, not getting the humor, and returned to his toys. It had been way too long since they'd been a real family, Grace thought. She liked them better this way.

After she ran through the day's schedule and gave Faith some last-minute updates, Deke arrived at the office. One look at her and a brow rose.

She crossed her arms over her chest. "Go ahead. Ask where the real Grace is. I've been getting it all morning."

"Actually, I was thinking the casual you is rather appealing. I like it."

Tendrils of pleasure sent heat up her neck. She glanced at Faith's knowing grin, then quickly grabbed her sunglasses from her purse. "I'll have my cell with me if you need anything, but once we get into the forest it may not work."

"Go." Faith shooed them out. "I've got everything covered here."

With a bit of a bounce in her step, Grace followed Deke out into a sunny, temperate morning. Once they were deep in the woods the temperature would lower a bit, but so far it was a great day for hiking.

She nodded to the backpack Deke tossed into

the back seat of the Jeep. "You have the first-aid kit?"

"Check."

"Bottled water?"

"Check."

"Trail mix?"

"Grace, this isn't my first hike."

"Sorry." She climbed into her seat, discovering boots worked much better when traveling in his vehicle than heels. "Since this was thrown at me last minute, I just want to make sure we're prepared."

"We are." Once he had the Jeep on the road out of town, he glanced her way. "Think you can just relax and enjoy yourself?"

"To be honest, I don't know. I forget what that feels like. If I ever knew, that is."

He chuckled. "How about you let me be in charge today?"

It was on the tip of her tongue to argue. Deke was right, she did have a hard time giving up control. But seeing him ready for the outing, dressed in cargo shorts, long-sleeved shirt and hiking boots, she knew she was in good hands.

Leaning back into the seat, she closed her eyes. "You got it, boss."

She heard his chuckle, savored the wind in her hair and enjoyed the remainder of the ride to the falls.

DEKE PEERED OVER the group—a ragtag assembly
of teens ranging from twelve to fifteen—detect-
ing right away who the leaders were. The kids
were straight out of Atlanta's inner city. They
loitered around the bus, laughing and boasting
how easy the day's hike would be, until Grace
escorted them to an open area beside the fast-
moving stream rushing over mossy rocks. He
divided the group of twenty into smaller groups
of five, picking one teen to be in charge of each
group. After fifteen minutes of instruction and
going over safety checks, the group ventured
to the entrance of the path leading to the forest.

Grace strode beside him as they lumbered
over the bridge to the other side of the stream,
where the forest spread out before them. "I've
always enjoyed this trail."

"So far it's my favorite out of all the different places you've sent me."

The pumping of his heart had less to do with
the adventure before them and more to do with
Grace's smiling face.

Crystal Trail began on the south side of the
welcome station, meandering in a mile loop
through the lower section of the mountain until
leading back to the original starting point. Once
completed, they'd take a break for lunch in the
park. From there they would walk the paved
path up the half-mile hike to Crystalline Falls.

As they settled into the trek, dried leaves crunched under their feet. Large stones were scattered throughout the landscape of tall, majestic trees. Fallen logs and low-hanging branches added to the picturesque scene. A crisp, woodsy scent filled Deke's lungs as they plodded up the slight elevation.

"You know your muscles are going to twinge by the end of the day," he told Grace.

"My arms got over the strain when we went canoeing so I'm sure I can handle a little dull ache here and there."

He chuckled. "We'll see."

Once all the kids had made it over the bridge, Grace stopped. She'd be taking up the tail end of the group. "See you later."

He nodded, missing her company immediately, then led the group, slowing once to make certain Grace was in position. Sure she had things well in hand, he started forward again. The path was worn, sometimes uneven, but not particularly difficult. He knew the kids were unsure of their surroundings, so he set a leisurely pace. They stopped to examine rocks, bushes covered with berries and wildflowers. At one point, Deke had to break up an impromptu sword fight involving long twigs. When the kids heard scampering sounds in the brush behind the trees, they were concerned about wildlife, but Grace eased their fears with stories about growing up near here. She was knowledgeable and kept the kids enthralled the entire time. An hour later they returned to the bridge, the kids already digging into their backpacks for lunch.

When he waited for Grace to produce hers, a sheepish grin curved her lips.

"I forgot my lunch."

"No, not the Prepared One?" he teased in mock horror.

"I was so worried about the other supplies it slipped my mind."

He opened his pack and removed two bags. "Never fear. Your leader remembered to make you a sandwich."

She took the bag he held out and tilted her head. "You really make a good partner."

"Was there ever any doubt?"

Her lips trembled. "Modest, too."

"Just stating the facts, ma'am." He paused as a thought went through his head. "We do work well together, Grace. It's not something you find every day."

Her smile faded. "Maybe, but not everyone is looking."

She then walked over to a group of girls, taking his heart with her.

They eventually settled on the picnic benches located beside the stream. Once they had the kids seated, the entire crew went quiet as they wolfed down lunch. When finished, the group grew restless, indicating it was time for the last leg of the tour.

"It's a fairly easy incline," Deke told the assembled group at the start of the trail up the mountain to the falls, "but make sure you stop if you get winded. We aren't in a hurry."

The group took off, spirits high again. Some of the braver boys hopped from boulder to boulder, ignoring the taunts of their friends when they missed the mark. Some banded together to take pictures of native birds. The swordplay started up again, which Deke shut down for their safety.

Watching all the high energy, Deke and Grace walked side by side. "You're really good with the kids," he said as they followed.

"They're lots of fun." She adjusted the strap of her backpack. "I remember those days."

"Thought those years were hard for you."

"Not always. You've had me recalling a lot of memories, and, to be honest, there were some good times mixed in with the bad."

Her admission surprised him. "So you're saying my walking into your life had a positive effect on you?"

"I don't know about that, but you've encouraged me to take stock of my life, and I appreciate it."

The stream gurgling beside them grew louder the closer they neared the falls. Even though the path was moderate, he adjusted his pace when Grace slowed.

"I forgot how the incline sneaks up on you." She stopped, dug a bottle of water from her pack and took a long drink. She pointed the end of the bottle toward the bend just before the falls. "But it sure is pretty up here."

He couldn't take his gaze from her. "That's a fact."

She sent him a puzzled look, then they resumed their stroll. More and more Deke was learning to accept the unmerited peace that he felt whenever he came up here. Or did the tranquility come from sharing the experience with Grace? "I keep thinking I wouldn't mind this being my office every day."

She adjusted her backpack straps. "Wouldn't you miss your real job?"

"I suppose. Over time. I'll be the first one to admit I'm a science geek." He stopped to pick up a twig and hurled it at the stream. "If I could combine the two it would be a dream come true."

"I'm not sure there's a big need for forensic forest cops."

He chuckled. "Maybe not the cop part."

"You'd consider changing careers?"

"Maybe. If a certain woman in my life would admit she really likes this place."

Her forehead creased. "I like Atlanta, too. That's where my job is."

Yeah, he knew.

She picked up her pace, moving ahead of him. He swallowed a sigh, wishing he'd kept his mouth shut.

As they turned the bend, the sight of the falls came into full view. A multilevel waterfall, the first section plunged over an outcropping starting high up on the mountain. There was a break in the middle where natural rock formed a ledge, then the water swerved to the right and cascaded over slick boulders, this time wider and faster, into a shallow pool. Wooden viewing decks had been built around the pool where the water dropped into the stream and raced down the remainder of the mountain, ending in a lake owned by a resort property.

The youth group scattered between the two tiers of decking, their phones out to take pictures of the beautiful vista. Other tourists lingered as they viewed the masterpiece of nature. Deke couldn't deny that he was moved every time he brought a group up here.

After taking a quick head count, he joined

Grace where she rested her arms on a wooden railing. The water swirled violently in the pool, forming foamy eddies that dispersed as the pressure from above kept the stream moving at a swift pace. The trees created a natural canopy overhead, keeping the brunt of the early-afternoon sun from burning their skin.

"You aren't taking any pictures," he commented.

She tapped a finger to her temple. "My pictures are all saved in here."

He leaned close, his shoulder brushing hers. He didn't dare move, not wanting to shatter this moment. He took it all in, Grace, her cherry scent, the way she smiled at the beauty around them, creating lasting snapshots in his memory.

Grace inhaled deeply, keeping her eyes on the falls. "We always wondered what was on the top of the mountain. Mama was too afraid to let us climb up that high, but I always suspected that Daddy took Nathan anyway. They just kept it on the down-low so she wouldn't find out."

"Probably wise." A small smile curved his lips. "Sounds like something my brothers and I would do." They'd gone on plenty of adventures when they were young, their mother warning them off, but came home no worse for wear. That was a different time. Now they were keeping their mother out of the loop for what they believed was her own good. To protect her. Wasn't that their job now that their father was gone?

"Still, it makes you wonder," Grace continued. "Who was the first person to actually discover this area and hike to the top? Did a family settle here? How did they learn to rough it in the wilderness? We always played 'what if' when my folks took us here."

She turned, resting her lower back against the railing. "As much as this place is in my blood, I have to see where my career leads, Deke."

So, they were back to the previous conversation.

Curious, he said, "You don't think it's possible for circumstances to change your projected path?"

"Sure I do. But what I'm telling you is that I don't want to change. Not now anyway. I've worked too hard to get to where I am in the firm."

Here was the part where a smart man would close the subject. Lately, around Grace, he questioned his wisdom. "What if this was meant to be?" He pointed between them. "You and me."

"My career is what's meant to be, Deke." She turned her head to face him, confidence etched on her face. "I get that you're struggling right now. Trying to figure things out. But I know where the future lies. In a law office in downtown Atlanta."

He couldn't blame her for wanting to return to her life. Just because being in Golden had given his troubled heart a rest didn't mean she should stay. But what about him? The thought of returning to Atlanta gave him pause. Was he ready to give up the measure of peace he'd found here? Would returning to his home and job send him back into the dark place he'd desperately needed to escape? Slipping into the bad memories that continued to give him nightmares? No, for his own well-being, he needed to stay in Golden until he was healed, or at least as restored as he'd ever be; his recovery was something he was unwilling to sacrifice. Even if it meant losing Grace in the process.

Stuffing down his regret, he turned to lean against the railing. From here he could keep an eye out for the kids. A movement caught the corner of his eye. An older couple they'd passed on the way up finally finished the trek, hand in hand. The woman's mouth hung open with awe as she viewed the waterfall, but the man had eyes only for his wife. He led her to an empty bench, making sure she was comfortable before sitting beside her.

The familiar band around his chest that had loosened since coming here tightened with a vengeance. Since he'd found Grace, he'd discovered he was tired of being alone. And was over being solitary. It took every bit of strength not to convince her to give them a chance, but he wouldn't beg. Either she wanted them to be a couple or she didn't.

An image of his parents' wedding picture flashed in his mind. He'd admired their marriage. They were partners until the end. Not only that, they truly enjoyed each other's company. Were each other's best friend. Deke always thought they modeled what a good marriage looked like, even if he never pictured it for himself.

Until now. Until Grace.

"I want that," he said in a soft voice.

Grace looked at him, then followed the direction of his interest.

"Deke—"

He held up his hand. "I'm not saying with you, Grace. You've made your position clear. I'm just saying, one day I want to walk through the woods with my partner." He met her gaze. "Is that too much to ask?"

Clearly she didn't have the answer. Her conflicted expression said it all. He was ready to move forward; she was not.

Thankfully, on the heels of his blurted admission, a couple of the boys started roughhousing. He and Grace wrangled everybody together and started them down the trail, one at each end of the group. About halfway down, the fighting started up again, only this time one of the boys lost his balance, tumbled into a girl and sent her sprawling. Seated on the ground, the girl began crying, pointing to the blood staining her ripped jeans.

Hurrying over, Deke had the first-aid kit out just as Grace knelt beside the teen.

"It's okay, Heather. We'll get you cleaned up."

"It hurts," the girl whimpered.

"I'm not going to lie, this will sting," Grace said as she pulled out a small bottle of peroxide and dabbed the scrapes.

At this point some of the girls started yelling at the tussling boys and Deke had to act as referee to get them to calm down. Pointing downhill, he escorted the rest of the kids while Grace took care of her patient, talking to the few girls hanging around their friend. About ten minutes later Grace and her group appeared. Heather walked gingerly but at least she was smiling at something Grace said. Disaster averted.

He jogged over to Grace. "Everything okay?"

"Yes. I applied my first-aid skills with expertise."

"Grace is the best," Heather giggled.

Deke agreed but kept his opinion to himself, because yeah, Grace was the best.

Right on time, Mr. Newton returned with the bus. The kids piled on as Deke explained what had happened. Thankfully, Heather was no worse for wear, even though her knees would smart tomorrow. As they drove away, hands waving out the windows, he and Grace waved back.

She blew out a breath. "What a day."

"Ready to get back to town?"

"Yes. I want to see if Faith needs any help. If not, I'm heading home for a long shower."

They walked to the Jeep.

"You did well under pressure," Deke said.

"I've handled a crisis a time or two."

Before starting the ignition, Deke angled to face Grace. "Listen, what I said at the falls? I didn't mean to put any pressure on you."

"I know, Deke. And while I will freely admit I have feelings for you, I still have to focus on my family while I'm here, and then my career. You understand that, right?"

"I guess I was hoping to sway you in my direction."

"Let's not rush things. The Summer Gold

Celebration is just around the corner, so we'll be super busy. There is the bigger picture to think about."

Bigger than him and Grace becoming a couple? He didn't think so.

CHAPTER TWELVE

SATURDAY MORNING, GRACE stepped out of the office restroom and peeked around the corner. "Is anyone here?" she stage-whispered to her sister.

Faith turned from the filing cabinet, her lips trembling to hold back a smile. "It's safe. You can come out."

Picking up the long skirt from the 1800s-style costume, Grace walked to the desk in tight leather booties. The reams of cotton swirled around her ankles, the waist was a tad too tight and the neckline was way too constricting for a summer day in June. "I can't wear this."

"Why not? It's so you," Faith teased, tilting her head to look Grace over. "I like it."

"Says the girl wearing a short skirt and sleeveless blouse." She cringed, gazing down at the calico-patterned fabric. The tiny flower print made her dizzy. "It's embarrassing."

"The tourists truly enjoy it."

The Summer Gold Celebration had officially kicked off. The sidewalks were filled with tourists soaking up the sunshine, enjoying the merchants' displays and food offered by some of the best cooks in town. Every time the door opened, the savory scent of barbecue or the yeasty smell of baked goods floated in. From outside the front window, Grace could hear the strains of music from the band set up in Gold Dust Park. Traffic had been a bear, but who could complain really? Tourists meant business and business meant working on a weekend. All in the name of putting Golden on the map.

The festivities would last a week, with a dance featuring a country band scheduled tonight in the city park. With all the publicity, there'd been an uptick in business. Grace had Faith take calls and book outdoor adventures while she readied for the first walking tour this afternoon. Nathan and Deke were busy, which came as a relief. Her brother was good with people and could easily be the face of the company if he'd stay grounded.

Grace sighed. "When did Mama go old-school?"

"A few years ago. Visitors were losing interest in the walking tour so she thought the costume would inspire curiosity."

This getup was so the opposite of the professional persona Grace had carefully cultivated over the years. Once she stepped onto Main Street, her reputation would take a hit for sure. As she fussed over her outfit, it suddenly dawned on Grace that their mother was missing. "Where is Mama, by the way?"

Faith gathered up some loose papers from the desk. "She decided to stay home with the kids. Her friend Donna is stopping by to spend the day with them."

"On opening day of the celebrations? That doesn't seem like her. She loves all this hoopla." Grace brushed a few stray strands of hair back into the makeshift bun she'd fashioned to go along with the severe look. "Is she bringing the kids later?"

Her sister tugged on her lower lip with her teeth. Grace recognized her tell. Something was off.

"Faith, what's going on?"

Averting her eyes, Faith replied, "Mama sort of fell again."

"Sort of?" Grace's stomach knotted. "When?"

"Yesterday." Fear shimmered in Faith's eyes when she turned back to Grace. "She lost her balance and pitched against the counter. Her hip is badly bruised."

"Why didn't she tell anyone?"

"She probably wouldn't have said anything at all if she hadn't lifted Lacey to her hip. I caught her cringing and asked what was wrong. She tried to blow if off, but I hounded her until she confessed." Faith blew out a breath. "I know

I've been caught up in my own drama lately, but Grace, I can tell she's scared."

"She should be. This is beyond blaming broken steps for her tumble." Her mind switched into overdrive. "Her balance must be off. Maybe there are neurological problems. We need to get her to the doctor for a complete physical."

"I agree."

Guilt and surprise seared her. How long had it been since she and Faith had agreed on something? A matter this important? At the sight of her sister's pale face, Grace walked over and hugged Faith tight.

"There's more," her sister mumbled against her shoulder. Grace pulled back, hands gripping Faith's upper arms. "While she was staying at the cabin, I noticed her lose her balance more than once. At the time I didn't think much about it because John was underfoot, but now..."

Grace squeezed her sister, needing the connection of her sibling. "How long do you think she's kept this a secret?"

Faith shrugged.

A sudden sense of mortality swept over Grace. The idea of Mama having serious health issues was more than Grace would ever have imagined when she came home. Nor had she thought she and Faith would be a team, bonding over their mother.

"We'll handle this," Grace said, infusing as much confidence into her voice as possible. "As a family."

Faith moved away and wiped her eyes. "And Donna doesn't mind staying with Mama."

Pulling herself together, Grace said, "There's nothing we can do today, but first thing Monday morning, I'm calling Mama's doctor."

"If she'll go for it."

The oldest-sibling bossiness took over. No one would ever accuse Grace of pussyfooting around a topic. "Oh, she'll be going, even if it's kicking and screaming."

Faith laughed, the worry lines on her face easing.

"And we'll need to tell Nathan. He should be a part of any decisions we make to help Mama through this."

"Look at us, the Harper clan working together."

Grace grinned. As much as she was nervous about what was going on with her mother, she couldn't recall a time when she was secure in the knowledge that she and her siblings would strive together for a greater good.

The phone rang and Faith jumped back to work. Grace picked up her mother's script from the desk. She'd read it over a dozen times. For the most part, it gave the same information

Grace had written when they first came up with the idea for the historic stroll. Her mother had embellished with some of the local history, but Grace had to admit, it added a fun element. If only she didn't have to wear this restrictive, long-sleeved dress with a muslin apron.

The back door banged open and before she had a chance to run back to the bathroom to hide, Deke and Nathan strolled into the office.

A wide grin curved Nathan's lips. "Nice look, sis. Plannin' on churnin' up some butter for dinner tonight?"

"Shut it, Nathan," Grace warned. Other than the twinkle in Deke's eyes, he wisely kept his opinion to himself.

"I don't know why you're so crabby. The tourists are going to eat this whole period thing up."

"We already sold out the two tours scheduled for today," Faith piped in.

While Faith and Nathan discussed a tour, Deke nodded to the front door. He and Grace stepped outside to the busy sidewalk. Leaning against the building in hopes of blending in—doubtful—she looked up at Deke. "Everything okay?"

"That's what I wanted to ask you. Have you given any thought to your siblings taking on more responsibility since our chat?"

She smoothed her skirt. "You gave me a lot to think about and, to be honest, I'm working on it."

"I noticed Faith opened the office this morning."

"Yes. You were right on the mark about sharing the load."

"I'm hearing a *but*…"

"It's tough." She glanced over her shoulder to peer through the window. In the office Faith was jotting something down while Nathan paged through the appointment book. "I get they have to work this out. Together."

"It's a process, Grace. They'll appreciate running the business more if you give them some space."

She shrugged.

"When's your first tour?" he asked.

"In thirty minutes. I'll need to be at the north end of the park to meet up with the group."

His eyes swept over her. "You know, you look like part of Golden history come to life."

"Please. I can guarantee the temperature is going up and I'll only resemble a sweating tour guide."

"What? No perky bonnet to protect your pretty face from sun damage?"

She groaned. "I almost forgot the bonnet. It's inside."

"Admit it."

She cocked her head. "Admit what?"

"You love your family. Otherwise you wouldn't have let your mother talk you into playing dress-up."

True. This wasn't exactly what she'd envisioned happening during her leave of absence.

"Loving them isn't the problem."

"Still, I think deep down you really like this festival stuff."

Probably more than she realized, since she'd gone along with her mother and Lissy Ann's request so easily. "Don't you have a group to take somewhere?" she huffed.

"I do." He glanced at his watch. "In ten minutes. But first, I have an idea to run by you."

Interest piqued, she pushed away from the wall. "What kind of idea?"

"I was down at the warehouse early this morning and found some newer camping equipment packed up in boxes. It all looks in good shape. What do you think about adding overnight trips up the mountain and back to your list of adventures? A combo of hiking and camping, but short excursions so as not to take up too much time."

"I'd forgotten about the camping gear." She curled her finger under the neckline of her dress and tugged. "We stacked it away a few years ago and, to be honest, once I started co-ordinating with the other businesses in town, it slipped my mind."

"What do you think?"

"I'd have to crunch the numbers, figure out logistics on a camping area, add in supplies and time constraints…"

"You don't have to do it right now," Deke said. "Besides, I thought maybe I'd run it by Nathan and see what he comes up with."

She looked at him with suspicion. "Is this part of the plan to get Grace's hands out of the business?"

Grace had to admit, Deke was right. If she wanted to make a life in Atlanta—assuming she got back there—she had to let go of some of the control here in Golden.

He grinned. "Definitely."

"Actually, I like the idea. I'm okay with you presenting it to Nathan. I'm just not sure about letting him do all the prep work. I've always handled that end."

He shot her a look that clearly conveyed "let go."

"I can't completely abandon the reins, Deke."

"You won't succeed unless you try."

Why was this so hard? Most likely her reluctance stemmed from both Faith and Nathan's being less than reliable over the years. They were here now, she told herself. That's what counted, right? She knew she couldn't have it both ways, no matter how much she tried. "Look, we'll discuss this later. Right now I have—"

"Grace, is that you?" came the female voice she dreaded hearing under any circumstances. Worse when she was dressed like this. Sneaking a glance, she went still. Lissy Ann and a few of her friends.

"Why me?" she mouthed.

Moving around Deke, she swore she felt his body tremble in silent laughter. Mostly, though, she was thankful for his presence. He slipped his arm around her waist and she absorbed some of his solid strength. He sensed she needed someone to lean on right now.

"Hey, Lissy Ann." She nodded to the other women, who looked familiar but she couldn't recall their names.

"You remember Beth and Francie?"

She didn't, but pasted a smile on her face.

"I'm so glad to see your mama resurrected the historical tour," Lissy Ann said. "It will really add to the color of the celebration."

Grace blinked. No snarky remarks?

"It was a brilliant idea to add the period costume," Beth said.

Francie nodded. "When your mama suggested a candlelight tour, the planning committee was thrilled."

"Planning committee?"

"Your mama is on the board." Lissy Ann frowned. "Didn't she tell you?"

No, she hadn't. That, among other important matters. Grace opened her mouth but Lissy Ann waved her off.

"What am I thinking? After her fall, she's not herself." She turned to Beth. "Give Wanda Sue a call and tell her we're thinking about her."

Beth nodded.

"Now, we've been walking through town, checking in with the merchants and those involved in the celebration to see if you need anything."

"An escape plan from this outfit?"

Lissy Ann laughed. "Grace, you're always so funny." Then her face went all business. "I'm not kidding. Put Your Feet Up has its place in the festivities and we need to make sure everyone is doing their part. This is an important week for Golden."

So she'd heard. But why? She hadn't thought to question it before, but with Lissy Ann on a mission, she wondered what was up.

Lissy Ann snapped her fingers. "Earth to Grace. Everything's in order?"

Grace found herself straightening up. It was

all she could do to keep from saluting Commander Lissy Ann. "Yes, ma'am."

"Your sister has my cell number if there are any problems."

"Good to know."

Lissy Ann's attention turned to Deke. "And you'll be participating?"

Grace squeezed Deke's fingers at her side.

"Of course," he said, humor lacing his tone. "Looking forward to the celebration."

"Excellent." Lissy Ann turned to her posse. "Let's move on, ladies."

As the three marched away, Grace watched them go. "That was…freaky?"

"What? People taking an interest in the town?"

She reluctantly moved from his hold, missing the closeness. For a few moments it had been nice to not be in charge of everything. Plus, Deke smelled good and standing that close gave her shivers. Oh, no, she had it bad.

"I suppose." She looked up at him. "What about you? When did the future of Golden turn into your concern?"

"I might have come here for my own reasons, but since I've been here, I feel a part of the town. I've made some friends."

She raised one brow.

"I shoot the breeze every morning with Delroy. Been to the lake fishing with Buck. I've even done some work in your uncle's cabin."

She tugged in a breath. Uncle Roy was extremely fussy about his cabin.

His lips quirked up. "With his approval."

"So, you're becoming a Goldenite?"

He looked down the street and back at her. "I believe I am."

Grace shook her head. "My siblings doing their jobs. Lissy Ann in charge. You liking it here." She rubbed her temple. "Okay, this day just officially became weird."

Deke chuckled. "Before I leave, I need to ask you something."

"Shoot."

"Care to go to the dance with me tonight?"

Oh, she hadn't expected this. Yes, she was very attracted to Deke. He'd started getting under her skin, but like she'd told him yesterday, she didn't want to begin a relationship when she wasn't even sure how long she'd be here. Or if she'd have time to spend with him once she got back to Atlanta. With her mother's health up in the air and her need to get back to her career, she didn't want to make Deke think things were moving forward in the romance department when she had reservations.

"It would be a good way to spend time together. Get to know each other better."

His words whispered through her head. *More time with me.* Here was her chance.

"Deke, I, ah, don't mean to turn you down, but I need to spend time with Mama tonight. There are some things going on…" Like a family intervention in her immediate future. But until they spoke to Mama, it wasn't fair to mention her health issues to anyone else, no matter how much she felt she could trust Deke.

He studied her in a way that made her think he could read her deep, dark secrets. "Sure that's the only reason you're turning me down?"

Brushing her hair from her eyes, she hurried to say, "Between Mama's injuries and my job…life is moving so fast I can't keep up. And you and me? I'm not sure what to make of us."

He held up a hand. Shuttered his expression so she couldn't read his reaction. "You know how I feel."

Her stomach dropped. She really wanted to say yes. "Maybe we can arrange another time? After I've had time to think?"

"Right." He took a few backward steps. "Duty calls. Gotta run."

He pivoted on his heel, walked to the end of the block and disappeared around the building.

"What is wrong with you?" she asked herself just as Nathan opened the door.

"Talking to yourself, sis?"

She shook off her regret at turning Deke down and faced her brother. "Nathan, we need to talk."

He nodded, looking more grown up than she'd ever seen him. "Faith beat you to it. C'mon in and join the discussion."

THE STRING OF white bulbs draped from tree to tree created a magical quality in the park. Given the way the lights sparkled, the name Gold Dust Park was particularly apt. The large grassy expanse was scattered with benches and picnic tables. Loud chatter and laughter energized the dusky shadows as Deke strolled the periphery of the exuberant crowd who'd gathered for dancing and fun. The last trace of the barbecue dinner lingered in the air, replaced by perfume worn by women dressed up for the occasion.

Judging by all the couples waiting for the band to start up, it was definitely date night. As usual, Deke was alone.

What had he been thinking, asking Grace to join him tonight? She'd quickly backpedaled when it came to getting close. Yes, they'd kissed. Twice. And yes, he'd revealed parts of his life to her that he hadn't even shared with his family. So what, that made her want to date him? He barked out a rough laugh, kicking himself for showing up here at all. Hanging out in the cabin would have been preferable over this misery.

He should have been relieved, really. Hadn't he decided early on that getting involved with a lawyer who put her career first was a bad idea? Yes, using her profession as an excuse to build a wall between them was narrow-minded on his part, especially after the last trial. It was hard to picture Grace as an attorney since he'd only seen her managing the family business in Golden. So, against his better judgment, he'd let his guard down.

You would have fallen for her no matter where you met her.

The unvarnished truth hit him in the gut. Yeah, he might not like most lawyers but he was a big fan of Grace Harper. And where would that get him? She'd been clear that she wasn't sure what to make of their relationship, and although for the first time in a very long time he wanted to pursue a romantic relationship with a woman, he would never press her into making a decision she wasn't ready for. It would ruin the friendship they'd cultivated before it had a chance to grow into something meaningful. He didn't want to risk tainting what they currently had, even though his heart yearned for her.

Surprise walloped him as he stepped around

a group of people, only to realize Grace was standing in the middle.

Gone was the pioneer woman, replaced by a thoroughly modern woman dressed in a white swirling dress, her hair shining under the lights, eyes aglow. She took his breath away. Made his pulse race. Painted him the fool.

Because here she stood, after turning him down.

Feeling an unusual heat crawl up his face, he'd just started to move away when Grace called his name. He took a bracing breath and faced her, schooling his expression to not convey his disappointment. "Grace. I thought you weren't coming tonight."

She grimaced. "I didn't think I was going to make it, but we had our family meeting and afterward Faith insisted that Nathan and I come to the dance."

"Everything okay?" he asked, mentally kicking himself. Not that it was any of his business, but she looked troubled, and like it or not, he'd become invested in the Harper family.

She glanced over her shoulder at the group she'd just left. He recognized Nathan, the Wright brothers and a few other merchants. She took a few steps away from the rowdy group and nodded at him to follow.

"Sorry about being so vague earlier. Seems

Mama had a few more tumbles than she let on. We sat down with her to voice our concerns and get her to agree to a thorough doctor's evaluation."

Deke pictured Wanda Sue, stubborn to the last. "That couldn't have been easy."

"No, but we made her promise."

"Sorry you're going through this."

Torn between giving Grace the space she needed and wanting to soak up every minute with her, he was about to excuse himself when she took his hand in hers and twined their fingers together. "For the first time, we're working together as a family. So while Mama's health is a concern, it feels good not to be the only one handling the situation."

"If I remember correctly, didn't a friend of yours make a recommendation to get your siblings more involved?"

"Yes, and he's also gentlemanly enough not to toot his own horn."

Deke chuckled. His chest was still tight, but with Grace's hand in his, the night was looking up.

A shout sounded as the band took the stage, tuning their instruments before launching into a raucous number that had the entire crowd on their feet.

Grace tugged his arm. "Care to join the others?"

Panic made him sweat. "Uh, Grace, I don't dance."

"What do you mean you don't dance? Everyone dances."

"Not me."

She fisted a hand on her hip. "So that's a no?"

He nodded, swallowing hard.

"I don't think so. You made me get into a canoe when I didn't want to. You owe me a dance, buddy."

She tugged again and this time there was no arguing. "I have two left feet."

Once at the edge of the dance floor, she turned. Shot him a cocky grin as she placed her hands on his shoulders and said, "Then I'll guide you through this."

Before he realized what was happening, she got him into a one-two-three, one-two-three rhythm. Between her laughter and instructions, he lost his fear and began to enjoy the process. Like anything he did, once his mind grasped the mechanics, he could carry through. Soon, he was twirling her about with ease.

"Look at you, taking the lead," she teased, her eyes alight.

"What can I say? I have a great teacher."

He repeated the steps in the next dance, finally

getting into the swing of things. Then the tempo slowed to a sultry ballad meant to woo couples onto the dance floor. Grace dropped her arms, taking a step back, but Deke chanced grabbing her hand to keep her there. She gazed up at him, uncertainty in her eyes. When she finally nodded, he pulled her close, inhaling the intoxicating scent that was Grace, and Grace alone. She rested her head on his shoulder, and they swayed to the old-as-time love song, the guitar strumming tender notes that lifted and lilted in the air.

With Grace this close, Deke figured she could feel his erratic heartbeat, but he didn't care. He'd never truly felt like he belonged with a woman, not entirely, until Grace. She'd slipped past his guard, made him open up without fear of losing himself. He didn't know how she accomplished it, just knew her smile slayed him every time. They hadn't known each other long, but they clicked in a way that felt natural. It scared and electrified him, and he was okay with both emotions.

The song slowed. Loath to let go, Deke tucked her in his embrace. When the music ended he finally let go. The mere inches between them felt like miles of space.

Her cheeks pink, she said, "I'm thirsty. How about we get something to drink?"

"Lead the way."

The band took a break as he and Grace navigated through the crowd. He stopped short when Colin Wright reached out to clap him on the back. "Hey, Deke. Good to see you tonight."

"Seems like everyone in town is here."

"Yeah. The Tremaines made sure to impress upon us how important this celebration is, so we're all in for the cause." He grinned. "Although I would have shown up anyway."

His brother, Adam, leaned over. "Where there's a party, my brother is in."

"What can I say?" Colin held up a cup. "I am the party."

Grace laughed, shaking her head. Then, after scanning the area around the drink table, she said, "Where did Nathan run off to?"

Colin looked over his shoulder. "No clue."

Adam shrugged.

Deke asked for two iced teas, then delivered one to Grace. "Thanks," she said, distracted as she continued to search the crowd.

Leaning closer, he said, "Want to go look for him?"

Relief crossed her face. "Would you mind?"

"As long as I'm with you, I'll go anywhere."

She lightly elbowed him. "Sweet talker."

"It's the truth," he said, his voice rough.

She sent him an appraising glance, as if questioning the veracity of his words, then they stepped away from the group and began to walk around the park. Five minutes later, Grace pointed. "There he is."

Deke couldn't make out who Nathan was talking to. The other person was hidden in the shadows, but the conversation seemed pretty intense. Then, with a sharp turn, Nathan returned to the crowd.

"That answers your question," he said close to Grace's ear as the music started up again.

A wrinkle crossed her brow. "I hope he's okay." Then she visibly shook off her concern, smiling at him. "Thanks."

"Why? Because I walked with you?"

She waved her hand toward the band shell. "You could be dancing or talking to some of the single women instead of hanging out with me."

"You suit me just fine."

The band launched into another toe-tapper. Taking his cup to place inside hers, Grace threw them both into a nearby trash can and they returned to the dance floor. They'd just started moving to the beat when Adam poked Grace's shoulder. "Mind if I cut in?"

With a comical expression, she stared at Deke, like she was asking his opinion. Or begging for mercy. He shrugged, and before Grace could decide what to do, Adam swooped in, moving Deke out of the way. Annoyed at Adam's high-handedness, Deke took a few steps back and almost bumped into Serena.

"Hey," he said, grateful to be near someone he knew. He felt like a fool dancing alone. "Fancy meeting you here."

"I don't think there's a stranger in the bunch," she shouted. The woman he'd seen in Serena's store the other day danced beside her. Deke stayed with them, moving to the beat.

Serena had some impressive moves of her own.

"I love to dance," she said.

"I can see."

Caught up in the song, Deke didn't notice that Grace had moved closer to him until she nearly stepped on his foot. When he glanced at her, she shot him a help-me look.

Adam worked his way between them, so Grace turned toward Serena. "Hey there. Having fun?"

"Yes," she yelled over the loud music and lively crowd. "It's nice to get out of the store once in a while."

"We haven't really had a chance to hang out. We should get together some time."

Surprise lit Serena's pretty face. "I'd like that."

"Count me in," Adam said, making sure everyone heard his comment over the band's boisterous rendition of the upbeat song, his eyes on Grace.

"Great," Grace said. "We'll have a group night out."

Deke nearly choked at the disappointed expression on Adam's face. Deciding to rescue Grace, he made his way closer to her. "Want another drink?"

"Yes." Grace nodded to the others. "See you later." Deke motioned to the table where they each had another cup of iced tea.

"Thanks for the save," she said.

"For both of us. I noticed you reaching out to Serena."

"Only way to find out what's going on is to get to know her. Then maybe you'll have more information to go on."

"And Adam? I read the SOS."

"Adam's a nice guy, but…" She took a long drink. "Maybe it's because I've known him for so long. I just know he's not for me."

Relieved, they strolled to an area tucked away from the lighting. "So does the fact that I'm not from here play to my advantage?"

Grace stared down at her drink. Looked up again and caught his gaze. "You really like it here, don't you?"

He propped his shoulder against the nearby

tree. "I feel at home here. Like I'm a part of something special."

"More than your real home?"

"Yes."

"Because of everything that happened?"

He watched the people gathered in the park, enjoying the night and each other's company. "I've made friends here. Earned a measure of peace that was missing when I arrived. It's been good for me to get away from the job that consumed my life. And the trial that derailed it."

"Deke Matthews, forensic cop?"

"Yes. I've realized I can't be defined by my title alone." He took a sip of the cold tea. Organized his thoughts before speaking again. "When I started working, I got so caught up in the job that I didn't have many friends, and the ones I did socialize with were people I worked with. My friend Britt pointed out that I needed a fuller life, but instead of listening, I did my own thing."

"And she was right?"

The feeling of loss strangled him. He spoke around the tightness in his throat. "Britt was the voice of reason in my life. As her own family grew and I was out in the field more, we didn't talk as frequently. I worked too much, and because of it I was part of a mistake that set off the chain reaction that took her life. I couldn't bear the thought of getting close to anyone again, for fear of losing them." He paused. Stared into the night for a beat. "I thought I was better off alone after what I'd done."

"And you don't want to be alone now?"

A wealth of emotions simmered in his chest, at the forefront the knowledge that he wanted Grace in his life for the long haul. "Not anymore."

She inched closer, placing her hand on his arm. "Are you saying you've given yourself a break? That you can't totally take the blame for what happened?"

"The part I played will always haunt me. But with time and perspective, I'm seeing that coming to Golden has given me a chance to forgive myself. Life, and death, isn't a thing we can control. Happiness and tragedy strike without warning and it's better to accept both and learn from each experience. I get what it feels like to be overwhelmed by circumstances, Grace."

"Wow. You gleaned all that from being in Golden?" She must have read the depth of his emotion because she turned away and gazed out at the crowd. "I could see you settling down here. You do fit."

"But not you?"

A flash of uncertainty came and went in her

eyes. "I couldn't wait to get out of Golden, yet I keep being drawn back."

"That's a bad thing?"

She ran her finger over the rim of the cup. "I honestly don't know."

He waited a moment before saying what was on his mind. "And if I decided to stay here?"

She slanted a glance his way. "I told you I can't make any promises, Deke."

Sadly, he knew that. Instead of pushing, he said, "Then let's make the most of the time we have together."

Their gazes met and held. Deke ran his hand around the back of her neck, his fingers tangling in wisps of hair, savoring the satiny-soft skin beneath his touch. His heart triple-timed at her gasp when he touched her. As if under a spell neither could break, she leaned in and Deke lowered his mouth to claim hers.

Their first touch sent his blood racing. This kiss was different from the others. Before had been exciting and new, the first thrill of attraction. This was deeper. Significant. He didn't think he was alone in his estimation, and when Grace placed her hand on his chest, as if she needed to feel his heart beating under her palm, he hoped she felt the same way. His heart ached, but in a good way. Like he'd finally found his true north. And just like that, he realized he was falling for a woman he had initially vowed never to get involved with. Fate laughed and set this path before him, one he didn't have to think twice about traveling down.

Hating to end the kiss but needing air, Deke broke the connection. Amazement, and a tinge of bewilderment, crossed Grace's lovely features. Deke caressed her cheek with his finger.

"Wow," she said, voice jittery. "That was…"

"Life-changing?"

"I don't know if I'd go that far." She playfully slapped his arm. "We have to stop."

"Why?" He looked up. "There's nothing I'd rather do than kiss you under the stars."

"I mean it, Deke. With my life up in the air, I'm not sure of the direction I'm headed."

"Fair enough."

"You understand?"

He did. Didn't like it. But understood that life threw curves when you were happily walking down the straight and narrow. The best thing to do was go with the flow, even if it meant losing your heart in the process.

CHAPTER THIRTEEN

BY MIDMORNING MONDAY, Grace, Faith and
their mother sat in the chilly examining room
in Dr. Collier's office. Grace had made an
early call and, after much wrangling, secured
an appointment time. Faith had made arrangements for the children to stay at a friend's house
for a play date. Her mother sat on the examining table covered in white paper, fidgeting
with the edges, gently flexing her still-injured
ankle. Getting her in the car to visit the office
was a study in patience, but between the two
of them, Grace and her sister had pushed the
issue enough that a mutinous Wanda Sue went
along.

"You know I hate doctors," Mama complained. "They poke and prod and can never
figure out what's wrong with you." She wrinkled her nose. "Plus, it smells like antiseptic
in here."

Yes. A study in patience.

"When was the last time you had a complete
physical?" Grace queried.

Her mother shrugged. "A year or two ago."

"Try five," Faith corrected.

Their mother sent her a flinty stare. "How would you know?"

"It was when you had that upper respiratory infection. I know because I drove you to that appointment."

"Oh, right, now I remember." She sent a sheepish glance Grace's way. "I stand corrected. Five years."

Biting back a retort, which wouldn't help the situation, Grace said, "This is a good thing. If nothing is wrong, you'll be happy. If the doctor finds something—" she waved a hand between her and Faith "—we'll deal with it."

"Humph."

"Mama, please keep—"

The door opened and a middle-aged man with soft brown hair and tortoiseshell glasses entered. He walked straight to their mother and shook her hand, impressing Grace immediately. "I'm Dr. Collier, Mrs. Harper. We haven't met, since I'm new to the practice." He looked down at the chart. "I understand you've had some falls?"

"It's nothing," their mother protested.

With a brisk movement, he set the chart aside. "How about you let me be the judge of that?"

Wanda Sue pouted.

As he checked her bruised ankle and then

her joints, the doctor asked, "How many times have you fallen?"

Her mother shot Grace a cagy look, then said, "About six times."

Six? Why hadn't she told them? Now more than ever, Grace was glad she'd forced the issue to bring her mother here.

"Is this right after you stand up?"

"Sometimes."

He went on to ask more questions, which Mama answered in what Grace thought was complete honesty. Had she been more shaken by the falls than she let on?

The doctor nodded, made notes, then looked at his patient. "When the nurse's assistant took your blood pressure this morning, the reading was very low. I wouldn't be surprised if this is the problem. To be sure, I'd like you to have a blood test. This will determine if there are any underlying problems causing the low pressure."

Wanda Sue's displeasure radiated across the room. "A blood test?"

"It'll only take a few moments but the results will give me a better idea of what we're looking at. You can have the draw done here and, after I review the results, we can get you started on a treatment plan. How does that sound?"

"Horrible. If you take blood out of me, I can't

guarantee I won't fall flat on your incredibly clean floor."

The doctor chuckled, then assured her, "You'll be fine, Mrs. Harper. I'll have one of my staff take you back to the lab." He turned to Grace and Faith. "Any other questions?"

"No," Grace said. "I'm just thankful you could see her."

The doctor nodded and left, Grace hurried over to help her mother lower herself from the table. "Happy now?"

"Yes," Grace and Faith responded in chorus, to which Mama rolled her eyes.

A woman dressed in scrubs arrived to take Wanda Sue to the lab. Faith walked out to the main office but before Grace could follow, her mother grabbed her arm with a death grip.

"I'm scared," she whispered.

Grace forced a smile to her lips. This was Mama, a bit pale and unnerved, leaning on Grace as always, but her resentment dried up in the face of this real threat to her mother's well-being. She understood Mama's fear. No one liked to be sick, but when the cause was unknown, it led to all sorts of conjecture, right or wrong. And since Mama didn't take bad news well…this could be tricky. Grace held her mother's cold fingers in hers and squeezed.

"I know, Mama. But once the doctor figures out the problem, you'll be good as new."

"You can't make promises like that."

"You're right, but I know you. You may not think so, but you're a fighter."

Her mother's teary gaze met Grace's. "How can you say that, after I put so much responsibility on you? I was a mess after your daddy left."

"But you pulled yourself up." Grace straightened her shoulders, as much a show of confidence for her mother as for herself. "We Harper women can take our lumps and still come out on top. Don't you forget it."

Her mother patted her cheek. "You're a good daughter, Gracie."

Swallowing the emotion lodged in her throat, Grace said, "So go have the test and then we'll deal with whatever the results are. Together."

The nurse acknowledged Grace and then said, "Are you ready, Mrs. Harper?"

"No, so let's get this over with."

Blowing out a sigh of relief that her mother hadn't insisted they leave, Grace went back to the waiting room. Still jittery about what the test results would reveal, she forced herself to stop pacing and sit. Faith, on the other hand, had grown very silent. *Another concern*, thought Grace.

"What's up, Faith?"

Faith straightened her shoulders. "I'm going to move in with Mama."

Not bothering to hide her surprise, Grace said, "Really?"

Faith clasped her hands together. "Since the day she confirmed another fall, I've been worried. I'll admit, moving back home was not what I'd planned, but then, nothing is going my way lately." She shook her head, like she was revving up to give herself a pep talk. "Anyway, Mama should have someone there and Donna can't be there all the time. You'll be going back to Atlanta soon, so I need to step up."

"That's very adult of you."

Faith seemed offended. "Are you mocking me?"

"No, I'm being honest." And with one look, the animosity Faith had targeted toward Grace since they were kids returned. So she quickly added, "You're right. Mama needs all hands on deck and I will be leaving."

Pushing her tangled hair from her face, Faith said, "I know she'll love having the kids around. And I can keep an eye on her until the doctor determines what the problem is."

"It's a wonderful idea, Faith. The office is running smoothly and once Mama's back on track, you two can keep the business going.

Maybe expand." She paused. "I know I've tried to get Mama to sell, but with you and Nathan engaged, we won't have to."

Determination gleamed in her sister's eyes. "We can do it."

"I know you can."

The door opened and another patient was called to an examining room. Grace settled back, feeling optimistic for the first time since she'd been home. Mama would get better, her siblings would pick up the slack and she could go back to what was left of her career. Smiling at the thought of making a comeback, it took Grace a moment to realize Faith had spoken.

"Sorry. What did you say?"

"I asked if you'd help me move our things to Mama's house today."

"Sure." Another thought surfaced. "What will Lyle think about you moving in with Mama? Will he join you?"

Faith averted her gaze, looking at everything in the room except Grace.

"Faith?"

"Things aren't working out between me and Lyle." Her voice broke. "I think maybe I should file for divorce."

As tears began to shimmer in her sister's eyes, Grace pulled her into an embrace. Just the fact alone that Faith and her kids had moved into the cabin was proof that there had been problems, but to this extent? True, she'd never liked Lyle, but she hated her sister's heartache more. They hugged for a long moment, then Faith pulled back, swiping her eyes.

"Are you sure?" Grace had to ask. Faith had a way of making decisions, then bailing before carrying through.

Faith raised her shoulders, uncertainty written on her face. "It's been over for a while, Grace. Lyle's never wanted to be tied down or accountable, and the more he stays out, the more I pressure him, and the more I pressure him, the more he stays away. I hung in there for the kids, but Lyle… He won't be happy with the news. I have to do better. For the kids and myself."

Grace took Faith's hands in hers. "And you will. I'll help anyway I can."

A bitter laugh escaped Faith. "Can you refer me to a good lawyer?"

"The best." Grace hitched a thumb in her direction. "I'll handle your case."

"You'll be in Atlanta."

"Doesn't mean I can't file the paperwork and do what needs to be done."

"How about you just refer me to someone local."

Faith's request made sense. Grace would be busy once she got back to the firm, but she couldn't ignore the little jab of hurt. It shouldn't bother her, but it did.

The door opened again and their mother limped across the threshold, muttering as she rolled her sleeve down.

"All finished?" Grace asked as she rose.

"For now. The doctor popped his head into the lab and said he hoped this would answer his questions so I didn't need any more tests." She hooked her purse over her good arm and pointed to Grace. "This better do it."

Grace held up her hands. "Hey, I have no control."

"Since when?" Faith teased.

"Well, with this."

Faith wrapped her arm around her mother. "Remember this day. It's the first time Gracie admitted she can't handle everything."

"Hey, no ganging up on me," Grace said, following her family out of the office into the bright summer day. Hope brimmed inside her, for the future of the business and that at least they were getting to the bottom of what ailed her mother.

On the ride through town, Grace noticed Faith hadn't told their mother she was moving back home, but figured her sister was going to discuss it later. Mama dominated the conversation, talking about the Summer Gold Celebration, the historical tour she missed leading and how happy she was that all her children were working together.

Grace dropped Faith off at the Put Your Feet Up office and then dropped her mother off at her house, promising she'd be back later to check in. Driving back downtown, Grace parked behind the office and hurried to the back door. When she went to yank it open, it didn't budge, forcing her momentum forward, and she slammed against the glass.

"What on earth?" she muttered, digging in her purse for her keys. She opened the door and stepped inside. "Faith, you forgot to unlock the back door."

Her heels echoed as she walked up the hallway, stopping short. The office was empty.

After dropping her purse on the desk, Grace quickly checked the restroom and storage closet. No Faith. Puzzled, she took her phone from her purse and dialed Faith's number. A muffled ringtone came from the other side of the room. Grace rounded the desk and opened the top drawer. Inside, her name, visible in bold letters, flashed on her sister's phone screen.

Hanging up, she removed Faith's phone and set it on the desk. She tried not to panic as her mind flashed from one scenario to another. What had happened to her sister? She'd left her only twenty minutes ago, but other than the phone, there was no trace that Faith had even been here.

With shaking fingers, she dialed Nathan, hoping to catch him before his next tour.

"It's Nathan. Leave me a message."

"You have got to be kidding me." She left a quick message for him to call her.

Grabbing her purse, she locked up the office and headed to the cabin. Since Grace had driven everyone to the doctor's office, she didn't know how Faith would have gotten out here unless she called a friend, but she didn't know where else to look. Sure enough, Faith's dusty van was still parked in the same spot. She ran inside, calling her sister's name. Silence greeted her.

Panic rising, she called her mother. Moderating her voice, she asked, "Is Faith with you?"

"No, she and Lyle just dropped the kids off. Faith said she'd be back later."

Faith had taken off with Lyle?

"Did she seem okay?"

"Why wouldn't she?" Her mother moved the phone from her mouth as she told John not to tease his sister. "She said she'd be back in a few days." Grace heard the pleasure in her mother's voice. "Gives me some time to spoil my grandbabies."

A few days? But Faith was scheduled to work. What happened to being responsible? Stunned, Grace lowered herself to the couch as her legs gave out. "Thanks, Mama."

She sat there staring into space for what seemed like forever. What about the divorce? Had Faith taken her husband back? Was she still moving in with Mama? Her phone rang in the middle of her attempt to figure out what had happened.

"Deke," she said after reading the caller ID.

"Hey, where is everyone? There are clients waiting at the door."

Not good. "I'll be right there," she said, slowly rising. She didn't know what was up with her sister, but it couldn't be good. And there was no way Grace could help her, since she'd fled to parts unknown with Lyle, just like she had years ago. Was this history repeating itself?

She made it back to the office in record time. Deke had the clients in the office, chatting them up before heading to the lake. He sent her a questioning glance, but she shook her head. Maybe later they'd have this discussion, but not in front of tourists. As he herded them out to the parking lot, she snatched his arm to stop him. Worked hard to keep her voice calm. "Have you talked to Nathan?"

"He's with a group at Deep North Adventures."

"You're sure?"

"Pretty sure." He frowned. "What's up?"

"Probably nothing."

Lines of concern formed between his brows. "Are you okay?"

"I'm not sure. Nathan's not answering his phone."

"Maybe he's busy."

She let out a shaky breath. "Let me know if he contacts you."

His eyes went tight at the corners. "Count on it."

Once Deke left, she was about to call her brother again when the office phone rang. "Put Your Feet Up."

"Grace. It's Colin. We have a problem."

Her stomach sank. "What kind of problem?"

"Your brother got a phone call, then got in the van and took off."

She ran a trembling hand over her brow. "How long ago?"

"About an hour. The zip-line tour is almost over."

"Any way I can borrow your van to get the clients back here to their cars?"

"Sure." He paused. "Everything okay?"

She would be so glad when there was no

need for anyone to ask her that question. With a firm tone, she said, "I'll be right over."

But as soon as she hung up, she swallowed a hysterical sob. Where were her siblings? How had things gone from good to bad in a matter of an hour? She left the office, afraid that her life was coming unraveled.

DEKE KEPT AN eye out, waiting for Grace to come home. She'd been rattled when he returned from the lake, asking again if he knew where Nathan was. Beside herself, she'd paced the office, wondering out loud what had made her brother leave clients behind at Deep North Adventures. Fifteen minutes later, Nathan strolled in through the back door, humming under his breath, like he hadn't a care in the world. After demanding an explanation, Nathan told her he'd gotten an important call he couldn't ignore. Said he left a message with Colin asking him to return the clients to their cars.

Grace confirmed his story with Colin, who explained that his employee at the front desk hadn't given him the message until much later. But instead of looking relieved, Grace had let out a harsh breath and disappeared into the restroom. Deke hung around, his concern for her growing. A frazzled look he didn't recognize, along with her shoulders slumped in what could only be defeat, told him she wasn't holding up well. When she finally emerged, her eyes were red, her mascara streaked. She grabbed her purse, told Nathan to lock up and stomped off.

Nathan looked at him and shrugged. "Chicks."

"Don't disrespect your sister."

Nathan's eyes had gone wide at his clipped tone. Deke knew something weighed heavily on Grace and he wanted to discover what it was. He was prepared for her rebuff, but he'd acquired just the thing he hoped would loosen her tongue.

Now, the sun had nearly dipped into the horizon when he heard the crush of gravel under tires. Peering out his window, he saw Grace's car. He swallowed his relief. His heart became a little lighter. She was home.

Grace emerged from the car, but abruptly stopped on the path and turned toward the firepit. Good, just what he'd had in mind.

He grabbed his bag of supplies and strode outside. The temperature had dropped, perfect for a pleasant evening. Insects buzzed around him as he crunched over the dirt path to the firepit. The shadows were long and filmy. A soft breeze darted through the pines as he drew close to find Grace seated in an Adirondack chair, head back, eyes closed, feet bare and resting on the edge of the brick wall of the firepit, shoes tossed haphazardly nearby.

"Tough day?" he asked, sinking into the chair beside her.

"Tough is a piece of cake compared to everything going on." She expelled a long sigh, but her eyes remained closed.

"Did you eat dinner?"

She nodded. "At Mama's."

The sudden whir of an engine, probably a boat on the lake, cut through the night. He could just make out the water through the trees as the sun set faster now.

"How about I make a fire?"

She moved her feet. "Have at it."

He rose to grab a few pieces of cut wood from the stack and in minutes had a small flame started. Bits of ash floated upward as the wood caught fire. Time to bring out the big guns.

"Since you already had dinner, how about we share dessert?"

One eye slit open. "What did you have in mind?"

He dug into the bag to produce a box of graham crackers, chocolate and a bag of marshmallows. "S'mores."

She flung her arm toward him, fingers wiggling. "Skip the crackers and fluff. Hand over the chocolate and no one gets hurt."

He chuckled. "Now I know it was a bad day."

When he handed her the bar, she sat up, unwrapped the treat and took a dainty bite. She closed her eyes and chewed. They sat in silence as she devoured the chocolate. Judging by the heavenly look on her face, she savored every second.

"This almost makes up for a truly horrible day," she said as she licked the smeared remainders from her fingers.

"Care to share?"

"I knew when you offered chocolate it came with a price."

He frowned. "I only meant to make you happy. Take away some of the stress dogging you."

She gave him a thumbs-up. "So far so good."

"Your day?" he reminded her.

Tucking her feet under her, she rested an elbow on the wide arm of the chair and dropped her chin in her palm. "Took Mama to the doctor, Faith ran off and, as you know, Nathan left clients stranded at the zip line." She shrugged. "All in a day's work."

"Faith did what?"

"Took off and left her kids at Mama's."

He glanced over his shoulder at the dark cabin. "Explains why it's so quiet at your place."

"One minute Faith announces she *thinks* she should file for divorce, the next she takes off with the husband she says she isn't happy with."

Deke didn't even know how to reply to that piece of news. "And your mother?"

"The doctor took blood for tests. Hopefully we'll find out something soon." She stared at the fire. As the dusk settled around them, Grace's face became pensive. "And I'm pretty sure I'll be moving back to my mother's house."

This statement surprised Deke the most. "What? Why?"

"Faith offered before she took off. Until we get answers from the doctor, Mama shouldn't be alone."

"Who is with her now?"

"Nathan and her friend Donna, who's been helping her out with the grandkids Faith dropped off before hightailing it. And get this, after hearing Mama had been to the doctor, Lissy Ann and her committee stopped by with dinner." She finally looked in his direction. "Uncle Nathan offered to play with the kids. I guess it's his way of saying sorry."

"His hanging around doesn't seem to make up for what he did today."

She scowled. "What is wrong with my family?"

"I'd say normal operating procedure, but I have to admit, they do manage to surprise."

Tilting her head up, she stared into the night. In a quiet voice she said, "I'm never going back to Atlanta and my career, am I?"

The way things were going, it didn't look like that would happen anytime soon, but he said, "You can't give up hope."

She turned toward him. "Hope? Really? I thought for one glorious moment that my family was finally under control, only to have them revert to form." She ran her palms over her eyes. "I either need to give up my career at the law firm to run the family business, or talk my mother into selling. After today, I don't know if I can trust Faith and Nathan to keep the business above water."

Deke leaned forward, resting his elbows on his knees, fingers spread out toward the flames. "Maybe you should walk away."

Her eyes went wide. "Are you crazy? Who will take care of them all?"

"I don't get it, Grace. You say you want your own life but you aren't willing to leave your family to do so. If you want your career so badly, go for it."

"Really? This coming from the guy who

walked away from his own career? Are you going back or will you continue to hide from your emotions?"

He blinked as the breeze blew smoke toward his face. *Good question.* So far everything he'd done—accepting his role to research a lead about his mother's boyfriend, which he was doing a supremely bad job of; taking on work that was more settling to his mind and soul and less about his cover; and falling for a woman who was more determined to take care of the world than live her own life—was all a big excuse not to face the truth. He'd messed up. A friend died. He'd live with the guilt, but hoped he was finally honest enough to admit he couldn't carry the burden alone. He wanted to share life's ups and downs. With a partner. Grace.

"I'm sorry, Deke."

"No, you're right. I'm in no place to judge. But I also know something's got to give."

"I know you think I'm wrong by not letting my siblings stand on their own feet. Reap the consequences of their actions, good or bad."

"Not like I'm any less wrong about trying to find out about my mother's boyfriend behind her back." He took the stick by his feet and poked at the smoldering logs to get the flame burning brighter. "I suppose loving our families isn't a bad excuse for our behavior."

When she held out her hand again, he reached into the bag and handed her another bar of chocolate. They sat in silence, listening to the fire crackle. Another white plume wafted his way, cloaking him in smoke.

Grace groaned. "Tomorrow morning, I'm going to be sorry for eating that second bar."

"I'd say you earned it."

Tossing the wrapper into the fire, she angled her body toward him. "So what now? What do we do?"

"One step in front of the other has worked well for me so far."

She shook her head. "I'm too impatient."

"You can't make things change just by sheer force of will, Grace."

"Okay, then I should set down ground rules. If they aren't followed, there are consequences."

"Which means you have to stand by those decisions. Can you honestly do that?"

Her face turned glum. "Probably not."

He held out his hand. She glanced at it, then up at him.

"Let's make a pact."

"Will it include chanting vows and a blood sacrifice?"

He gaped at her.

She shrugged. "Sorry. My mood is dark."

"You think?"

With the barest hint of a grin, she laid her hand in his. He savored the soft touch, the connection to the woman who had grown important to him over a short period of time. "I'll admit I can't do this alone, if you agree, as well."

She pressed her lips together.

"Asking for help doesn't make us weak, Grace. In fact, it takes much more courage. It's easy to be an island, much harder to open our hearts and admit we can't control everything, no matter how much we convince ourselves otherwise. We aren't in this life alone."

He lifted her hand to his lips to place a kiss. In the firelight she appeared so vulnerable, so sad and unsure of herself. If he hadn't thought he was in love with her before, he knew for certain now.

"I don't know if I can," she whispered.

"Maybe it's because you don't want to."

"Just like you can't let go of the guilt over your friend's death?"

The tension in his chest tightened. He wanted to let go. He did. Found himself failing every time he tried.

Grace stared at him a long moment. Her voice cracked when she asked, "Do you want to?"

He ran his palm across his chest.

"You loved her." A statement, not a question.

"I thought so. Years ago." He reached across the space between them to place his knuckle under her chin and turn her head his way. "Everything changed when I met you."

Their gazes caught and held. He wasn't sure she believed him, but before he had a chance to assure her that the feelings he'd once had for Britt were eclipsed by what he felt for her, she unfolded her legs and stood. "I need to get home."

"Grace, I wasn't finished."

She held up a hand. "I don't want to know the rest." She gathered her shoes and purse. He reached out to stop her, surprised by the anguish in her eyes. "Grace, what is it?"

"I can't compete with a ghost, Deke."

"Ghost? No, Grace, you've got it all wrong."

"Really? Because sometimes you get a look in your eyes, like you miss her."

"I do. She was my friend and I'll always grieve the way she died. But you? I can't imagine not talking to you every day, watching that look of happiness when you sip your first soda of the morning. The way your hair shines in the sun or how you get a determined look in your eyes when you singlehandedly take care of a problem. You dressed up like a pioneer to keep your mother's vision for the historical tour

alive, for Pete's sake. I want us to share everything life has to offer, Grace. More than I've
wanted anything in my life."

"My life is messy and uncertain right now. I
want there to be an us… I do, but until I figure
out how to balance every aspect of my life, I
don't think I can do this."

She tugged her arm free, slipped on her
shoes and hurried across the drive to her cabin.
A fierce longing welled up in Deke. He'd been
trying to help. Make her see she didn't have to
carry her burden alone. How on earth had his
gesture turned so spectacularly wrong? In trying to make her see she didn't have to take care
of everyone alone, he'd managed to raise the
hurdles of a relationship between them even
higher.

He watched the last glowing embers of the
fire fade and burn out, wondering if Grace
would ever realize no onc had complete control of their lives, no matter how much they
willed it to be true.

CHAPTER FOURTEEN

STILL STRUGGLING WITH the turn of events the night before, Deke rose early after barely sleeping and went for a run to clear his head. The pounding of his feet against the hard earth, the whistle of the wind as he weaved in and out of the trees, did little to alleviate his troubled thoughts. Since he couldn't seem to get a single thing right with Grace in the romance department, he might as well do what his family asked and gain more intel on Serena. At least his brothers' request was clear and to the point, unlike his fuzzy and confusing relationship with Grace.

After a bracing shower, he grabbed a protein bar and locked the door to the cabin. First, a visit to Serena Stanhope. Then he'd stop by the office, hoping Grace would be alone and they could finish last night's conversation. He'd jogged the short path to his Jeep when his cell rang. Pulling the device from his pocket, he recognized the number and accepted the call.

"Hey, Dylan. Sorry I haven't checked in sooner. I was going to call you later this morning."

"No need. I have some news."

"Good or bad?" Deke asked, slipping on his sunglasses.

"Both."

He continued walking to the Jeep as he talked, his boots crunching over dry ground. "Okay, lay it on me."

"In the pictures you sent me, I recognized Tate with Serena. I had my friend Max extend the search on him."

"He found something?"

"The picture opened an avenue. Turns out Tate is an alias. His real name is James Stanhope."

Deke swung himself up behind the wheel. "Stanhope? Like Serena?"

"His daughter."

In his wildest imagination, Deke hadn't expected this revelation. "Unbelievable."

"He did a good job covering his tracks, but my guy is better."

"Let me guess. His one weakness was being unable to cut ties with his daughter."

"Partially. There were other ways Max dug up the truth, but the bottom line is we have conformation."

"So what's the deal with the guy?" Deke asked, resting his free hand on top of the steering wheel. "Why the secrecy?"

"He's a con man."

Deke leaned back in the seat. "Did you say con man?"

"Yep, you heard me right."

Unsure he wanted to hear the answer, he asked anyway. "And you told Mom?"

A pause. "Not exactly."

"What, then?"

On the other end, Deke heard Dylan's frustrated sigh. "She refuses to talk about what she may or may not know. James's past is off-limits and she's sticking with her position. So much so she's refusing calls from Derrick and Dante and won't speak to me when I stop by to visit her."

Deke pictured the scenario in his mind. Dylan asking questions, dogging their mother's every step while she remained mum. Honestly, that was Jasmine Matthews to the core. Independent to a fault. She always trusted her instincts. Even if it meant keeping her sons at arm's length. "When Mom digs her heels in she's unshakable."

"Which is why we need a different tactic."

Mulling that over, Deke said, "My cover isn't blown, per se, but if Serena's father has given her a heads-up, there's no way she'll talk to me now."

"Just what I was afraid of."

"What about going back to my PI buddy, Logan. He's from around here and owes me a favor. I'll call in my marker. Maybe he can get further than I can at this point."

"Sounds like a plan."

Deke felt better knowing they could put an alternative idea in motion. "I'll call him when we hang up."

"I'll let the others know."

Deke's mind then took him in a different direction. One he didn't want to face. Their mother might be mixed up with a con man. Bad. Even worse? She might already know the truth and have decided to keep seeing him anyway. Jasmine could be stubborn, especially if she felt her sons were pressuring her. Or maybe Tate, er, Stanhope, had bamboozled her with his lies?

It was time to head south and insert himself in the situation.

Dylan cut his musing short. "Deke?"

"Yeah, I'm here." He glanced over the surroundings he was coming to love. Leaves swaying in the gentle breeze. The sun breaking though the tree cover to shine on the ground in wavering patches of light. The nearby lake and mountains. "Once I hand over the reins, my work here is done. I can head to Florida."

"Will that be a problem? You can only take a leave of absence for so long."

He was nowhere near ready to get back to work. Not when he was finally coming to grips with his part in Britt's death or while things were up in the air with Grace. If she refused to acknowledge the fragile bond forming between them, there was nothing else he could do. Since this was her home, no matter how sporadically she might visit the mountains, he wouldn't stay if they parted ways. Atlanta or Florida would be the best alternative for him.

"I'll let you know what I decide," was all Deke could promise his brother.

"I'm here if you need me."

"Thanks, Dyl, but some things a guy has to figure out on his own."

Deke heard a soft chuckle on the other end. "Must be a woman."

"One worth fighting for." He paused. "And promise you won't tell Derrick. I won't hear the end of it."

"We've all suffered through his brotherly advice. It's your turn."

Deke shook his head as he ended the call. Talking to Derrick felt more like brotherly ribbing than advice, but he knew his brothers had his back. Always. One constant in life that never changed.

After leaving a message for Logan Masterson, his PI connection, Deke started up the Jeep and exited the main drag from the cabins, kicking up gravel as he turned onto the asphalt road. He was thinking about how to digest this new information when his cell rang. He glanced over to see a call coming in from Derrick.

"That had to be record time," he muttered, ignoring the call. Hands tightly gripping the steering wheel, he focused on driving to his destination. Until he figured things out with Grace and talked to Logan, he didn't want any well-intentioned advice.

Dylan's phone call had changed the direction of his morning. He should give Serena some room until a new plan went into play. As he drove down Main, he glanced into the Put Your Feet Up office. There was a group of people inside. So much for talking to Grace alone.

Might as well make a pit stop for his daily coffee fix. As usual, the jolt of caffeine got his blood moving—not that he needed much of a boost after Dylan's phone call. He stood on the sidewalk, shooting the breeze with a few locals, trying not to look in the direction of the tour office. Procrastinating didn't matter. Grace never wandered outside. After determining he'd killed enough time, he headed to the warehouse.

Spending the morning unpacking camping equipment would be a good way to focus on the matters at hand. Busywork to keep his mind free to brainstorm solutions. He didn't have a tour until this afternoon, when he would take a group on a hike to the highest mountain summit in the area. Afterward maybe he'd get Grace alone. Invite her to dinner. Someplace romantic. But for now, he was still employed by Put Your Feet Up and had a job to do.

Nathan's truck was parked to the side of the warehouse, the large roll-up door open. As he strode inside, Deke's feet echoed on the concrete floor. "Nathan?"

"Be right there," came a voice from out back.

Pushing up the sleeves of his long-sleeved T-shirt, Deke began hauling the boxes to the floor. He was using his pocketknife to slit the tape when Nathan materialized.

"You don't have to unpack all that. I was going to get it done this morning."

"I'm free and need something to do."

A ghost of a smile passed over Nathan's lips. "Did you stop by the office?"

Suspicion had Deke frowning. "No. Should I have?"

"You usually check in."

"My group doesn't leave until later, so I'm good."

"Good, huh?" came his reply, heavy with humor.

He shot Nathan one of his hard-line cop glances. "Got something to say?"

"I do." Nathan squared his shoulders. "What are your intentions toward my sister?"

Deke's hands stilled on the box of equipment. "Intentions?"

"I see the way you look at her."

Deke straightened. "What way is that?"

"Like you can't decide whether to argue with her or kiss her."

No way was Deke admitting to Grace's brother that he'd already kissed her or that it was the most incredible experience of his life. Then the first part of the statement stopped him. "Why would I argue with her?"

"Because she's the boss and knows it."

True, but that was one of the things Deke found appealing about Grace. Clearly Nathan was the one with the problem. "And that bothers you?"

The other man scowled. "I didn't say that."

"You didn't have to."

Nathan clammed up, hefting another box from the corner and tearing open the packing tape. Just as Deke hoped, the conversation switched from his attraction to Grace to the real problem.

Voice tight, Nathan blurted, "She doesn't trust me."

"She has every right not to after what you pulled yesterday," Deke admonished, putting as much authority in his tone as he dared. It was time someone spoke to Nathan, man-to-man.

"That was unavoidable. And in my defense, I did let Colin's front desk help know I was leaving."

"But you never should have taken off until you finished the job."

Nathan looked contrite, then conflicted. "It won't happen again. Not that it'll change things with Grace."

As one brother of four, Deke realized a dare was needed here. "Then prove her wrong."

Interest spiked in Nathan's eyes. "How?"

Deke pointed to the gear scattered around them. "Come up with a plan that shows Grace you're committed to the business."

"By what? Adding a tour or something?"

"Not something. Exactly that. Come up with a plan."

Surprise, then excitement crossed Nathan's face.

"Go for it."

Nathan backed up. "Be right back."

While Nathan raced off to his truck, Deke continued unpacking. He'd hold off discussing his hike/camping idea with Nathan until he heard what the younger man had to say. Then his phone beeped with a text. Grace, admonishing him for working when he didn't have to be, but asking how it was going.

So she was being all business? Deke could reciprocate. I'm working with Nathan, he texted back.

He's been avoiding me.

Can't imagine why.

With a chuckle, Deke set the phone aside. Nathan returned with a notebook and held it out to Deke.

"What's this?"

"My ideas."

Curious now, Deke flipped through page after page of Nathan's outdoor adventure concepts. Granted, some were a bit grandiose for a small team like the Harper family, but there were a few nuggets of gold. Deke focused on one in particular.

"Wilderness survival trips. What did you have in mind?"

"Taking kids up the mountain for a few nights. Bare basics to teach them how to survive on their own. I had some clients ask about this kind of thing the other day."

"A good start, but what if parents aren't secure with this kind of trip for their children?"

"Then we make it a family outing? That's more of what Put Your Feet Up does anyway."

"Start with family, see if there's interest and then maybe just kids somewhere down the road."

"Right." Nathan took the notebook back and jotted down a few lines. "I'd have to figure how much equipment we have…"

"We're doing inventory right now."

"And costs. Food. Time."

Deke could see that developing his own tour had piqued Nathan's interest. The next step would be convincing Grace that his idea had merit. While Nathan put details to paper, Deke opened the last box, removed the equipment, then sorted it.

Calling Nathan over, Deke said, "By my count you have enough gear for eight guests, plus two guides right here."

An odd expression flitted over Nathan's face.

"Am I incorrect?"

"No, I was just, ah…thinking about my dad. He wanted to do camping trips but it didn't pan out."

The infamous drug dealer. "Grace told me about him."

Surprise lit Nathan's eyes. "She did? Huh. It's not something we share with strangers." Nathan regarded him closely. "But then I'm guessing you're more than an employee to my sister."

He was working on it, not that his efforts seemed to be gaining any traction. Instead of admitting to making a mess of things with Grace, Deke said, "Your dad. Do you ever hear from him?"

Guilt flickered in Nathan's eyes.

So he had. And kept it a secret. "I'm guessing you haven't told the others."

With a sigh, Nathan unfolded a nearby lawn chair and sank down. "No, it's just…they wouldn't understand."

Deke leaned against the wall, crossing his arms over his chest. Instinct told him that Nathan's story was bigger than he let on. "You think they wouldn't want to know how he's doing?"

"His request."

Which didn't raise his already questionable, low esteem in Deke's opinion. "When was the last time you saw him?"

"A month ago," he said quietly.

"When you took off?"

"I only wanted to help. To make Mama's life easier."

"By doing what, exactly?"

Nathan ignored his question.

"Are you afraid to tell me what you were doing before you came home?"

Nathan seemed conflicted. "Grace said you're a cop. Why would I tell you anything?"

"Because I can help you."

"Trust me. You can't."

As much as his desire to protect Grace kicked in, she needed to know what her brother was up to, now rather than later. All Deke could do was be there to offer a shoulder to cry on or advice after the shoe dropped. From the expression on Nathan's face, that shoe was more like a big, heavy boot.

"This have anything to do with leaving clients behind yesterday?"

Nathan averted his eyes.

A car door slammed outside. Deke walked to the open door, anticipation and dread filling him. "It's Grace."

SMOOTHING HER BLACK skirt after climbing from the car, Grace noted her heart skipped a beat when she glimpsed Deke standing in the open doorway. She'd overreacted last night. Big-time. But in her defense, she had felt adrift by the events of the day, unsure what to do about her future, so she deflected. Accusing Deke of being in love with a ghost was jumping to conclusions, but the devastated look on his face when she'd brought up his old friend made her doubt herself even more. He'd been honest with her, telling her she meant more to him than Britt, so why was she putting up a roadblock?

After driving to Mama's last night after fleeing the firepit, she realized she owed Deke an apology. She'd sat down with an old family photo album, thumbing through the pages of memories. Stopped at pictures of her parents when they were young and happy. Had the fracturing of her family after Daddy was arrested made her lose faith in love? Was she afraid to love, and lose again?

Grace decided there was a lot of truth in what Deke had said. She couldn't continue making excuses for her family, had to stop believing she could handle all the family problems alone. She couldn't, no matter how often she had delusions that she could do otherwise.

So she'd stopped for takeout, hoping to butter him up with a nice lunch. Oh, and also to tell him she wanted to see where this attraction was taking them. Because he wasn't alone in thinking there was something between them. Her attraction to Deke was starting to outweigh her family commitments and she needed to be honest with him. Hadn't he laid it all on the line with her? It was time she admitted the truth to the one person it mattered to the most—Deke.

"Hey, how are my two hardest workers doing?" she called out, carrying a bag heavy with heavenly smelling food and a drink holder from Laurel's Corner Café.

"You mean the *only* hardworking guys?" Deke countered, his steady gaze glued to her.

Controlling a runaway shiver at the intensity of his stare, she pulled a smile. "That, too. Thought I'd bring by lunch and see what you've unearthed here."

Nathan walked up beside Deke, a patent look of guilt on his face. Sensing that she'd interrupted more than just work, she glanced from Deke to her brother. When Nathan turned away, her smile faded. "Something wrong?"

Deke kept his expression neutral. Waiting for Nathan's lead? Judging by the caged expression on her brother's face, something big, and probably unpleasant, was about to be exposed.

Grace dropped the bag and drinks on an empty table against the wall. "Well?"

Nathan walked over, handing his notebook to Grace. "We were discussing ideas about what to do with the camping gear."

Taking the notebook, she scanned the notes.

"This is well thought out, Nathan." Her smile returned, and her stomach settled. Maybe she'd read him wrong. Maybe her brother was nervous about revealing his ideas to her.

Nathan ran a hand through his hair. "Thanks. That means a lot to me."

"Look, I know I give you a hard time, but you really have a head for business. I'm excited to implement your ideas. After we sit down and get this initial proposal conceptualized on paper, Put Your Feet Up will offer a new tour."

She handed the notebook back to him. Even though she'd hoped the notebook wasn't a stalling tactic, her stomach continued churning at the regret on Nathan's face.

"There's more," he said. "You should sit."

He pushed the lawn chair toward her and opened another for himself, placing it directly in front of her. Deke leaned against the wall.

"You know how I took off last month?" Nathan started.

"You never did explain why."

"Things were going good for the business. But Mama's personal finances? I hadn't kept up to date on them like I promised. She got behind on the mortgage."

Grace closed her eyes, then opened them again. "What did you do?"

"I kinda borrowed money from some guys.

Then I tried to gamble it back so I wouldn't owe them."

"Oh, Nathan."

Her brother glanced at Deke, a pleading expression on his face. To his credit, Deke kept his expression schooled, but said, "Might as well get it all out in the open. Your sister deserves the truth."

Grace's eyes went wide. This could not be good.

"I went down to Biloxi," Nathan continued. "Know some guys who run a card game down there. Only I got in deep and they wanted me to run a delivery with another guy."

Shadows of the past rose up to haunt her. "What kind of delivery?"

"I didn't ask. Just took the box and went to meet the guy."

"And?"

"The other guy turned out to be Dad."

So stunned by his answer, Grace could barely come up with a coherent response.

"How…" The crushing pressure in her chest made it hard to speak. "Why didn't you say anything?"

"You know Mama. She would have insisted I take her to him. He may be our father, but no way would I let him get anywhere near her," Nathan said fiercely.

While Grace appreciated the loyalty—because he was right, Mama would want to see Daddy—she was starting to get miffed by all the secrets and tiptoeing around the truth.

Deke pushed away from the wall.

"You knew about this?" she accused.

"Not the details. Yet."

She believed him and turned her attention back to her brother. "Nathan, just tell me."

"I trusted Dad. Turned out to be a mistake." Nathan jumped up from the chair and began to pace. "We were outside this run-down building where the games are held. He told me to wait while he got the car. Once he pulled up, he popped the trunk and I placed the box in the trunk. Before I had a chance to get in the car, he burned rubber out of the parking lot."

Astonished, she yelped, "He left you?"

Nathan nodded, cheeks flushed. "I panicked. That's when I came home, hoping to forget the whole thing."

The details sank in. Grace was startled when Deke spoke.

"During the dance at the park, who were you talking to?" he asked, his tone calm in comparison with Grace's racing pulse.

"One of the guys from down south. The package never reached its destination and they wanted answers."

Rising slowly, Grace placed a shaky hand over her mouth. Her eyes flooded with tears. "Did they threaten you?"

"Not exactly. More like they want the money I owe plus the value of what was in the box."

"Drugs?" Deke asked.

Nathan shrugged. "Probably. I didn't look."

More like he didn't want to know. Grace eased back down into the chair as her legs gave out.

"They want me to do some more jobs for them until we're even."

"You don't honestly think you'll ever be even, do you?" Deke asked.

Nathan didn't bother to give the obvious answer.

"How could Daddy do this to you?" Grace whispered, her throat dry with fear.

"He's never changed, Grace."

"How do you…" A thought skittered into her mind. "Wait, you've seen him more than that trip?"

"A few times."

Silence settled heavily over the warehouse. Deke clapped a hand on Nathan's shoulder. "I don't have jurisdiction in Mississippi, but I could contact some people I know. Whatever illegal activity is going on, you can stop them."

Nathan's tanned face went pale. "By what? Turning on the guys I owe money to?"

"Nathan, be reasonable," Grace said, all signs of unease gone as she faced her brother. "You dug yourself in deep. Those guys followed you here. That means they'll find you no matter where you go. You'll always be on the run or forced to work with them. Neither one is a good option."

"Not if I don't rat them out."

"It's either pay up or work with the authorities," Deke said calmly. "You don't have the money, do you?"

He shook his head.

"This isn't going away, Nathan. We have to get ahead of this," Grace said, all attorney now.

"I'm not a kid, Grace, so quit treating me like one."

"Really? You could have fooled me. Why couldn't you just focus on the business? Contacted me if you needed money for Mama. Your schemes never work, Nathan."

"And you never make it easy to follow in your footsteps. Grace Harper, who never makes mistakes. Oh, wait, until you got our father arrested and our lives changed." He glared at her. "You aren't going to do the same thing to me."

At her wounded gasp, Nathan stomped out of the warehouse. Grace started after him, but

Deke stopped her. She tried to pull from his grasp, then went slack. There was no point fighting.

He tugged her close. Oh, how she'd love to sink into his strength right now. Let him fix this latest disaster.

"Going after him will only make matters worse, Grace. He needs time to figure out how to handle this."

"And if he runs?"

Deke didn't speak immediately. That's what she loved about him, how he thought a situation through. Acted on fact, not emotion. Kept a level head when everything was crumbling around them.

Wait. She loved him? Her heart nearly unraveled with the truth.

Before she could wrap her mind about this unexpected realization, Deke said, "I don't think he will. Look, he wants to come up with new tours and ways to advance your business. He made a mistake and he has to learn from it, Grace. He's not a boy any longer, he's a man."

"Yet he's blaming me."

"He's lashing out. It's easier than accepting the truth."

She gazed up at him, turmoil making her eyes burn with unshed tears from both her un-

timely realization of love and her brother's fool-
ish actions. "What now?"

"Nathan knows he screwed up. But he also
knows he has a family who loves him."

"I do," she agreed, voice barely above a whis-
per. *And I love you, too.* But look what happened. By falling for Deke, she'd started letting
go of her family, and disaster struck. To be
fair, Nathan's troubles started long before Deke
came into her life, but was she wrong to want
to focus on Deke and herself? It was becoming difficult to split her attention between her
family's needs and her longing for a serious
relationship with Deke. It brought her back to
square one.

"I came to Golden at my brothers' request,"
Deke said in a hushed tone, "wanting to escape the consequences of my last case. I never
imagined I'd find myself smack in the middle
of the Harper clan's messy business. But I'm
here, Grace. And I can help. If you want me
to." He bent at the knees so their eyes were on
the same level. "There's no way I'm walking
away. You're over your head with this newest information. Let me keep an eye on your
brother. The fact that he started opening up to
me, knowing I'm a cop, is a big step, Grace."

"It is."

He placed a gentle kiss on her forehead.

"Then you should suggest he go to the authorities."

"And be the reason another member of my family goes to jail?" She trembled at the thought. "I can't. I won't."

"Do you think any other way is going to work?"

If only she had never left Golden. Maybe she could have steered her brother from going down the wrong path. Or helped her sister make better decisions. She'd let her family down yet again.

"If he somehow works with the police, you can't promise he'll be safe."

"No, but he has a chance. If not, you'll be defending him when he goes to jail. Because he will get caught, Grace."

Grace couldn't breathe. She thought she might hyperventilate on the spot. "I can't think. I need to get back to the office."

Releasing his hold on her, he stepped away. She swayed toward him, then snapped back. After a moment's hesitation, she turned on her heel until Deke called out, "Grace."

She stopped, closed her eyes for a brief moment and turned.

"All your skills as a lawyer won't help if those guys get to him first."

CHAPTER FIFTEEN

LATER THAT NIGHT, heavy knocking on the cabin door jerked Deke from his comfortable position on the couch. Engrossed in a fiction thriller, he hadn't heard anyone approach. Worried it might be Grace, he strode to the door and yanked it open.

"Nathan."

Under the single porch light, the younger man shifted from foot to foot, running a hand through his already messy hair. "Sorry to bother you but I didn't know where else to go."

Deke stepped back. "Come in."

Nathan stormed inside, pacing the living room.

Closing the door, Deke braced himself. "What's wrong?"

"Those guys I was telling you about? The ones in town last week?" If possible, his face went even paler. "They're back. Looking for me."

So it was worse than they'd thought.

"Where are they right now?"

"At the park, I think. I was closing up the office when I noticed a car idling on the street. I turned off the lights and watched from the dark. This big guy got out and I recognized him." He stopped pacing to pull his phone from his jeans pocket. "Here. He sent me a text."

Taking the device, Deke read the short, but succinct note.

Meet at park. Now. We know where your mother lives.

A chill ran down Deke's spine. "Did you call your mother? Or the police?"

"I called Mama, but it went straight to her answering machine." A look of terror came over Nathan's face. "And I don't want the local cops involved. I lit out of the office and came straight here." He ran both hands through his hair. "You gotta help me."

Deke walked to the coffee table to retrieve his cell phone. Hit the speed dial for his brother.

"Awfully late to be calling," came Dylan's groggy voice.

"I have a situation." Deke quickly explained the issue at hand.

"I need names."

Deke shifted the phone away from his mouth. "Nathan, do you remember those guys' names?"

"One of them." He rattled it off and Deke relayed the info to his brother.

"Can you check into this? These thugs are serious and I'm afraid things are going to get dicey around here."

"I'm on it."

Dylan hung up.

"Who'd you call?" Nathan stopped moving long enough to ask.

"My brother. He works for the DEA. Hopefully he can get some answers."

"And until then?"

"We do what we can." Deke went to his bedroom to remove his firearm from its hiding place. Checked the chamber and rejoined Nathan. The younger man's eyes went wide at the sight of the weapon.

"You, ah, think you might need that?"

Deke sent him a *really?* look.

"Yeah. Those guys probably have guns, too."

"Where is your sister?"

"At Mama's. Faith came home sooner than expected. Grace was spending the night."

Deke froze. Grace was in danger? He grabbed his phone again, calling her. "Straight to voice mail."

"Grace and Mama were playing with John. Maybe they got involved in a game or something."

A cold resolve filled Deke, momentarily eclipsing his alarm. He needed to keep a cool head, needed to get to Grace and the others. Now. "We have to be there before your friends."

"My friends?" Nathan sputtered.

Deke yanked his arm. "Let's go."

They ran to the Jeep and jumped in, gravel spraying as Deke took off. All he could think about was Grace. She had no clue she was in danger. None of the Harper women did. And just like a few months ago, when his best friend had unknowingly walked out of work into the sights of a murderer, he couldn't help feeling he was living out his worst nightmare.

"I'm sorry," Nathan yelled over the engine. "I never thought."

"Let's just keep a level head," Deke advised, even though he was less than calm. If Grace got hurt... He couldn't go there. She was safe. She had to be.

Ten minutes later Deke screeched to a halt in front of Wanda Sue's house. As soon as he cut the ignition, he jumped from the Jeep and ran to the door, Nathan on his heels. The door flew open before they reached the steps. Faith stood there, silhouetted in the bright light, the baby on her hip, tears on her cheeks.

"They took Grace," Faith cried.

Deke's heart seized. When he could breathe again, he asked, "Who?"

"I don't know. Two guys I've never seen before."

Deke made his way into the house. Wanda Sue sat in an armchair, tissue in hand as she wiped her face. "They wanted me," she told Deke in a choppy voice, "but weren't happy that I couldn't walk fast enough because of my bruised ankle. Grace volunteered herself instead."

Of course she did. If putting her own safety in jeopardy meant protecting her family, she would jump in, eyes wide open. And give Deke a heart attack in the process.

"I called the police," Faith said, bouncing the whimpering baby.

Deke nodded. He didn't think he could talk, his throat so clogged with fear. When his phone rang, he snatched it up immediately.

"Talk to me, Dylan."

"Your guy has been on our radar for some time. I notified the New Orleans Division and they're getting right on it. Atlanta's closer, so they're sending some agents. Afraid I can only give you an ETA."

"That's better than nothing."

"Look, don't go rushing into this. Let the agents handle it."

"I can't, Dylan. They have Grace."

His brother uttered a few choice words. "Then be careful."

"I will."

Deke rammed his emotions down deep into that dark place where they couldn't affect him or his ability to save Grace. He had to get to her. "Did they say where they were taking her?"

"Gold Dust Park." Faith shot a nervous glance at Nathan. "They said they sent you a text and would meet you there."

Nathan's voice trembled. "What do we do?"

Deke went deadly serious. "We bring Grace home."

If Grace's heart beat any harder, she could almost imagine it jumping through her chest. She'd never been this scared in her life.

When the two thugs had shown up on Mama's doorstep, shock and fear had coursed through her veins. She'd known Nathan was in trouble, but had hoped they'd have time to come up with a plan before the situation got ugly. Turned out these guys had other ideas.

The taller of the two men shoved her toward a park shelter located far from the main road, draped in shadows. She lost her footing and nearly fell until she quickly righted herself.

"What do you want with Nathan?" she asked for what seemed like the twentieth time.

"I think it's pretty clear. He owes us money and product. We're here to collect."

The taller man pushed Grace down on a picnic bench. She wrapped her arms around her middle, hugging herself tightly, her legs shaking. "Do you honestly think he's going to show up?"

Taller bent down to get in her face. "You'd better hope he does."

She swallowed hard. His eyes were soulless.

"What if I give you the money?" She'd already been thinking about ways to come up with the funds Nathan needed. At this point she just wanted to bail him out of trouble and deal with the consequences later.

The other man laughed. "I doubt you got that kind of money, lady."

"How much?"

"Twenty grand."

Her stomach sank. Okay, that tactic wasn't going to work. What could she offer them to make them happy? She knew the answer was Nathan, but tried to come up with a different, less horrifying solution.

A piercing ringtone tore through the night. The heavier man answered. He nodded his bald head a few times before ending the call.

"Boss wants results."

Taller cracked his knuckles and sent Grace a menacing smile.

Pressing her lids shut, she tried not to panic. Impossible. The only thing that kept her from falling apart was the knowledge that her mother and sister were safe. By now, Mama would have called the police. And hopefully Deke.

Hot tears pinched her eyes at the thought of Deke getting involved. Because he would. She had no doubt. As a police officer, he understood the gravity of the situation. Knew anything could go wrong, just like it had with his best friend. Was he reliving that nightmare right now?

Squeezing her hands into fists, she inhaled shaky breaths. Help would come, somehow, some way. She had to hold on to that assurance. Golden might be a small town, but people would rally in her defense. Wouldn't they?

Time ticked slowly by. The waiting was almost as excruciating as imagining what the final outcome would be.

The two men kept to the shadows, moving restlessly, watching for her brother. Taking advantage of their distraction, she inched her way to the far end of the bench. Maybe she could make it into the woods. It was dark. If she could only—

"Hey. Where do you think you're going?"

The taller man yanked her collar and jerked her back to the middle of the bench.

"Don't even think about going anywhere."

Okay, but she could shout as soon as she saw someone. Anyone who could get help. Except it was late and this was Golden, so the streets were deserted.

Time stretched. Grace blinked away tears, needing to stay alert. Once the rescue started— *please let there be a rescue*—she'd make her escape.

If anyone was coming.

Holding back a sob that desperately wanted to escape her throat, she noticed movement. From the direction of the parking lot, a figure strode their way. Squinting, she saw it was Nathan and she barely held back a cry.

Taller moved beside her, his frightening tone cold as ice when he said, "You're a smart woman. Keep quiet."

Nathan stopped ten feet away. His gaze met hers. "You okay?"

As she opened her mouth to answer, the man gave her a hard push. Her side jammed into the picnic table, the contact painful enough to send tears to her eyes. She got the message and clamped her lips shut.

The bald man stepped forward. "You got what we asked for?"

"Yeah. But not until you let my sister go."

A sneer formed on his lips. "Nice try. Not gonna happen."

The taller thug pressed a heavy hand on Grace's shoulder, as if to keep her in place in case she tried to run.

"Then follow me to my car. The stuff is there."

Grace could tell Nathan was trying to sound tough, but caught the slight tremor in his voice.

"Think I was born yesterday?" the bald man asked.

"No, really. It's in my car trunk," Nathan explained. Grace almost believed him. "You can get it and take off."

Bald guy turned to his partner. "Keep her here. I'll get the goods, then we'll leave." He sent her a look. "With you, honey."

Grace almost passed out.

Nathan turned on his heel, leading the hulking man away.

"It's just you and me now," Taller said, his words sending a shiver over her skin. When he pulled a pistol from his pocket, she lost her breath.

Forcing herself not to panic, she decided to try to reason with him when a thud, then another, sounded from behind him. He whirled, gun drawn, to determine what had caused the noise.

Grace thought she caught sight of a shadow in the nearby woods, but Taller turned back to her.

Suddenly Deke appeared out of nowhere. He barreled into the tall man with enough force to throw him off balance. As Taller went down, his gun raised, a flash of white flame fired from the weapon.

Grace reared back and cried out in pain.

"No," DEKE SHOUTED, launching himself toward the gun. He managed to pry it out of the struggling man's hand before another shot fired. As they tussled, Deke tried to get a glimpse of Grace. Had she been hit? Was she hurt? Worse?

Taking care of the bad guy took Deke longer than he'd hoped but after a well-aimed punch, he had the creep on his stomach, arms behind his back. Local law enforcement streamed from the tree line, guns drawn. Once Deke made sure the perp was in the hands of the locals, he raced to Grace, who lay slumped against the picnic table, her beautiful face pale in the moonlight. She squeezed her upper left arm with her right hand. Deke could see a dark trickle between her fingers.

"Grace. Talk to me," he said as he sank to his knees before her.

"I'm fine," came her answer, spoken around chattering teeth.

"I don't think so," he countered. "You were hit."

"I…can't tell if the bullet…"

"We need paramedics," he shouted to the police officers nearby. Someone immediately radioed for assistance.

As Deke hunkered before her, Grace's entire body began to shake.

It took everything in him not to hug her close, but he couldn't risk it until he knew the extent of her injury. "Help is on the way." He cupped her face. "Can I look at the wound?"

Eyes wide, pupils dilated, she managed to get out, "Nathan?"

"I don't know, but there were officers positioned by the car."

She sent him a jerky nod. He reached up to take her pulse, concerned by the rapid pace.

"Cold."

Shock. He gently pried her hand away to inspect the damage the bullet had caused. Grace winced but allowed him to look. The skin was puckered, red and steadily bleeding, but Deke didn't want to jostle her to find out if the bullet had penetrated. Prayed it hadn't. But he could tell it hadn't hit an artery.

Tearing the bottom of his T-shirt, he formed a makeshift bandage to at least stanch the blood flow until help arrived. Once he had the torn fabric in place, he hauled her into his arms. Held on to her with all his strength. "I've got you."

She tried to hug him and gasped.

"Stay still. I won't let go of you."

Grace pulled back. Blinked at him. "You came."

"Of course I came."

What if Nathan hadn't gone to the cabin? Handled these guys on his own? Grace could have suffered far worse and he wouldn't have been able to do a single thing about it. As it was, he was appalled that she'd been shot while he was so close.

He shuddered as he recalled the shot—ringing in the night. The muzzle flash. Grace's cry of pain.

"Not—not your fault," she stuttered.

No, but he might not have made it to her in time. And then where would they be? "I should have insisted Nathan go to the authorities right away."

A half-hearted laugh escaped her lips. "You can't make Nathan do anything."

"And you shouldn't have put yourself in danger."

"It was either Mama or me."

He gazed at this amazing woman as if she were the most precious gift in his life. Which she was. He admired her loyalty—even if he didn't agree with it 100 percent—the way she took care of others with no thought to herself. He loved her spunk. But most of all, he loved the way she'd filled a gaping void in his heart. Filled it with love and laughter.

And he'd almost lost her.

In the distance, sirens blared, red and blue flashing in the dark, starless sky. Grace shifted beside him and moaned.

"You're going to be fine, Grace."

"Easy for you to say."

Soon, there were paramedics asking him to move away from Grace so they could evaluate her. It was all he could do to let her go, but he stayed out of their way. All that mattered was Grace. Once her vitals were taken and her arm stabilized, they helped her onto a stretcher and rolled her to the ambulance.

As they moved, she reached her hand out. Deke ran over, squeezed her moist fingers. "I'll see you at the hospital."

Nodding, she closed her eyes and her arm went limp.

GRACE WOKE TO the sound of beeping and an antiseptic smell that made her nose wrinkle. She opened her eyes, scoping out her surroundings. Hospital, for sure. But what had... Oh, yeah.

She'd been shot. Before she could stop them, the events of the night crashed over her.

Moving, she felt a searing pain shoot down her left arm. She tilted her head. Thick white gauze bandaged her upper arm. When she tried to sit up, a heavy hand against her shoulder stopped her. Turning her neck, she met Deke's gaze.

"You were shot, Grace. You're at the hospital."

"I already figured that out." She squiggled around as Deke adjusted the pillow so she could sit up. When the motion winded her, she paused to catch her breath.

"The bullet caught the outer part of your arm, a little deeper than a graze but no major damage. Doc says you'll need to take it easy."

"And Nathan?"

"He's okay. With the authorities."

"You let them take him?"

"I didn't have any choice. Besides, they need his help."

She closed her eyes. Swallowed. "To testify against those men who took me tonight?"

"Yes. And their boss."

Tears trickled from her closed lids. "I'd hoped to avoid that."

"He wants to, Grace."

Her eyes flew open. "Even knowing the danger?"

"Because of his actions, you could have been killed tonight. It rattled him, Grace."

"He can't handle this alone." She went to flip off the covers and escape from the bed but Deke—and the side rails—stopped her. The IV needle pinched her hand when she inadvertently tugged it too far.

His voice sounded oddly strangled when he asked, "Where do you think you're going?"

"Nathan needs a lawyer."

"And he'll get one. But not you."

"Yes, me. I have to talk to him. Make sure he doesn't do or say anything the authorities can use against him."

"Grace, relax. You can't fix this."

She huffed and then slumped back onto the mattress. "I can try."

A thin smile curved his lips. "Stubborn to the end."

The room grew silent, except for the monitoring machine noises Grace found annoying. Deke stayed by her bedside, his woodsy scent overpowering the antiseptic hospital smells.

"Thank you," she said.

"I did what I could."

She blew out a breath. "By inserting yourself in our problems. I never asked you to."

"But I would do it all again."

She couldn't meet his gaze. "I don't know how to repay you."

"How about giving us a chance?"

Oh, how she wanted to. But there were too many Harper issues she had to deal with first. "Deke, I can't. Not right now."

His voice went flat. "Ever?"

"Let me take care of family matters. Then when I get back to Atlanta, we'll see."

"Until there's another excuse?" He took her hand in his. "I almost lost you tonight. Do you know how scared I was?"

She shook her head.

"Family problems will always exist, Grace. But you don't have to solve every single one of them. Our time is now, if we're brave enough to take it."

She bit her bottom lip, unsure what to do. She'd always taken care of her family. How could she do anything else? But Deke was offering her a life full of love. Did she dare take it?

"I want there to be an us, but…"

"You'll always put your family first."

She nodded.

A flicker of emotion flashed across his face, then it was gone. "That's not good enough for me."

She reached out her hand but he stepped back. Before she could say anything else, her mother and sister rushed into the room, full of concern and questions. The moment was lost.

As her family fussed over her, she looked over their heads. Watched Deke, his shoulders rigid, walk out of the room, and she realized she'd just made the worst mistake of her life.

CHAPTER SIXTEEN

Three weeks later...

DEKE EXITED THE federal building in Atlanta, loosening his tie as he went. Squinted against the bright sun beating down on him. He reached for the sunglasses tucked in his jacket pocket, then put them on. It would be a scorcher in the city today. He unbuttoned the top button of his dress shirt and stretched out his collar. Finally, he could breathe. The suit he'd worn restricted his movements, much like the oppressive mood that had descended over him while driving downtown this morning.

He'd been called in for questioning on Nathan's case. Ready to throw him under the bus—well deserved in his mind since Nathan had unwittingly put Grace in danger—he'd had second thoughts after hearing Grace's opening comments.

Yes, she was there to advise her brother.

No, he and Grace hadn't spoken to each other since the night in the hospital.

He'd entered the cool room on the third floor, quickly taking in the scene as he'd been trained.

Federal agents reviewed notes and discussed the case. Grace, dressed in a power suit, reading a document while Nathan, in an ill-fitting suit, sat beside her, fidgeting in his chair. Taking a seat in the corner, he waited for Grace to notice he was there. She looked at her brother, then stopped and scanned the room. Their gazes met. Regret swam in her eyes.

She'd made good on her choice. Family first. Deke accepted her decision. Fighting her wasn't going to earn him any points, so he'd pretty much stayed out of her space. Mostly because he didn't want to hear any more reasons why she'd chosen her family over him. He understood, to a point. Had hoped that the feelings between them would have taken precedence. He was wrong.

The questioning went on and on. Deke finally had a chance to see Grace in professional action and had to admit, he was impressed. And surprised. She didn't downplay her brother's role in the events that had led to the perps' showing up in Golden. In fact, she stressed that once Nathan finished helping the police, he'd accept his punishment. Within reason.

Her caveat earned her a small smile.

Then Deke was called to answer questions about the night in the park and was free to go.

Free to go where? he wondered.

Shrugging out of his jacket, he'd taken a few steps toward the parking lot when someone called his name. Not just someone. Grace.

"Deke. Wait up."

He paused. Schooled his expression. Grace had torn up what was left of his heart, but he didn't have to disclose the power she held over him.

"Hey." Dressed in her pinstriped suit and those high heels she loved to wear, she stopped to take a deep breath. A lingering result of the bullet wound? Probably. But other than that, she looked good. Still beautiful as ever, sunlight brightening her blond hair, her green eyes sparkling, her face full of healthy color, unlike the gray pallor he'd worried over the last time he'd seen her in the hospital room.

He acknowledged her greeting. "Grace."

She lifted the hand not holding her briefcase. "I'm sorry I haven't talked to you since…well, you know. It's been a hectic few weeks."

He nodded, finding himself unable to speak. If he'd thought seeing her again was going to be easy, he was dead wrong.

Her confidence slipped at his silence. "So… uh… I wanted to thank you for continuing to work for Mama. It's been a big help and she appreciates it."

He shrugged. "With Nathan gone she still

needs a guide and I'm happy to stick with the job."

"Still deciding if you'll go back to GBI?"

His job, like his life, it seemed, was on hold. "Something like that."

She shook her head. Seemed to search for words. "I'm actually surprised at how well Mama and Faith are doing together."

"Once her ankle healed your mother was ready to work."

"I think knowing you're there has made Mama feel safe. And Faith seems focused." Grace let out a short laugh. "I have to hand it to her. As much as I was ticked that she took off with Lyle, it made sense that they went away to talk. Figure out where they stood with each other before making any big decisions."

"She'll be fine without Lyle. Your mother's fantastic with the kids and Roy is back in town."

"Imagine that. The Harpers getting their acts together."

"Which means they don't need you, Grace. You can finally focus on your career."

An emotion he couldn't name passed over her eyes. "About that—"

Deke held up a hand to stop her. "It's okay, Grace. You made your choice. Live your life and be happy."

"I would, if—"

"Great seeing you. I need to get going." Because really, he didn't want to know what the *if* was. *If* she'd wanted to get together, she'd had three weeks to call him. *If* she'd had second thoughts about working in Atlanta, she would have moved home. He hadn't seen her car at the cabin, so he assumed she'd gone back to her apartment in Atlanta. Either way, there'd been only silence. He got the message loud and clear.

Sending her one final nod, he turned and strode to the Jeep. Seeing Grace was like losing what they'd started all over again. He didn't want the rug pulled out from under his world a second time, which made him decide he couldn't stay in Golden indefinitely. He'd be sure to run into her again and, after this brief talk, knew his heart wasn't up to it. He'd go back to the office, give Wanda Sue his notice and assist in finding a replacement. Let Roy know he'd be moving out of the cabin. Then he'd be on his own again.

He'd just slid behind the wheel when his cell rang. Glancing at the caller ID, he picked up.

"Logan. I was going to touch base with you later."

"Just wanted to give you a heads-up. I'm headed to Golden this afternoon. I did as much background research on Serena Stanhope and her father as I could get my hands on, which wasn't much. Her father has a way of staying under the radar."

"But you think you can get to the bottom of who the Stanhopes are?"

"Dude, how long have we been friends?" Logan chuckled. "I'll get results. Count on it."

"Good. We'll meet up in town and go from there."

"Sounds like a plan."

Deke ended the call, then started up the Jeep. Once Logan had his investigation under way, Deke would leave Golden knowing he'd done his part to uncover the truth about James Tate, i.e., Stanhope. Then he had some serious decisions to make concerning his future.

Driving through city traffic frustrated him to no end. He finally relaxed once he saw the mountains in the distance. Traffic thinned out. His chest ached with a longing he recognized as a love for the small town he'd become a part of. Made him realize how much he'd miss Grace once he was gone.

In hindsight, he should have known better than to get involved in people's lives when he first arrived in Golden. Solitary had worked just fine for him. Why did he have to go and mess with success? *Because Grace gave you a glimpse of what happiness and being a partner with someone you loved could be like.* Being alone didn't hurt as much as putting yourself out there. Or falling in love. He'd forgotten that fact and wouldn't make the same mistake in the future.

GRACE ARRIVED BACK at the high-rise glass building that housed the law firm to find a lop-sided stack of files on her desk. The hustle of the busy office overwhelmed her: coworkers making calls, discussing strategies. Deadlines. There were always deadlines. After spending so much time in her small office in Golden, she'd forgotten how distracting all this activity could be.

Removing her jacket, she winced as she pulled her still-healing arm from the sleeve. She stored her purse in the bottom desk drawer and lightly rubbed her arm. The outcome of that night in the park could have been so much worse than the reality, she'd put up with a little discomfort.

Grace focused on the remainder of her day. With so many details to catch up on, she won-dered if she'd ever make a dent in the pile of cases threatening to topple over on her desk. This was what she'd wanted, right? Her goal had been to return to the firm and here she was. She should be happy, yet deep down she had a sense she was missing something important.

After her injury, her family had taken over the reins of the business that she'd slowly started releasing during her leave of absence in Golden. Mama's doctor had discovered her dizziness and falling episodes were due to an underactive thyroid. Now on medication, she went to the office every day without difficulty. Nathan was working with the authorities. It was too soon to tell what the outcome would be. The authorities hadn't found her father, which was probably for the best. The Harpers didn't need him in their lives. And Deke had been right. She needed to live her own life. That night in the park had been a wake-up call, for everyone.

Deke. Oh, how she missed him. The way he'd brushed her off earlier as they stood outside the federal building, well, it wasn't unexpected. He had every right to back off, just as she'd done to him that night in the hospital. In her defense, she hadn't been thinking clearly. Pain, drugs and the drop in adrenaline had her falling back on old habits, thinking she alone could solve all the family problems. Only, she'd had time away from him to consider her choice, and honestly, the gravity of her mistake grew more real every day. She never should have let him walk out of her hospital room. Should have revealed what was in her heart. But after his cool reception today, did she still stand a chance? And if so, how in the world did she make this right?

The elevator bell dinged and she glanced around the office.

What am I doing here?

For all her attempts to escape Golden, she'd finally succeeded. Had reached her goal. That all changed when one tall, handsome man entered her life and made her think that maybe there was more than what she'd always dreamed of. A guy who was the opposite of her usual suit-and-tie type, who embraced the outdoors she'd tried to escape from for years. Questioned her motives while making her heart race whenever they were together. Deke saw what she couldn't. Put Your Feet Up was truly a part of her, but wasn't there room in life for more?

She genuinely liked him. Liked that he challenged her. Liked his take-charge attitude. Sure, he had baggage, but who didn't? She'd never met a guy who made her laugh, made her think on her feet and, most important, made her consider moving into a serious relationship.

She loved him.

"Earth to Grace."

Grace jumped at her coworker's greeting. "Stacy. Hi."

"Where were you?"

"Just thinking." She smoothed her unwrinkled skirt. "What's up?"

"Great news." Stacy lowered the files in her arm to her side, looked over her shoulder and lowered her voice. "We just took on a major client and I've been asked to work on the case with Mr. Franks."

Grace's stomach flipped. Mr. Franks had told her she'd be the next in line to assist in a big case. "Congratulations." She paused. "But I'm curious why he didn't talk to me."

"I happened to be in his office going over a brief when he found out about the case. I've been working lots of overtime, making myself available to the firm. I guess since you just got back and need to get up to speed, he decided to ask me instead."

How had Grace forgotten how competitive working in a large firm could be? Obviously, Stacy was going to take advantage of Grace's absence. As associates, it was in their best interest to put in long hours and do as much as possible to impress the partners. And Stacy was ambitious…

"I even got my own office down the hall from the partners. Granted, it's small, but it's a step up."

That news didn't sit well. This open-concept desk space didn't work for Grace.

Stacy glanced at Grace's desk. "I see the files I passed off to one of the new hires were returned to your desk."

Those and a few more, Grace was sure. "I should have come back sooner."

Stacy waved off her concern. "Don't worry so much. I'm sure another big client will come your way. Just pick up where you left off and see what happens."

If only it was that easy.

Glancing around the room, Stacy said, "I'd love to chat, Grace, but I have to start researching right away."

"Maybe we can grab dinner and you can fill me in on what's been going on."

"Sure. I'll probably need a break after the long hours I see myself spending here." She pulled the files closer to her chest and practically danced in glee. "Take care."

Grace's stomach churned. She could have had that opportunity, yet she chose to take care of her family. She'd never get assigned to special cases if she didn't spend endless hours working to get ahead. Taking every deposition thrown her way, writing up as many motions as she could reasonably manage. She felt like she was starting from scratch, proving to the partners she was committed after the time she'd taken off.

Having a seat at her desk, she let her gaze stray from the files to the window. The sky was a pure, cerulean blue, not a cloud as far as the eye could see. A bird flew by, wings wide with freedom. And here she was, holed up in the office on a beautiful summer day when thoughts of hiking to Crystalline Falls seemed so much more pleasurable.

Did she want to spend her days buried in the law library at the firm, looking up precedents and finding ways to acquit clients instead of actually working with people to better their lives? Where was the excitement she'd experienced when she first started working here? The surge of adrenaline when presented with a new case?

More than once the fleeting idea of opening a small practice in Golden had crossed her mind. She'd laughed it off, thought perhaps if she was home, she could keep a closer watch on her family. But could it be more? There were plenty of people in Golden who could benefit from her services. Could she do it? Leave the firm of her dreams and open her own practice? She couldn't ignore the nagging sense that her life was at a crossroads.

She needed an antacid. Her hunt through her desk drawer was interrupted when her cell rang. Closing the drawer with a slam, she felt her heart pick up when she read the caller ID. Uncle Roy.

"Where have you been?" she asked her uncle.

"Enjoying my life, which is more than I can say for you," came his raspy reply.

"And how would you even know what I've been doing? I haven't seen you in weeks."

"That's what happens when you fall in love."

She held back an eye roll because, sure, she'd had her chance, blown it and didn't need her uncle rubbing it in.

"Is everyone okay?"

"Just peachy."

"Then why are you calling me during work hours?"

"Just wanted to let you know your boy is movin' out of the cabin. Gave me his notice today."

"Deke? Why?"

"Didn't say. Gave your mama his notice, too."

Stunned, she leaned back heavily against the chair. *What did you expect him to do, Grace? Hang around Golden waiting for you forever?* "Mama will be heartbroken. She was thrilled when Deke agreed to stay on. Why did he change his mind?"

"Didn't say."

So this was it. She and Deke were truly over.

"What're you gonna do about it?" Uncle Roy pestered.

"Do? It's his decision."

"Come on there, Gracie. You're a bunch smarter than that."

Indignation made her voice squeak. "He's leaving because of me?"

"I got eyes. Boy doesn't say much, but I can read between the lines."

"So what do you think I can do about it?"

Her uncle chuckled. "I'd say use that big ole brain of yours and figure it out."

After the call, Grace still held the phone to her ear. The sounds in the office suddenly diminished. Movement blurred as if in slow motion. And Grace finally knew what she had to do. Even if it backfired on her big-time.

DRESSED IN SHORTS, a pale blue T-shirt and sneakers, Grace jogged through the woods the next day to the lake. The shady trees enveloped her in a comfortable sense of serenity. She inhaled the scent of damp earth as she neared the water's edge. Guests staying in the cabins were out and about, roaming the paths through the woods or hanging out by the water's edge. She waved and said hello. In the distance, boats zigzagged on the lake as folks were making the best of the sweltering summer day by escaping to the cool water.

When she reached the clearing before the dock, she stared out over the water. The scenery here was magnificent. She'd let her past experiences cause her to look through jaded eyes. A shame, really, but also a hard truth. It had made her more determined to stay away from Golden.

No more.

Deke stood at the end of the dock, the golden light of the sun burnishing his dark hair. Tall, shoulders broad and steady, he remained stock-still. Taking in the view for one final time? His hands were shoved in his shorts pockets as he surveyed the lake spread out before him. He belonged here, she realized. Had since the day he walked into the office asking about the outdoor guide position.

She knew he hadn't left when she pulled up the lane and saw his Jeep still parked beside the cabin. Took it as a sign of a second chance.

Suddenly nervous, she hesitated. What if he wouldn't hear her out? Had decided she was too much trouble? That he was much more suited to the solitary life? What would she do then?

He turned. Took a step, saw her and froze.

Taking a huge breath, she pressed a hand against her stomach and powered forward. It was now or never to change her future. Their future, if he'd listen.

A flash of surprise lit his eyes. "Grace. What're you doing here?"

"I had to get out of Atlanta for a while."

One dark brow arched. "Problems?"

"Clarity."

He pulled his hands from his pockets and crossed his arms over his chest, legs planted in a wide stance. "You'll have to explain."

She licked her lips. "Uncle Roy called. Told me you were leaving."

Shrugging, he looked away. "There's really nothing here for me now."

"And that's where you're wrong."

His eyes swung back and pierced hers. "Enlighten me."

She took a step closer. Inhaled his familiar scent. Didn't want to go a day without him in her life ever again. "I've been under the misguided impression that I'm in control of the universe. It took one brave man to point out how totally outlandish and mistaken I was."

His lips curved just the slightest bit.

"Being at a big firm was the dream, Deke. Until I realized that some dreams are really excuses." She paused, searching for the right words. "I needed an excuse to leave Golden because if I didn't have one, I'd never go. I'd never try. I'd never see what was out there. It wasn't about the job, although I do love my career. It was about being away from Golden, so that I could fully realize how much I'd miss it."

"You miss Golden?"

"Every day." She stepped around him and waved her hand in the air, the gesture encompassing the lake and mountains. "It didn't click until you reminded me just how beautiful my home really is. How there's a simplicity in being in tune with nature." She turned to look at him. "You also made me see I'm not the boss of everyone, and to be truthful, I don't want to be."

Arms still crossed tight, he asked, "So what are you suggesting?"

"That we both stay in Golden. See where the relationship I made a mess of takes us." She reached out. Touched his strong arm and felt the resulting quiver beneath her fingers. "I love you, Deke. And honestly, if Golden isn't for you, that's fine. If we give us another chance, I'll be happy wherever we go."

He tilted his head. Studied her for so long her knees grew weak. "Are you sure you're up to this? I don't want to be your second choice, Grace. Equal partners or nothing."

"I'm ready."

He ran a hand over his chin. "I'll be honest.

I haven't decided if I'll go back into law enforcement."

"So we'll figure it out together. As you once told me, we make a good team. There's no rush." She grinned. "Well, except that I need to know what you're thinking right now."

His smile spread, revealing the dimples she loved. He took a step closer, circled his arms around her waist. "I'm thinking there's only one Grace Harper and I'd be happy to continue this journey with her." He leaned in for a quick kiss. "I love you."

She rested her hands on his chest, relief sweeping over her. "Then here's to discovering what life has in store for us. Together."

* * * * *

For more great romances from acclaimed author Tara Randel, visit www.Harlequin.com today!

Don't miss Logan Masterson and Serena Stanhope's story, coming in August 2019!

Get 4 FREE REWARDS!

We'll send you 2 FREE Books plus 2 FREE Mystery Gifts.

Their Family Legacy
Lorraine Beatty

The Rancher's Answered Prayer
Arlene James

Love Inspired® books feature contemporary inspirational romances with Christian characters facing the challenges of life and love.

FREE Value Over **$20**

YES! Please send me 2 FREE Love Inspired® Romance novels and my 2 FREE mystery gifts (gifts are worth about $10 retail). After receiving them, if I don't wish to receive any more books, I can return the shipping statement marked "cancel." If I don't cancel, I will receive 6 brand-new novels every month and be billed just $5.24 for the regular-print edition or $5.74 each for the larger-print edition in the U.S., or $5.74 each for the regular-print edition or $6.24 each for the larger-print edition in Canada. That's a savings of at least 13% off the cover price. It's quite a bargain! Shipping and handling is just 50¢ per book in the U.S. and 75¢ per book in Canada.* I understand that accepting the 2 free books and gifts places me under no obligation to buy anything. I can always return a shipment and cancel at any time. The free books and gifts are mine to keep no matter what I decide.

Choose one: ☐ **Love Inspired® Romance Regular-Print**
(105/305 IDN GMY4)

☐ **Love Inspired® Romance Larger-Print**
(122/322 IDN GMY4)

Name (please print)

Address   Apt. #

City   State/Province   Zip/Postal Code

Mail to the **Reader Service:**
IN U.S.A.: P.O. Box 1341, Buffalo, NY 14240-8531
IN CANADA: P.O. Box 603, Fort Erie, Ontario L2A 5X3

Want to try 2 free books from another series! Call 1-800-873-8635 or visit www.ReaderService.com.

---

*Terms and prices subject to change without notice. Prices do not include sales taxes, which will be charged (if applicable) based on your state or country of residence. Canadian residents will be charged applicable taxes. Offer not valid in Quebec. This offer is limited to one order per household. Books received may not be as shown. Not valid for current subscribers to Love Inspired Romance books. All orders subject to approval. Credit or debit balances in a customer's account(s) may be offset by any other outstanding balance owed by or to the customer. Please allow 4 to 6 weeks for delivery. Offer available while quantities last.

Your Privacy—The Reader Service is committed to protecting your privacy. Our Privacy Policy is available online at www.ReaderService.com or upon request from the Reader Service. We make a portion of our mailing list available to reputable third parties that offer products we believe may interest you. If you prefer that we not exchange your name with third parties, or if you wish to clarify or modify your communication preferences, please visit us at www.ReaderService.com/consumerschoice or write to us at Reader Service Preference Service, P.O. Box 9062, Buffalo, NY 14240-9062. Include your complete name and address.

LI19R

MUST ♥ DOGS COLLECTION

SAVE 30% AND GET A FREE GIFT!

Finding true love can be "ruff"— but not when adorable dogs help to play
matchmaker in these inspiring romantic "tails."

YES! Please send me the first shipment of four books from the **Must ♥ Dogs
Collection**. If I don't cancel, I will continue to receive four books a month
for two additional months, and I will be billed at the same discount price of
$18.20 U.S./$20.30 CAN., plus $1.99 for shipping and handling.* That's a
30% discount off the cover prices! Plus, I'll receive a FREE adorable, hand-
painted dog figurine in every shipment (approx. retail value of $4.99)! I am
under no obligation to purchase anything and I may cancel at any time by
marking "cancel" on the shipping statement and returning the shipment. I
may keep the FREE books no matter what I decide.

☐ 256 HCN 4331   ☐ 456 HCN 4331

Name (please print)

Address   Apt. #

City   State/Province   Zip/Postal Code

Mail to the **Reader Service:**
IN U.S.A.: P.O. Box 1867, Buffalo, NY. 14240-1867
IN CANADA: P.O. Box 609, Fort Erie, Ontario L2A 5X3

PETSBPA19